THE FIFTH AGENDA

THE FIFTH AGENDA

Peter Clements

ATHENA PRESS
LONDON

THE FIFTH AGENDA
Copyright © Peter Clements 2006

ISBN 1 84401 602 1

First Published 2006 by
ATHENA PRESS
Queen's House, 2 Holly Road
Twickenham TW1 4EG
United Kingdom

Printed for Athena Press

I would like to dedicate this book to Val, my wife, who has had to suffer my absence over many years and, offer thanks to Kevin for saving the book from a computer virus, also Pam for her help and encouragement.

London

George Dolby closed the door to his office and took the lift down to the basement garage. It took only twenty minutes from Vauxhall Bridge, through the mid-afternoon traffic to drive the distance to a meeting of the Intelligence Strategy Team. Such meetings had become an essential part of his daily life since integration. The merging of MI5 and MI6 had reduced the once venerable British Intelligence Service to a penumbra of its former self. The merger had been a political coup with vengeance aforethought, ensuring that the Machiavellian machinations of both services would never again embarrass or threaten the privileged halls of Westminster. It had been a hundred years in the coming and was viewed as a triumph for open government and accountability. The aim was to strictly subordinate and centrally unify the vast labyrinth of Britain's security apparatus, which, perforce had distinct chains of Bureaucratic command, defending divergent interests. Now Dolby, a loyal and faithful servant of both crown and master, was embroiled in an operation the strict legality of which was impugnment. With the merger, 'The Game', as Summers called it, was simply being played out on different grounds, each with its own set of rules, with rogue and officially certified elements practising their trade in parallel, but each with official blessing from on high.

Terrance Albert Summers was the Convenor of the Intelligence Strategy Team that met, when politics and interest required, in a safe house off the Gloucester Road. He viewed the large fortress that was now headquarters for British intelligence, standing sentinel across the Thames, from which the newly combined British security apparatus carried out its paternal duties, as both compromised and structurally flawed. Summers had avoided the August cleansing that arrived with the merger, a cleansing that had forced so many experienced field officers, sulking into premature and unwelcome retirement. As Convenor he was now chair-bound, excluded from adventures, destined only to watch as others sought out the adrenalin rush he once shared. Few within the newly constituted service possessed such a charmed if not distinguished and iniquitous record as Summers. To those at the head of the new service he had been the proscribed man. As a junior officer in Washington, a shadow of association had been cast briefly over his fledgling career after working alongside the now infamous Guy Burgess. Although innocent of all wrongdoing he had been posted back to London. After a short spell at the London School of East European and Slavonic Studies, he was masquerading as a trade official with the Moscow Embassy when he became the hapless subject of a Soviet sting and was again forced to return to London, only to fall under the influence of George Kennedy Young, a retired vice-chief of MI6. His subsequent embroilment, along with others of middle ranking within MI6, in the overthrow of the democratically elected Prime Minister, Harold Wilson, should have spelt the end of an already faltering career. Fortune, it is said, smiles on such people and a fortuitous posting to Her Britannic Majesty's Embassy in Athens, again as a trade official, provided the setting for an intelligence coup that was to save and revitalise the career of Terrance Albert Summers. Space, if not interest, however, precludes the telling thereof. Suffice it to say that, after events in Athens his future within MI6 seemed more assured and was further enhanced when he was selected as one of the few within MI6 granted access to Anthony Blunt, following the latter's confession to MI5 and the FBI.

The nondescript red-brick Victorian safe house, indistinguishable from so many others in West Kensington, with its urban ambience, was more to the Convenor's liking than the Thames-side citadel, near Vauxhall Bridge. It belonged to the world he knew and understood, something that looked like one thing, but in reality was another. No longer paid to stand in the shadows of Moscow or Athens, he was one of a diminishing group of Cold War dinosaurs, waiting for his pension and the hope of just one more 'game' around the fires of which he could warm his liverish hands.

'Thank you all for coming,' he began, calling the meeting to order, followed by the usual warnings about note-taking and the need for utmost security.

Dolby viewed the others assembled around the oval table. Summers at one end, with only a closed reference file before him. To his left sat Phoebe Strongman with her armoury of dossiers and the ever present lap top. A woman of Rubensian proportions, she was an old member of the team, someone with whom the Convenor had stood against the common enemy, on a number of occasions. A lady of the highest standards of probity, neither young nor old – she had hovered around forty for many years – she had been part of the strategy team since its inception following the demise of the 'Evil Empire', a Reaganism beloved only by those who didn't play the game. A spinster of no fixed parish she had been a biochemist before joining the service and had studied at the East Anglia University's John Innes Institute, Norwich, beside the infamous Dr Rihab Taha, otherwise known outside of her native Iraq as Dr Germ, or Toxic Taha. She had been on the MI6 special task group that evaluated the material from 'Truncate', the code name given to the defecting microbiologist Dr Vladimir Pasechnik. Now something of an expert in biological warfare, Phoebe could explain the difference between botulinum toxin and wet anthrax to a two year old. A skill much in demand for a number of those involved in the project, including Dolby whose entire knowledge of BW and their delivery systems, had been gained from Ministry reports of the Iran/Iraq war and a slim volume on germ warfare from the Kensington Public Library.

The service watchdogs from B branch were absent, mute testimony to the irregular nature of the meeting and the subsequent operation. In their place sat Simon Trench, sprawled in his chair beside the upright Major Thurston, a man Dolby viewed with suspicion, as indeed he viewed all who had graduated through military intelligence. Next to the Major sat the effete John Barrington-Brown, an Arabist, wearing a crumpled linen suit, looking less like an Arab than anybody present. A trio of unknown eager young recruits, not invited to sit at high table, were perched on hard wooden chairs against the wall beside a fireplace, long since bricked in. Through academic excellence and endogenous contacts, they had found themselves, after much screening, employed by a combined yet fractured service and were

9

now straining to become operational. Their role did not stretch beyond that of observing the performance of their betters. Seen but not heard. Mary Stone completed the ensemble. A small brittle lady, of almost infinite power and with the ear of the Director-General, was present, for the record, in the role of E branch liaison. How much, from such anomalous meetings, she passed on to the D-G, remained known only to Mary Stone. Dolby had watched with interest, the verbal and physical manoeuvres of the two women now present. They seemed forever watchful and distrustful of each other, except when their interests coincided. On such rare occasions they were a phalanx not even Summers would challenge.

'I've called this meeting because of new developments that make it necessary for us to act, concerning the matter of Professor Vasily Batioushenkov, of "Hell's Kitchen". Our friends, the code-crackers at GCHQ, have intercepted a billet-doux from Baghdad, to the Prof, that would seem to indicate that the said gent is preparing to decamp and take up a new career in Iraq, possibly at the Salman Pak research centre, although John and his people think that it is more likely he is heading for Al-Hakam. He leaves Stepnogorsk within the week and will, in all probability, fly out via the Gulf. As you are aware, both the CIA and we keep an eye on the movements of certain key microbiologists and you will see, from the information in front of you,' he paused and looked around the table before continuing, 'that he ranks rather high on the list. I trust we have all done our prep. Even if Batioushenkov is not at the top of the list, this career change is disconcerting. Baghdad is awash with biochemists and microbiologists on fat retainers, but it could be that our Prof has something special to offer. He worked under Vladimir Pasechnik at the Leningrad Biopreparat Research Institute, a man who left his defection to us rather late, October 1989 as I remember. Having run foul of the Party, the Prof, for his sins, was sent to the Vector laboratories in Koltsovo, Siberia. Following rehabilitation he moved to comparatively more pleasant surroundings at Stepnogorsk in Kazakhstan – NATO designation, "Hells Kitchen" – and the largest BW production facility ever built in the world. There he has remained until now. It's all in the file. Yes, Simon?'

Having indicated a wish to speak, Simon seemed lost for words. The room fell silent. Along the wall the three eager young men sat poised, hanging on every word. Summers eyed him expectantly, over the top of his glasses.

Finally Simon said, 'All right if we smoke, Terrance?'

'Sorry, old chap. Terribly *verboten*. You'll just have to cross your legs.'

Phoebe Strongman, never one to let 'men's talk' take hold, shuffled her files noisily.

Taking advantage of the interruption Barrington-Brown felt moved to ask why the Professor had waited until now to leave 'the decaying ramparts of Hell's Kitchen.'

The Convenor patiently continued, 'With the collapse of the USSR the establishment was strapped for cash and bereft of purpose, as were similar institutions across the old USSR. Stepnogorsk had fallen into such a state as to be a health hazard to the local community, if not the whole of mankind and was marked for demolition. Trouble is, no one seems to know how to demolish such a place without causing a major health hazard to the environment. Those scientists who had remained were few and unemployed, their labour now forbidden by international agreement. The answer to your query, John, is on page five of your file.'

Dolby had always admired the thoroughness with which Summers prepared for such meetings.

He continued. 'There you will find two pictures, one of the Prof's son, Dimitri, named after his maternal grandfather, the other of his daughter, Zoya, the apple of the old man's eye. Dimitri has embraced fully the delights of the capitalist system and become part of the St Petersburg Mafia, about which, I should imagine, the Prof is none too pleased. It was Zoya that kept him in Stepnogorsk, her and his work. She has been in a drug rehab unit, in St Petersburg, for the past two years. Cocaine, if I remember correctly, supplied, no doubt, by her brother. Released last week she promptly went on a bender and ended up being knocked down by a lorry outside a MacDonald's restaurant and killed. Missing is a picture of the late Mrs Dorcas Batioushenkov. She, poor woman, was a victim of the last great purge. Being both a writer and Jewish proved fatal. She died in a Siberian Gulag. The Prof survived only because he was useful, but ended up doing time at Koltsovo. As with so many, he remained throughout, a loyal citizen of the state, at least until now.'

'Could never understand that,' added Barrington-Brown.

'Quite.' Leaning forward Summers spread his hands out on the table, as if to examine his nails.

'The plant in which he has been working at Stepnogorsk has, in the past, given us cause for concern. I should add that a Joint Intelligence Committee assessment of the Russian programme concluded that Russia's BW research capability and some production facilities, such as Obolensk, although in decay, remain relatively intact and could be reactivated with little effort. The Prof is part of that capability and whether in Kazakhstan, Russia or Iraq he is a problem. With the death of his daughter the dear fellow has nothing to keep him near mother Russia. Clearly he feels a change of climate would be beneficial and where better than with the Butcher of Baghdad? It would not be in our interests or for that matter anybody else's, for him to take up the position.' Visibly pleased with his presentation thus far Summers leaned back in his chair feeling sufficiently secure to ask if there were any questions.

'In what particular field of BW has Professor Batioushenkov been employed?' asked the Major.

'There you leave me, Major. It's more in Ms Strongman's bailiwick than mine. Perhaps, Ms Strongman, you would care to…' he trailed off, as if lost by the mere mention of the subject.

Phoebe Strongman possessed a voice that was surprisingly soft and low for a woman of her size, though the strength of which was not in doubt. 'We're unsure what he has been up to over the past twelve months. The Kazakhstan authorities have plans in place for the dismantling of the plant. Soil, air and water samples from around the plant have proved confusing because of the large amount of chemical dumping that has taken place over the years. His last known field of research was in aflotoxins, a mould called Aspergillus that grows on plants and can cause jaundice, internal bleeding and liver cancer. In the sixties he attempted to get a paper published on the subject, but his masters, not surprisingly, blocked publication. It's an unusual BW agent for any government to use against an enemy. Its effects can sometimes take years to show. Cancer being the longest to appear. It has the advantage over other agents in that the delivery can go undetected for so long and so it's difficult to know who to blame. Some of the toxin from Stepnogorsk has found its way to Iraq, not that they didn't have their own strain. UNSCOM inspectors discovered evidence, back in the nineties, that Iraq had produced approximately 2,400 litres of aflotoxin, at their Water and Agricultural Research Centre at Fudaliya. Iraq's expert in this field is, or was, a Dr Emad Diyab, who commenced working for the Iraq regime in 1988. He quite unwisely granted an interview to a British researcher in September 1995 and has not been heard of or seen since. Another BW agent that may make the Professor particularly attractive to Baghdad is his work on anthrax. Anthrax, as you know, has been with us a long time, since World War I. However, its spores are weakened and decay with exposure to the UV rays of sunlight, which, in the Middle East makes it a rather unreliable agent of destruction. However, as long ago as the mid-sixties, both the United States and the Soviet Union had developed a special organic compound that offers a protective coating to the spores. It's a process known as microencapsulation. North Korea is the only other country known to possess knowledge of microencapsulation. It may be that Iraq would like to move its anthrax programme forward in that direction. If so Professor Batioushenkov has the required knowledge. In his field the Professor is well respected.' Having spoken, she relaxed, her chair protesting at her weight.

'Thank you, Ms Strongman. John, perhaps you would like to come in here and inform us as to why the Prof finds Iraq so attractive.' Summers liked to be inclusive and felt that all should sing for their supper.

'Following Iraq's invasion of Kuwait, Saddam gave us all a bit of a scare,' John Barrington-Brown began, his lisp and weak 'r', an irritant to all. It was Mary Stone who suffered most. Such was her discomfort when listening to the Arabist, that she would drum her pencil on the table. An act all noticed, save the irritator, but none commented on. 'He ordered his BW team to commence the loading of Aspergillus aflotoxin, along with botulinum toxin and a few other nasties into the warheads of bombs and rockets. His air force commanders were ordered to take possession of the ordnance along with full authority to use them should America or Israel carry out a nuclear attack on Baghdad. The particular aflotoxin in question came from the lab of Professor Batioushenkov. Because of MAD – Mutual Assured Destruction – Iraq's BW weapons remained in their bunkers. Had Saddam engaged in BW, America had given warning that Iraq would suffer a nuclear attack. We believe that Iraq has rebuilt its chemical and BW stocks that the UN inspectors destroyed. The true scale of production and weaponisation remains unknown, but Iraq has failed to account for seventeen tons of biological growth medium. More recently it has experimented with camelpox and smallpox virus. The pool of foreign scientists in Iraq fluctuates, but has suffered some defections of late and they would welcome Professor Batioushenkov's particular research knowledge on aflotoxin.' Seemingly oblivious to the discomfort he had caused, Barrington-Brown offered, in conclusion, a weak smile. Mary Stone put down her pencil.

'Thank you, John. Where would we be without our experts We now come to the point of this little gathering. It is the considered opinion of Her Majesty's Government that we intercept the Prof, en route to Baghdad and invite him to Old Albion. Our task is to effect the diversion. If you get my drift.' Summers paused to let the words sink in. He continued. 'I should add that all attempts to contact him in the past have been rebuffed. We would naturally prefer that he came over to us voluntarily. Whatever the outcome, I think we would all agree that, Professor Batioushenkov would be better in our camp than that of Baghdad. As to our primary source, concerning his departure from Kazakhstan, it is GCHQ, so we must assume that our American friends and others, in particular AMAN, Israeli Military Intelligence, are also cognizant of his impending change of address, courtesy of one of their satellite stations and God knows what else. It's a given that Iraq will have its own welcoming committee of Mukhabarat thugs, to assist the

Professor on the last leg of his journey. We would prefer to work with Langley on this one, however, they have shown scant interest in cooperating, so we can take it that they'll be making a similar play. I've asked George to run the show. George.'

Dolby was aware that Summers wanted a 'show'. Something for the record. Something that would satisfy the scrutineers, in the event of a snafu. Something that would keep Summer's pension on track and pay for winter's fuel.

Dolby hesitated.

'George?' Summers insisted, removing his glasses and cleaning the lens with a red silk handkerchief.

'As the Convenor has said,' Dolby began falteringly, 'the Professor will be coming out of Kazakhstan via the Gulf which, given his choice of carriers rather limits the options, but we are still not sure whether he will use Bahrain or Dubai.' Dubiety rather than certainty had served him well in dealings with committees. There was, he reasoned, no need for all the facts to be displayed like a travel agent's itinerary. He would not encumber them with details, such as how the Professor would vacate Stepnogorsk. No doubt the aging scientist would fly out of the capital, Astana, on a domestic flight to Almaty in the south and then on to the Gulf, but such matters were best left unsaid.

'As the Convenor has said, we must assume that we're not alone, concerning our interest in the Professor's movements.'

'All of which makes for an interesting game,' Summers added enviously.

Dolby continued. 'He's an elderly man with only his work to live for, now that his daughter is dead. It's my opinion that he cannot be bought. As a scientist he'll be attracted to better and unfettered working facilities, wherever they are. I think we might be able to convince him that we can better whatever Baghdad is offering. Not, of course, in BW, but in some allied field. I would rather not go into any further detail at this time.'

Summers to the rescue. 'Quite, George. It's all on a need to know basis. Thank you for your input. Indeed, thank you all for your offerings and for your attendance. Our terms of reference are simply that we sanction a play that will bring the Prof to Old Albion. Once with us, Major, it will be your responsibility, along with our own boffins, to assess his worth to us and decide what should be done with Professor Vasily Batioushenkov and how he might best live out whatever time he has left. Does anyone have anything to add?' This was Summers's way of indicating that the meeting was now closed. The meeting adjourned. Dolby rose from his seat, but made no attempt to leave. Summers talked briefly with Mary Stone as the room emptied. Upon her departure the Convenor crossed the room to where Dolby stood examining a limited edition print of a Hitchens landscape.

'George, let's walk in the garden.' It was a typical Kensington city garden, consisting of a narrow grass strip, bordered on both sides by neglected beds. An attempt had been made to plant flowers along one side, but they had died due to high brick walls, constructed to prevent unwanted surveillance, but cutting out whatever sun might penetrate that private part of London.

'George,' his tone was solicitous. The counsellor was speaking. 'Bit of a tricky one this. Not sure how much to tell you.' The subtext of which was that the operation to bring the Professor out of the Gulf was unofficial. It was, as Dolby had supposed, a rogue operation.

'You will, of course, have the full backing of the department.' Subtext – you are on your own, if it all unravels.

'I think it best that you keep this one close. Get my drift?' Subtext – deal only with me.

'I don't have to tell you how much things have changed. We don't have the freedom to run our affairs the way we once did and there is not a lot of financial support available for what we are asking you to do. All in all, George,' the counsellor engaged, 'I don't really care whether the good Prof comes here or not. His usefulness to us is limited, given the BW Treaty our chaps have signed. Just as long as he doesn't arrive in Baghdad. Do you get my drift?' Subtext – if necessary the Professor should be permanently settled in the Gulf, where only the sharks could plunder his aging Slavic body, they having little use for the evil knowledge contained therein.

'I have asked you to take care of things because we cannot afford any snafus, George. With both the Americans and Israelis and God knows who else in pursuit of the same prey, the race will be somewhat crowded. The point to remember is, no embarrassing ends. By the bye, how are you? You've had a bit of a hard time of late.'

The solicitous tone fell from him as hot roast onto a cold plate. Dolby's stoicism had become something of a talking point in the office. Sympathetic secretaries brought him tea. Colleagues feigned interest in his well-being. The cleaning lady delivered home-baked cakes. But for the few who had known his late wife, the recently departed Emma Dolby, George's stoical behaviour could be viewed in a different light. What had passed for love between the Dolbys of number 65a Carrington Street had, for many years, been replaced by an emptiness that for George had been filled, first with work and then meaningless affairs with women, many of whom he was unable to remember. Emma the barren woman, the service wife, destined to live out a marriage of normality inside a world of abnormality, had increasingly sought solace for both her barrenness and failed marriage in the stuporous relief offered by a bottle of gin, behind the net curtains of their Chelsea tenement. Her few friends and acquaintances had gradually dropped away, either embarrassed or bored by her decline into alcoholism. Dolby had only watched, as if from outside of his own body, at the huddled pathetic creature his wife had become. Unable, or was it unwilling, to help. At times there had been a closeness, when her drinking engulfed him, throwing up the love he once had for her in mock drunken relief, until the shared inebriation ended in vituperation. Her death from injuries sustained in a drunken fall, while dressing for a solitary dinner, had come to him at a strategy meeting in Oslo. He had expected relief, anticipated freedom, but had experienced only apathy.

'You should have taken leave when it was on offer,' Summers advised. 'Never mind. When this is over you should get away. Go fishing or something.'

'Thank you, I'll have to settle for the "something". Fishing and I are not compatible,' he replied.

'You should try it. You never know what you may catch.'

Dolby stuck his hands in his pockets to ward off the early evening chill.

The Convenor continued, 'We don't know for sure when he

intends to make his move, so you should be in position as soon as possible, George. We cannot afford to let him slip through to Baghdad. Have you thought who you will take with you?'

Dolby had indeed made up his mind on the matter of who would accompany him to the Gulf.

'Is that advisable? Going alone leaves you rather exposed. The Americans probably have half a Marine Corps already in position. You will need someone to hold your hand through the desert nights.'

'I would rather not. Once I'm there and I've assessed things you can always send someone to join me. I can't see that numbers are what is required. If I can't persuade him to come to us then the alternative still requires only one person,' Dolby said.

'God, Dolby, not you. I don't want you—' the Convenor protested.

'No, not me. There is someone we can use from the old days who is already close by. For a small fee he will arrange to terminate the Professor's pension plan.'

The Convenor, visibly relieved, replied, 'In the old days we could have called on the local office to help. Not now. Damn cuts. Damn merger. No snafus, George! If your chap is still reliable then use him. Bringing the Professor back to the UK poses more problems than it solves. But I suppose we have to try. It's up to you. Your call, as they say. Good luck, George.'

The drone of traffic heading out to Heathrow was momentarily drowned by the roar of four Pratt and Whitney engines attached to the wings of a jumbo jet on its final approach. Both men looked up as the late afternoon shadow of the giant aircraft passed over them.

Washington, DC

Jose Miguel, the owner of the Rapid Grill, a small diner north of Pennsylvania Avenue, on 7th Street, prided himself on the cleanliness of his modest establishment. This he was able to achieve through the slave-like conditions he imposed upon his staff, most of whom were family and all from Costa Rica. New immigrants work the hardest, especially without the protection of a green card. It was a situation Miguel was happy to exploit. And so the clean windows of the diner, north of Pennsylvania on 7th Street, enabled Alex Kelday to view the erection, across the street, of a new building, which would shortly provide yet more office space for the capital's Bureaucracy. He had switched his patronage to the Rapid Grill having given up on Misha's Deli, after it appeared in a popular tourist guide to Washington city. Like so many others in the nations capital, beset by tourists, he asked only to be able to dine in the company of his choosing and, from time to time, when the necessity arose to leave some memories behind with the dirty dishes.

She had unexpectedly appeared one lunchtime, in a high state of Latin excitement, to find him colloguing with two staffers from Domestic Operations Division. He had failed to call her. In truth the time had come when retreat from what was becoming an untenable relationship had seemed the preferred option. His desire to move on, however, was not shared. An awkward silence had followed her sudden arrival, exasperated by her physical magnetism and postural defiance. Tall and elegant, in a 5th Avenue suit from Lord and Taylor, she had made a statement, even in Misha's. They were standing, four of them, at a table, without introductions or words of welcome, as around them the sophisticated lunchtime traffic continued to eat and drink, seemingly oblivious of their predicament. Kelday, confused and unable to break the impasse, had never envisaged that she would invade his world. They had agreed from the beginning that their own space would remain just that and that their illicit meetings would be on neutral ground. Once, they had met aboard a luxury houseboat, permanently moored near the Frances Case Memorial Bridge. Afterwards he had gone out for fresh crabs from Jessie Taylor's, only to find on his return that she had gone, leaving only her smell among the dishevelled bedding. On another occasion they had driven to Tangier Island, in the Chesapeake Bay, to a discrete guest house he knew. Each liaison had been somewhere different, as much for the excitement as for security. Now, for reasons he could only guess, she had broken the covenant and taken a personal risk that would expose a relationship that, for him, had already run its course. But her presence brought back the fever of their last liaison, strong and demanding. Among the lunchtime diners and the clatter of plates a strong intimacy returned. After what seemed like hours, he found the words that permitted his colleagues to escape with grace, aware of their sudden superfluity.

Three Manhattans later he helped her into a cab, promising to see her that evening, knowing that he would not. That had been three months ago. Shortly after, he had forsaken the celebrity ambience of Misha's for the more modest surroundings of the Rapid Grill.

His second cup of coffee had gone cold while he watched with detached interest the two mobile cranes working in concert, taking from the long trailer truck a large slab of concrete, bristling with re-enforcing rods. The expertise of the two crane operators was such that the slab was lowered into position at the first attempt, as a black worker bravely stood beneath the monolith guiding the slab as he would a jet landing on the deck of a carrier. Checking his watch Kelday left the diner and returned to his desk at CIA's Washington office, on Pennsylvania Avenue, also home to the Domestic Operations Division of Clandestine Services. A message from his pool secretary, one of the few black secretaries within the agency, and now out for lunch, informed him that he was required, upon his return, for a briefing with the Assistant Director of Operations. She had ruefully added at the bottom, 'Beware of Greeks bearing gifts.'

'Alex, come in. Take a seat,' the Director, Paul Damaskinos, beckoned him into his spartan office. John Weston was there, along with Garth Wolfowitz. The former, an old USSR hand, now with logistics, and the other from Special Projects. Wolfowitz was something of a BW expert these days and had been with UNSCOM. It was rumoured that he knew Baghdad like he knew Langley.

The Director opened. 'The BW Professor in Kazakhstan is soon to take flight. So it's time to tango. We've put together a small support team for you, Alex. They've been briefed. So go out there and persuade the SOB that he should terminate any plans he had for going on to Baghdad. Tell him we can offer a good life, right here in the US. Offer him the world, if you have to. The Agency is adamant that for him Baghdad is only a dream. Shangri-La, or should that be Scheherazade?'

'How do we know he's on his way?' Alex enquired.

'We don't. Well, not for sure. But if he hasn't gone he's about to. The boys down at the National Security Agency intercepted a message to the Brits telling them he was leaving. And before you ask, no, we are not going in with them. Since five and six jumped into bed together they don't know which one is the bride and which is the groom. We grab him for our side.' To the Assistant Director the world was a simple place with simple rules. It helped that he was a simple man, but one who had complicated his fifty-six years by acquiring, at varying stages throughout, three wives and a child.

'I thought we were on the same side, on this one,' Kelday protested. He had been briefed at the weekly session on the possible departure of Professor Batioushenkov, but had wrongly assumed that it would be a joint operation.

'Orders from on high. He's ours. To quote our President, "Go out and round him up and bring him in."' The Director rose from his seat and walked over to the water dispenser.

'Rounding him up might be the easy part. Bringing him in may be more difficult,' Kelday fielded.

Garth Wolfowitz took up the Agency's case. 'The Professor is too old to resist what we have on offer. All he wants is peace and quiet and a decent lab in which to carry on his dark work. We can provide all three. As you know, his family circumstances have now changed and he wants out. Your problem will not come from the old man. It's all the other bastards who want him that you will need to concern yourself with. In particular Israeli Army Intelligence, AMAN. After the William Buckley affair, back in the eighties, when MOSSAD screwed us real good, we prefer to look on our Israeli friends with a bit more scepticism, whether they're from MOSSAD, AMAN or SHABAK. We know that Jerusalem is very keen to get its hands on the Professor. The Brits we can outbid. They've got nothing to offer except bad weather and even worse coffee. The Israelis are something else and they can play hardball. That is why we are sending along some muscle. AMAN will terminate him before they'll allow him to go Baghdad-side. Perhaps we should just stand aside and watch the show. You can also expect some of Saddam's boys to be on hand. But we hope to have them neutralised before you arrive.'

Weston added, 'We have an Air Force aircraft standing by at Dullas International. The rest of your team are already at the field. A car will take you back to your apartment to pick up your things and from there to the plane.'

'Alex,' the Director intoned. 'It's a straightforward operation. You fly out to the Gulf. You convince this Batioushenkov guy that we can offer him all he ever wanted and you bring him home. As Garth says, it would be easier to let nature take its course, but we can't take the chance. Any problems along the way and you have the means to deal with them.'

'The Agency's Gulf office will be on hand to offer additional support if it's needed,' added Weston.

The Director returned to his desk and thrust out his hand. 'Have a good trip, Alex. Bring me back one of those cloth things they wear around their heads, for my son. He loves to play at being Lawrence of Arabia.'

Kelday left the office aware that either Weston or Wolfowitz was directly behind him. It was Wolfowitz, escorting him to the car pool.

'If, by any chance, the Professor should not find our offer sufficiently attractive, you're authorised to use whatever means necessary to prevent him reaching Baghdad.' His instruction was more adventitious than conspiratorial.

'This guy has been around the BW business too long to be allowed to run free. He's got enough knowledge inside him to destroy the world. From here on in he works for us or no one. OK? By the way, you'll have some additional company along for the trip. The drug boys from the Drug Enforcement Administration (DEA) have asked if they can hitch a ride for two of their agents. Routine rotational of their Gulf station.'

Kelday closed the car door and was driven away from his apartment. There had been no direct order or authority to act, should the operation not go as planned, just a casual instruction in the corridor from Wolfowitz, affirming that the Professor should not arrive in Iraq. Everything was to remain deniable. It was the way the agency liked to operate. Something he was used to and could live with.

He looked out of the car window at the homeless, huddled on the sidewalk, preparing for their night without benefit of the American dream. Central Washington, beyond the tourist areas and government agencies, was a city of the poor, most of whom lived on welfare. Some took their chances on the streets among the garbage bags and in summer on park benches, where the police sometimes took pity on them. Unlike LA, where arched seats made sleeping difficult intentionally, the city's fathers had not yet changed the design of the benches in the park, making a night's sleep under the stars still possible. Most were crowded into poorly maintained turn-of-the-century red-brick tenements. Crime remained endemic. A series of black mayors had failed to clean up the mess, just as their white forebears had failed. It was a system of governance that provided so much for so few, but denied the very basics of life to so many, in a society unwilling to blame itself. Amid the expense account affluence of Misha's, he had talked to her of the inequality that existed, not only in the capital but throughout these great United States. She, a woman from the Third World, had dutifully listened, but remained detached, like any good diplomat's wife. Her life on 23rd Street, north of Massachusetts Avenue revolved around embassy parties and official outings, a life far removed from the squalor that was the lot of so many in the District of Columbia, and for that matter, from the impoverished millions her husband had the privilege to represent. Dating an Ambassador's wife, even that of a friendly power, had proved to be more than he could handle. Especially one from whom he now felt under siege.

Outside of the rush-hour it takes approximately forty minutes to drive from downtown Washington to Dullas International Airport, situated in rural Chantilly, VA. The traffic was already beginning to build up and he settled down to think, not of Professor Batioushenkov and how he might inveigle the aging Russian stateside, but of her and that last, somewhat melodramatic meeting in Misha's. What had started out as a brief liaison had become something more turgid, a complication he could do without. Only once had he seen her since that day, a chance sighting as she got into an embassy car in front of an expensive Georgetown restaurant. The mind can be trained to prioritise, to move those matters of importance to the front and leave the remaining pieces of life to fend for themselves until required. But, even when lives depend upon it and the fate of a nation can hang in the balance, that part of us that makes us sweat, that deprives our mouths of moisture and importunately invades our consciousness, that part demands front row.

So it was that he was still thinking of her as they drove into the military compound, adjacent to the Presidential hangar that houses Air Force One. Standing on the tarmac was an aging Air Force Lockheed C141 Starlifter transport, around which ground crew worked, preparing the aircraft. The wings drooped, heavy with fuel for the long flight ahead. Inside the military departure lounge he met his team among whom he recognised some faces from previous operations. Of the five, Kelday had previously worked with three, including the team leader, John Mitchell, a reliable and discreet New Yorker. They had last been together in Afghanistan, 2001, following the ousting from power of the Taliban. On that occasion Kelday had been instrumental in saving Mitchell's life, during the suppression of Taliban prisoners at the mud-walled fortress at Qalai Janghi. The insurgency had caught them by surprise and had come close to killing more than just the one US agent who died in the line of duty that day. Mitchell had been wounded, unable to move from the small room in which he had sought shelter. Kelday had guided a small unit of special forces to his rescue. It was both comforting and reassuring to have some 'old hands' along. The two personnel from the DEA, were absent.

The DEA was one of thirty-five US agencies tasked with fighting the drug menace. As a government agency, eager to protect its budget, they frequently used military transport, when available, to move their staff around and it had been Kelday's experience, whenever their paths had crossed, that the men and women of the DEA marched to their own drum. That they were late came as no surprise.

'Mr Kelday?' the flight captain enquired. From the insignia on the lapels of his flight suit and cap Kelday identified his rank as that of Colonel. The man was tall and muscular with a Southern drawl. 'I'm Colonel Lancroft, flight commander. We're ready to go when you are.'

'Thank you. It's not every day I'm flown by a full Colonel.'

'It's not every day I get to fly, Sir. I'm reserve and this is my time away from the office.'

'Well, that makes two of us, Colonel. Lead on.'

Inside the Starlifter, the air force had installed two rows of economy class seats immediately forward of the freight, from which they were separated by a partition that did not quite reach the cabin roof. As he entered, Kelday observed two civilians already seated on the right-hand side of the aircraft. The punctuality of the DEA was not something you could rely on, but here they were, first aboard. One a dark-haired man of Latin appearance wearing a leather jacket, the other a young woman dressed in a plain cotton frock, the sort you might find in an old dime and ten cent store. They made no attempt to introduce themselves as Kelday and his team took their seats.

Somewhere over the Atlantic, he had awoken in the middle of the shortened night and gone forward to the galley where a Master Sergeant was holding court over a freshly made pot of coffee. The absence of windows in the main fuselage made it impossible to tell whether it was day or night. Dim cabin lights shone from an olive green interior lining making it difficult for Kelday to see the black face of the man with whom he now drank a mug of freshly ground Arabica.

'The Colonel says that any time you want to go up to the cockpit just let him know, Sir.'

'Thank you, Sergeant. Is this a non-stop flight or do we touch down along the way?' The monotonous drone of the four Pratt and Whitney TF–33 engines was a reminder of their vulnerability and he wondered about the glide range for such a machine, in the event of a complete power loss.

'We meet up with a tanker out of Spain over the Western Med in a few hours. It's just a routine air to air refuel. At all up weight out of Dullas we would probably have had to perform two air to air, but since you folk don't weigh much we'll do it with one.' A green light appeared on a panel above his head.

'Excuse me, I'm wanted up front.' As the airman departed his place was taken by the slender frame of the young woman in the cotton frock.

'I couldn't sleep,' she said, excusing her presence while running her hands through short red hair.

'Good morning or is it good evening? Without windows it's anybody's guess. Would you like some coffee?' Kelday responded.

'I think it's early morning. Thank you, a coffee would be nice. Black. I guess we have you to thank for our lift to the Gulf. Are you military?'

'No.'

'I didn't think so.' She clasped the mug in her two hands as if cold.

'And you?' he replied, knowing that each knew who and what the other was.

'Just two government employees grateful for a lift.'

Her verbal sparring intrigued him. Now that he could see her more closely he put her age in the late twenties early thirties. She had a small scar below her right eye, on a face that carried little make-up.

'In search of some sun?' he enquired.

'Could be. I'm Kate Cranley,' she held out her hand.

'Alex Kelday. Your friend seems to be sleeping easy.'

'He took a pill. I can get a few hours, but that's all.'

'Are you based in Dubai?' he enquired.

'In the Gulf.'

The defensive nature of her response left him wondering how far she would take the charade. DEA agents were not normally open about their identity. On the other hand, the FBI sometimes sent agents abroad utilising DEA slots. It would be of interest to know who paid her monthly cheque. As the senior representative of the agency sponsoring the flight he felt free to press her further.

'How long have you been with the DEA?'

'That, Mr Kelday is an improper question to ask a lady at 34,000 feet over mid-Atlantic, in the middle of the night.'

'Then let's pretend we're flying at one hundred feet over Kansas and it's midday, shall we?'

Before she could reply the Sergeant returned with a request that Kelday visit the flight deck.

In the sparsely lit cockpit the night sky could be seen, alive with stars. The red glow of the instruments offering a peaceful ambience for the four men who worked that sector.

'Come forward,' the Captain beckoned. 'Watch the step. What do you think? Isn't that the prettiest thing you ever saw?' His arm swept across the night sky like a conjurer with a new trick that could produce the universe. Beside and behind him, the three other members of the flight-deck crew worked silently. An air of casual professionalism prevailed.

'You a music man, Mr Kelday?' the Captain enquired?

'I play some piano.'

'I'm a Wagner man. If you want to hear Wagner at his best you need to do it at altitude, in a cockpit at night, with a star-lit sky and the purr of four turbo fans. It sure beats the hell out of a concert hall. When you look out at all those stars and listen to "The Mastersingers" or "The Dusk of the Gods" from *The Ring* then it's as near as you are ever going to get to heaven on earth.'

'Earth and or heaven being at 34,000 feet?' he replied.

'Yer dead right. We've just climbed to 38,000, about as high as we're going to get on this trip. As we burn off the fuel so we climb and this evening we are getting into better wind at altitude. We might have to descend for the refuel. Got a message for you from the office.' He handed him a note. 'Use the torch if you can't see.'

Kelday didn't need the torch to read, 'For Kelday. Have a great trip.' It was the prearranged signal that Professor Batioushenkov had left Stepnogorsk in Kazakhstan.

'Hope that's what you wanted to hear.'

'Thank you, Captain. And thanks for your hospitality.'

'You're welcome to stay up for the refuel if you want. It will be in about ninety minutes.'

'Some other time. I'll get back to the team. And thanks again.'

'Mind how you go. The Sergeant will see you back to your seat.' A hand took him gently by the arm and guided him back to the relative brightness of the main cabin.

The young woman had returned to her seat and was deep into a paperback. Her colleague remained asleep beside her.

Kelday motioned John Mitchell to the comparative privacy of the galley.

'Can I help you, Sir?' asked the Sergeant, who was preparing a meal.

'Would you mind giving us some space, Sergeant?'

'Certainly.' At this he left and headed towards the flight deck.

Kelday handed the note he had received in the cockpit to an expectant Mitchell.

'He's on his way, John. Let's hope we arrive before him.'

'I think we'll have the drop on him. If he's using a local carrier chances are the damn aircraft will break down a dozen times before it reaches the Gulf.' Mitchell's lack of faith in Third World airlines was well founded, having experienced and survived two crashes.

He continued, 'Presumably the local office will hold things in place until we arrive, that's if he beats us to the draw. There is just the one target?'

'Just the one and with the right persuasion he'll be a fellow-traveller, rather than a target. Are you happy with our team?'

'No problems. I've worked with all four and they are reliable. The office has given us enough equipment to stage a small war of our own. I supervised the loading of it myself.'

'Right.' Kelday was unsure how much Mitchell knew, or indeed wanted to know. He was a good man to have by your side when it got rough and he asked few questions.

'We're not sure what we're walking into. It may be that past friends become foe, on this one. So keep the team at the ready. What do you make of the Princess and her sleeping partner?'

Mitchell looked back into the cabin.

'If he's her sleeping partner he's one lucky fella. Who are they?'

'They're from the DEA, on a rotational exchange of their Gulf station. The office told me they would be coming along.'

'OK, gents?' the sergeant enquired upon his return. 'I've got a meal to serve you people. Can't have you getting hungry and blaming the air force for not feeding you.'

Kelday and Mitchell returned to their seats on the port side of the aircraft. Shortly after a small meal appeared in front of them on an olive green air force issue tray.

'Sorry about the lack of wine,' the Sergeant said, 'Air force regulations, she's a dry ship.'

Later he returned to remove the trays. Kelday noticed that the male DEA agent had not touched his food and remained asleep. The other rose from her seat and headed towards the small washroom at the rear. Kelday intercepted her upon her return.

'Did you enjoy your air force meal?' he asked.

'I've tasted worse,' she replied, settling back into her seat. He crouched down beside her.

'You never answered my question.'

'And what was that?' Her tone was defensive.

'I asked you how long you had been with the DEA?'

'And I didn't reply,' she answered.

The Sergeant appeared. 'Has he finished with his tray, Ma'am?'

'He hasn't touched his meal, but you can take it away.'

As the Sergeant removed the tray it nudged the right arm of the sleeping passenger off the arm rest so that it swung loosely between his chair and the bulkhead. Such a movement, even to one who is deeply asleep, would have, should have, roused him from his slumbers. His failure to awake caught the attention of both Kelday and the Sergeant. To Kelday it looked as though the Latin gentleman in the leather jacket would wake no more. He was dead.

They touched down at Bahrain International Airport six hours later. Their mission precluded any thought of a diversion, dead agent or no dead agent. They would proceed to Dubai and let the US military authorities deal with the problem. Throughout the remaining hours of the flight John Mitchell, along with a crew member, examined the body, having first removed it to a clear area at the back of the plane among the freight. There was nothing to indicate anything other than death by natural causes. Later, Mitchell remarked that he found it strange that a frequent flyer who took travel pills was bereft of a further supply. A casual search of the body and his hand luggage had confirmed his ID but failed to find pills of any nature. At one stage, the Captain had come back and asked questions of the deceased's companion. She had answered factually, with little display of emotion. Throughout, her demeanour had remained composed and professional. Whether she was DEA or FBI would be something Kelday was compelled to leave to another day.

The hot desert air on stabs of bright sunlight hit them as the side fuselage door was opened on the tarmac at the US air base, Bahrain. Waiting for them at the bottom of the steps was the Gulf resident officer, a team of US Navy policemen and a number of local officials. While the police impounded the aircraft, crew and remaining passenger, Kelday's team and equipment were driven to two army Iroquois helicopters and flown along the coast to the semi-autonomous Emirate State of Dubai. There they learned that not only had the Professor failed to arrive, but that John Mitchell had become something of a prophet. Kazakh Air 203, an internal flight, had not left the capital Astana, in the north, for Almaty in the south due to mechanical problems.

Stepnogorsk, Kazakhstan

Azat is a Kazakh word meaning liberty, not that Professor Vasily Batioushenkov could or would wish to speak the native language of the country in which he had spent so many years. Rather it was how he felt. The death of the young woman whose photograph he now held in the worn wooden frame had released him from his self-imposed internment. He had long ago lost hope that she might one day join him in Kazakhstan and leave the world into which she had degenerated. He had long ago lost hope that he would ever again live under the same roof with his daughter. The young face in black and white that stared up at him from the frame, no longer existed. Even before he had been informed of her death, the photograph was redundant. The woman with eyes that shone and skin so smooth, the child whose weight he could still feel sitting on his lap, the baby who could have grown up to be like her mother, had been removed by the criminal greed of others. Immured by her own weakness, the person he had visited in a Moscow clinic, years earlier, had not been Zoya Natalya Batioushenkov but a creature of doll-like proportions, the fetidness of whom had revolted him. As a micro-biologist he knew the structure and effects of the genus Enythraxylum on the human condition. Eighty-five per cent of the world's illicit cocaine is of the novogranatense species and Zoya was just another one of its victims. The drug had probably been supplied by her brother, Dimitri, whose affluent existence among St Petersburg's criminal fraternity had attracted her to the same city where their father and mother had first met on a bridge, over the frozen Bolshaya Neva.

His years at the Leningrad Biopreparat Research Institute, before his fall from grace, had been both productive and satisfying. He and Vladimir Pasechnik had carried out some of the early work on bacteria, including plague and tularaemia. They had been part of a research programme that at its acme stretched across the USSR, employed 60,000 and had an annual budget of nearly $1 billion. Those were heady days. Flattered by his recruitment onto the team at Biopreparat he was ignorant of the brief given to Pasechnik by General Ogarkov and the Ministry of Defence. In 1974, Pasechnik had been asked to set up a high-tech laboratory in Leningrad, no expense spared. The laboratory had been established to study the characteristics surrounding the stability of micro-organisms used in biological weapons. Once the scale of ambition had been lifted from Batioushenkov's eyes by a wife who questioned, in a country where it was safer to accept, he saw something of the true nature of his labour. But, in defiance of the gods, a belief in the Party and in mother Russia had driven him to continue the devil's work, buoyed on by its success and the anomic praise of his Moscow masters.

Following the publication in the West, of his wife's dissertation on 'Law and Reality', Pasechnik had failed to both support and protect himself and his family from the Moscow wolves, the result of which was their expulsion and deportation to the East. Both children, Zoya and Dimitri, were placed with his sister in Gorkey. Dorcas, his wife, had been sentenced to the obligatory twenty-five years in a labour facility for crimes against the state and he to a small research laboratory in Koltsovo, Siberia. His experience and knowledge would not be wasted. They would allow him to continue to serve the State, albeit in a less exalted capacity. There he had worked on the development of a broad spectrum antibiotic to fight anthrax, known as Ciprofloxacin.

It was not until after her death that he realised how close they had been to each other during the years of exile. Just two days' travel on a bus would have taken him from his laboratory to the wire fence behind which she lived and worked each long exhausting day, a day of physical labour for which she was neither anatomically nor mentally suited. Her whereabouts had been kept from him and all attempts to find her had come to nothing. The letters – she had been allowed to write once a month – arrived en masse one fine spring day, wrapped in a silk scarf, within an official brown envelope. They had been sent, not from the east but from Moscow. He found it impossible to read the letters. She had ceased to exist for him from the moment they had put her on the train, two days before his own journey eastward. Later, relatives in Israel wrote, asking for details. He had not replied.

Keeping alive some contact with the children, however, had been possible. At first his sister had dutifully written once a month and there had been the occasional photograph. This had trailed off over the years to the point where he only heard from her when money was needed. Then she wrote to say that she had remarried and that Zoya and Dimitri would have to move out to make room for their new step cousins, once or twice removed. Homes were found for them both, five hundred kilometres apart. Later he heard that Dimitri had gone into the army and that Zoya had contracted gonorrhoea. It need not have been so. Perhaps if he had not married a Jew he would have been able to stay in Leningrad and given Pasechnik a run for his money. If, as his teachers at school had wanted, he had become a lecturer, instead of a micro-biologist, they would still be together, living in Moscow or Leningrad, with a dacha for holidays. Had she not been a writer with a political conscience they might still be together. There had been so many ifs. The new so-called freedoms that had swept through the old USSR like the first snow, might even have brought a move to the West, to America or London in the steps of the traitor Pasechnik, lured to the United Kingdom as a Moscow street dog to a meat scrap. Not that he had himself been without offers. The British, on a number of occasions, had made less than discreet overtures concerning a future in the West. Once, on a rare visit to Almaty, he had been approached by a German oil engineer, whom he assumed to be working for the Stasi, but who turned out to be an agent of the CIA. It had been a moment of triumph, to send him packing.

With the death of his daughter a point of resolution had been reached that now allowed him to leave Stepnogorsk. Although he had been many kilometres from Zoya, while she was alive he had felt a closeness. It was something he could not have explained, had anyone been remotely interested. The conflation of emotional and physical distance had inexplicably relieved the pain of his isolation and his loss as a father. The futile but innate feeling of protection he had for her remained as strong as when she had been taken away by his sister, in another life. His need to take her in his arms, somewhere she would be safe, had turned into a pain that enclosed whatever feeling remained within him. For Dimitri, the errant son, there was nothing but a deep dark hole, where there should have been only love.

In Russia, in the mid-1990s, a small number of oligarchs had become fabulously wealthy during privatisation, while the worn-out populace endured corruption and the collapse of decent civil institutions. Dimitri had been on the periphery of the wealth, eager to take his place in the centre. His chance had come in 1998, with the collapse of the rouble, when he had made contact with an Estonian drug baron. By becoming a barterer, Dimitri worked his way into the centre, on the leaf of the coca plant. Cocaine, it is said, contaminates everything it touches, and becomes infectious. The son of Professor Vasily Batioushenkov and the late Dorcas Sara Batioushenkov, brother to Zoya Natalya, was more than eager to be contaminated and to infect others, if it provided him with power and a lavish lifestyle.

The Professor had not freely chosen to live in Kazakhstan. In that he was like many others. Most had come as victims, deported as anti-social elements. During the thirties, all Chinese and Koreans living in Eastern Siberia had been uprooted and shipped like cattle, under Stalin's orders, westward to Kazakhstan. Between 1959 and 1970 the population had been increased by forty per cent with Russians, Ukrainians and Belarussinas. It had become the human dumping ground of the USSR. So many came that Kazakhs made up less than half the population. After the collapse of the USSR, Kazakhstan achieved its independence. Since then little had changed for Russians living, as he did, in the north, where Russiafication was well advanced and Kazakhs were in the minority. But for those in the south, particularly in Almaty, nationalist sentiment was such that non-Kazakhs were being made to feel like foreigners, no matter that they had been born and brought up in Kazakhstan and that some families had lived among the Kazakhs for 250 years. The Kazakh tongue was the official language and everywhere there were signs of Kazakh revanchism. 'Kazakhization' was official policy.

In July 2000, the National Centre for Biotechnology of the Republic of Kazakhstan organised an international conference on

'Biotechnological Development in Kazakhstan'. Among its many aims was the evaluation of the dismantlement process of the former biological weapons facility at Stepnogorsk. The facility was in a state of advanced decay, Moscow having ceased to finance their work following the seizure of power by the reactionary Yeltsin, whose drunken sententious raving on the roof of a tank had spelt the end of all hope for his country. The failure of the army to rise up and crush the usurper Yeltsin had been the final betrayal. It had abandoned the Party and Russia to all that they had fought against for so long, forfeiting the sacrifices of three quarters of a century. That they had abandoned Stepnogorsk was but a postscript.

In Pushkin's *Mednyi Vsadnik* (*The Bronze Horseman*) the poor clerk Evgeni stands before the imposing statue of state power, in the form of Peter the Great and curses Peter's inhuman wilfulness, which he blames for his fiancée's death. Through an hallucinatory experience he is cured of his rebelliousness, after which, whenever he passes the statue of the emperor, his manner shows respect and fear. The Professor had his own statue, that of Lenin, erected in the grounds at Stepnogorsk. Unlike the poor clerk Evgeni, he was not rebellious. Against whom or what should he rebel? It was not the Party that had erred, but those within who, from jealousy, malice or personal gain, had conspired against him and his family. Because others had lost their way, was that an excuse to rebel? Like Pushkin, the Professor recognised, that Peter (the Party) had done Russia great service. Then one day, shortly after the closure of the laboratory, from the window of his small apartment, he watched the local Kazakh authorities remove his statue. It had been taken away on a truck, like so much garbage.

Many at Stepnogorsk had left for Russia or moved to surrounding towns. Fear of international investigation and retribution for labours past had motivated some to change their name and start afresh as someone who had not soiled their hands in the furtherance of BW. Although no longer paid he had worked to the end, until the doors of his laboratory had been sealed. Thereafter he continued in the home-made laboratory constructed within the small one-bedroom apartment in the drab

Stalinist block the state had allocated to him upon his arrival in Stepnogorsk. His emotional investment in Zoya had been both sustaining and draining for a life devoted to labour, the very nature of which had changed, yet the passion remained. He would leave Kazakhstan an old and tired man, but with the intellectual rights to half a century of satanic labour.

Dubai

Captain Avraham Guriel of Israeli Military Intelligence, otherwise known as AMAN, sat crammed among the other passengers aboard the crowded *abra*, as the water taxi made its way between the many trading vessels of the Creek, which separates the two towns, Deira to the north and Bur Dubai to the south. He had boarded at the Al-Sabkha terminal for the short journey across to Bur Dubai, for his meeting with Iqbal Patel. To his right the city skyscrapers cast early afternoon shadows over the Dhow wharf, a hive of activity, with all manner of cargoes being handled between boat and shore. Beneath the *abra*'s narrow canvas canopy the heat was oppressive and he was pleased to be rid of the winter suit, left behind in an airport locker, in Athens, the previous day. He could smell the spices from the Deira Souq and thought he could hear the sound of tin being worked by hand in the Murshid. He had last been in the United Arab Emirates during the time of unrest in Sharjah. Then, as now, he was working with the Indian Gulf community.

When Sheikh Muhammad Bin Rashed al-Maktoum built Dubai from the desert floor he created a need for labour that could not be satisfied from among his own people. As with other Gulf States the need would be met by, among others, Palestinians, Filipinos and Indians.

Indians make up the largest national group in the emirate, surpassing the local population. Along with their sweat labour they have brought wealth, their culture and enterprise to the region, with both Urdu and Malayalam, the language of Kerala, widely spoken. However, for all that they contribute to Dubai, non-resident Indians do not enjoy citizenship. Nor, until 2002, were they allowed to own property. Such deprivation is of little concern since, for over 200 years, the Indian population has been well treated and allowed to trade and make money in a free economy within a tolerant society. It was among such a community that AMAN had established a working relationship.

The water taxi slammed up against the wharf and Guriel joined the late afternoon crowd fanning out into the streets of Bur Dubai. Turning left he skirted the Dubai Souq and made his way towards the Bastakia Quarter. There had been much building since his last visit, but not so much that he could not find his way to the small office block in which the Patel family traded, away from the city centre and an early example of Dubai's rise from the desert. He took the stairs to the second floor and walked into the outer office in which sat a small, perfectly groomed sari-clad receptionist. In Jerusalem, he observed, it would be hard to find such a refreshing sight at the end of a working day.

'Mr Lindsay?' she enquired. 'Mr Patel is expecting you, please go in.'

Iqbal Patel rose from behind a large teak desk. He was short, with slicked-down hair and a small but well-manicured moustache. He displayed Anglomania, not only in his manner of dress, a tropical suit cut in the London style, but also in the way he walked, which he did with British military precision. Indeed, his every gesture was cultivated to display a love for the customs and manners of a country he had only visited, but been brought up to revere. At his briefing, Guriel had been informed that Patel could be trusted. It was something he would accept until disproved. An on-going trawl through the family's past and in particular through that of Iqbal's, had produced nothing that would raise any doubt. Over the years, the Agency had sought his help and that of the extended Patel family, on a number of occasions, never to be disappointed. But loyalty could be an ephemeral commodity. There existed one unique, if not eccentric, caveat. Patel was never to be prevailed upon to take part in an operation that was aimed at the United Kingdom or any of Her Britannic Majesty's citizens. Such a request, if made, was sure to be denied and would sully their relationship. Professor Vasily Batioushenkov was not, nor ever had been a citizen of Great Britain and as such was game for the hunting.

'Lovely to see you, Mr Lindsay. I trust you had a good trip?' The handshake was firm and short. 'It's always nice to have a visit from our American customers. Will you take tea? Or should I be offering bourbon?'

'Tea will do just fine. You have heard that our consignment has been delayed?'

'Yes, indeed. So very disappointing, don't you know. It does however give us more time to arrange for proper onward shipment. It is very good of your company to again place your business with the House of Patel. We are, of course, always ready to help.'

Looking around, he continued, 'We are perfectly safe here. This office is swept once a month and all communication equipment is serviced by my family. Feel free to say what you wish.'

'We're always grateful of the service provided by your company and we have the greatest regard for your business methods. I'm instructed to inform you that payment will be through our normal procedure.' The offer of unrestricted speech was not taken up.

'Thank you.' From an oryx box of exquisite craftsmanship, Patel, the patriarch, offered a Turkish cigarette. 'Perhaps you would prefer American?'

'No thanks.' The slap slap of the large ceiling fan carved into the sound that emanated from the street below. The fans were a feature of the House of Patel, for whom the convenience of air-conditioning was a modernity more suited to less traditional traders. The swish of a sari and the sound of leather sandals on tile heralded the serving of tea. He could smell the faint odour of a perfume he was familiar with, but could not identify. The door closed silently as she returned to the outer office.

'Mr Lindsay,' he began, 'you may have heard of the unfortunate accident experienced this morning by some visiting gentlemen from Beirut. The car in which they were travelling caught fire. In the Satwa district, I understand. There were no survivors. The Lebanese Consol seems unconcerned. Now why is that do you think?'

'I couldn't say,' he replied.

'My friend in the local police department informs me that they found, within the carnage, as well as a quantity of firearms, the burnt photograph of an elderly gentleman in a suit that could only be of Russian origin. I find that interesting, don't you?'

Guriel looked into the ingenuous face of his host. 'Accidents happen. How do you suppose it caught fire?'

The Professor's welcoming committee had been reduced. Whom he should thank for such a blessing was problematic.

'As you say, accidents do happen. It was, by all accounts, a conflagration of some magnitude. As our hosts would say, "Inshallah". Rest assured, Mr Lindsay, that your business will receive our undivided and individual attention. The consignment will be taken care of. Will you be staying in the Emirate long?'

'My business will be completed once the consignment has been forwarded.'

'Such a pity, there is so much to see in Dubai. Perhaps we will do more business together in the future and next time your visit will not be so brief.'

The House of Patel had many faces. They were respectable members of Dubai's prestigious India Club and traders with distinction throughout the region for over one hundred years. Their tentacles of commerce reached as far west as London and eastward to Hong Kong, as well as into the Indian Mafia that operates throughout the Gulf, from Kuwait in the north to Oman in the south.

'As you know, our company does quite a lot of business in the Gulf. I'm sure our paths will cross again,' he replied. Guriel, unlike many within the organization, understood the need for and approved of the new order in Jerusalem. AMAN, like its sister organization the MOSSAD, had taken to enlisting the help of foreign groups, for certain adventures. It followed a severe bout of cost cutting and a number of disastrous operations, commencing with the Lillehammer fiasco, when a Moroccan-born waiter had been mistaken for the notorious terrorist Ali Hassan Salameh and killed by the MOSSAD operatives, most of whom were subsequently caught and put on trial. AMAN suffered similarly in Japan, when the kidnapping of a Saudi assassin went spectacularly awry causing the agents to flee in disarray, only to reappear on the front page of every Japanese daily. Both organizations were safe within their milieu – the large cities of Germany, France, the United States and in their backyard among the nations of the Middle East. Norway and Japan had been salutary lessons.

Removed from their habitual surroundings, without an established network, they had been exposed to failure. In a world awash with terror groups and criminals it was both prudent and economical to utilise the skilled labour available. Kept at arm's length, through such fronts as the Patels, it provided a solution with few risks. It was only a short step from there to using such personnel nearer to home. And denial was so much easier if the miscreants were of foreign origin and, as with the Gulf Mafia, already tarred by the police of several nations, in the unlikely event of their use ever being traced back to AMAN. The contract was as simple as it was unambiguous. The House of Patel would, on behalf of AMAN and for an undisclosed sum, prevent Professor Batioushenkov from ever leaving Dubai, should he eventually arrive in the Emirate.

'Unfortunately British Airways do not operate from Kazakhstan to Dubai,' Patel continued disappointedly, 'otherwise we would have been able to transact our little business on schedule, Mr Lindsay. Even our own fine carrier, Emirates, sees little profit in such a route. We are reliant on Kazakh Air, a fate one would wish on few travellers. Who knows. They may end up doing our work for us. In such an event, of course, we would not expect remuneration.'

'I'm sure that my office would see that you were in no way financially disadvantaged, should the consignment go astray.'

'That is indeed most generous. You are, I believe, staying at the *Metropolitan*. Allow me to arrange for a car to meet you at the Deira *abra* dock.'

'Thanks, but no thanks. I prefer to walk.'

'At least let me send someone over with you in the water taxi,' he protested.

'That won't be necessary.' He rose to leave. 'I'll be at the hotel. You will contact me when you hear something?'

'The very moment. You will be informed when the aeroplane leaves Almaty and whether or not your consignment is on board. Perhaps we could meet for coffee in the morning. Shall we say ten o'clock, at your hotel?'

It occurred to Guriel, as he sat in the water taxi watching the skyscrapers light up the evening sky above the Creek, that to commune with Patel in the hotel coffee shop would be a display laid on for the benefit of his rivals and potential customers. A sophisticated and wealthy man such as Patel would not normally frequent such an establishment, whatever the brochure said concerning the Metropolitan's cuisine. Dubai was a small place in which to trade and the name of Patel was known by all. For Guriel, the delay of Kazakh Air 550 presented an opportunity to learn more about the Patel dynasty.

Sitting in the small boat he felt rested and at ease. The final call to prayer through a distant speaker phone echoed across the Creek. The boatman and all the other believers on board would have just a half hour in which to pray, the conditions being too cramped on the vessel. The sound of the water swirling by the *abra* in the evening air reminded him of fishing trips with his father, before the cancer had taken hold. Like father like son, but unlike his father he had beaten the disease. By the time his father's condition had been diagnosed sentence had been pronounced. Malignant cells had detached from the primary tumour and circulated into the lymph and bloodstream. His immune system, already depleted by a childhood spent in a Gulag, received further harm while serving with AMAN during the Iraqi invasion of Kuwait. There was nothing left with which to fight the cancer. He and others of a small Israeli infiltration team had been exposed to extreme pollution, following Saddam's senseless burning of the Burgan oilfield. The Burgan field was second largest in the world, after the Ghawar field in Saudi Arabia, and its destruction had caused an extreme environmental disaster throughout the region. For Guriel there was a reckoning with the Butcher of Baghdad that had yet to be transacted. His own battle with the disease had been won through an early intervention programme introduced within the service. It had been suggested, following surgery, that he might like to consider early retirement or a position behind a desk. Ruth had returned to work as a teacher and encouraged him to leave AMAN. The boys, Aarran and Moshe, were both at high school and close to independence. Soon they would be in the army and then university. With a small pension and Ruth's salary they would survive.

We are, however, if not the sum total of what has gone before, at least a part thereof. His grandfather had been one of the founding members of AMAN, but had gone down with his boss, Benjamin Gibli, in the aftermath of the Lavon affair. Only ten senior officers had ever been dismissed from their post. Having such a stain on your family is hard to carry in as small a nation such as Israel. He was never recalled to serve his country, the disapprobation turning him into a recluse, living alone in a caravan in the Negev, while his wife eked out an existence in their small apartment in Tel Aviv. He had been found by a German geologist, sitting under an awning, his dead eyes staring out across the desert. In his right hand he held a letter of commendation from President Chaim Weizmann. Neither Guriel's grandfather or father had been allowed to complete their service to Israel. His grandfather, due to excessive loyalty and, his father, through ill health. He, Avraham Guriel, if only out of filial piety, would correct the record.

Jerusalem, he surmised, would already know of the delay concerning the Professor's arrival. The elimination of Baghdad's reception team, if that was who they were, removed one obstacle. But there would be others who would attend the party, intentions unknown. In the past, he had worked with both American and British agents, but now Israel would act alone. Guriel had been briefed on the importance attached to the Professor's attempted transit through Dubai. Quite why Jerusalem was adamant he should not complete his journey did not concern him. There were rumours. There were always rumours, with every operation. What threat an elderly Russian could pose to his country was the concern of others. With the assistance of the House of Patel he would complete his allotted task and return to Israel.

The *abra* glided beside the wharf and Guriel set off for the Metropolitan Hotel. It was as he approached the roundabout by the Perfume Souq, that he saw in the mirror of a parked car, a slight figure wearing the traditional *dish-dasha*, on his head a lace skull cap, the taqia, rather than the more formal *gutra*. It was someone he had seen only a few minutes before, as he alighted from the boat. The man had been standing near the dock looking out across the Creek. One of the basic tenets of fieldcraft is to see that which is out of place. It may be the presence or absence of an object or a person. Inapposite behaviour. Such observations are often subconscious and can be retrospective. Whoever was following him must have known of his meeting with Patel. The Al-Noor Hotel appeared on his left and he stepped inside. To the right of the deeply carpeted reception area a lounge ran the length of the hotel front. He took a seat from where he would be able to see all who passed. The traffic was heavy along Al-Soor Street, its noise penetrating the double glazing of the hotel. The garish lights of the duty-free shops opposite coloured the pedestrians on the sidewalk. A large tourist bus glided by from which bored Asian travellers stared mindlessly into the hotel. After a while he left by the door he had entered and resumed his journey. The tail was there, keeping a full block behind. At the Metropolitan he recovered his key from a disinterested clerk and took the elevator to his room on the fifth floor.

As he entered the phone rang. The clipped accent of Mr Patel was immediately identifiable.

'Mr Lindsay. I'm glad you have returned safely. Even here in the jewel of the Gulf we have our miscreants. As our guest I would not like anything to happen to you.'

'Thanks for your concern. Was that one of your people that followed me back to the hotel?'

'Mr Lindsay, if you saw someone following you he was not from the House of Patel. No doubt the person who followed you back to your hotel was a policeman. I shall find out more from my friend, who is a police officer, in the morning. I look forward to our meeting. Good night.'

Bahrain

'Ms Cranley, until we find out what your partner died of, or we receive instructions from Washington, you are stuck right here with us at 5th Fleet Headquarters,' the Provost Marshall informed her. 'Your people at Arlington aren't being very helpful. So let's go over it again. You were passengers on the air force flight that came in from Washington earlier today, and you are on a rotational exchange with your office in Bahrain?'

'Correct. And, as a US Government employee, I demand the right to use a phone.' If she could make just one call to Washington she would be free to go.

'Here we are under military jurisdiction, Ms Cranley. As a US civilian, you have your constitutional rights, but we are technically on foreign soil. The Bahrain authorities would prefer that the US Navy handle the investigation. It was a military flight, everyone on board was an American citizen and the death occurred over international waters. But I guess we still have the option of handing you over to them, until this is all sorted out. Somehow I don't think you would like that. Do you want to talk to a Navy lawyer? They are the best in the world.'

'I want to use a phone,' she demanded.

'Perhaps if you would tell us who you want to phone we can consider your request.' A Latino Navy policewoman sat attentively by the door of the small room in which Ms Cranley had been detained. Outside she could hear the sounds of a busy airport, with aircraft taking off and landing continuously. The room was windowless and on her one visit to the toilet she had seen only an empty office and a cell-like door adjacent to the room in which she was being held.

'This can all be straightened out if you would just let me make a call. And in private.'

The Provost Marshall was a big man who, but for his age, with his cropped hair and starched white uniform, could have walked out of a recruiting poster. He sat opposite her, studiously moving a polystyrene coffee cup to the middle of the table.

'We have a problem. When we received notification of your flight from Washington, which we both know was not your all-regular air force movement, flight control were expecting six passengers. Not eight. Those folks you were travelling with were NCVIP.'

'What, in plain American, does that mean?'

'Non-combatant VIPs. High priority. However, you do both appear on the aircraft manifest, which means that you were legally on board.'

'That's a relief,' she interrupted sarcastically.

'OK so far. Obviously, whoever sanctioned your travel failed to notify air force movements, who in turn failed to notify us. Ms Cranley, who was it who sanctioned your travel?'

'If the Navy's communications are lousy that is their problem. I suggest you call in Bell Telephone to fix them.'

'It's a simple question. Your local DEA office says that both resident officers are out of Bahrain and can't be contacted. The Drug Enforcement Administration at Arlington, who you say you work for, don't seem to want to know you or your travelling companion. The documents you have shown us, well, frankly they don't add up to much. It's not exactly office hours back home so perhaps in the morning, when they come on deck, they'll give you the all-clear.' A knock on the door interrupted him. A note was handed to the policewoman who, in turn, passed it to the Provost Marshall. The latter rose from the table and moved to the door.

'I'll go and see about this phone call you want to make. Meanwhile if you can think of anything more you want to tell us, about you or your buddy, we would like to hear it.'

A few minutes later he returned and resumed his seat opposite her.

'You lied to the US Navy.' The accusation came out as a personal affront.

'What do you mean?' she replied.

'The business of you working for the DEA is crap. Right?'

'Who said?'

'Washington. You're with the FBI. Why the hell didn't you say so in the first place, instead of giving us all this salami about the DEA?'

'Like you, I do as I'm told. If you had let me use a phone this could have been... Never mind. Can I go now?'

'Yes. But we may want you to answer some more questions about your buddy. We still want to know more about him. Perhaps he was with your agency, as well? Our surgeons reckon he died of natural causes. But that has yet to be confirmed by an autopsy, which will probably be done Stateside. Let us know before you leave Bahrain.' His relief at being rid of a particularly thorny problem – anything to do with civilians was a problem – was tempered by a desire to see her incarcerated, if for no other reason than for the time the US Navy has wasted.

'If I leave the Gulf I'll be sure to let you know.'

'You do that. Remember, Ms Cranley, nobody takes the US Navy for a ride.'

An hour later she was on board a commuter aircraft for the short flight eastward along the coast to Dubai, where she booked into Le Meridian hotel.

Sleep was quick in coming, but not before she had thought through the events of the previous few days. When the phone had rung in her apartment she had expected it to be her mother, calling from Miami, with more complaints about the food, Cubans and the humidity. That it was her boss came as something of a relief. That he wanted her to report back to work was also a deliverance, extracting her from the solipsistic Dean Casey, a confident suitor whose ego matched the car he drove. It had been his British Jensen Mark III Interceptor, with the 6.3 litre engine, that had first interested her. Find first the car, then the man. Their relationship had revolved around the right-hand drive vehicle. A ménage à trois with a difference, but it was a relationship that still ran a familiar course.

Male agents often spoke of the social advantage that came with the secrecy surrounding their work. But for Kate Cranley, relationships outside of the aberrant world of the FBI proved problematic. Relating to someone, even the owner of a Jensen Mark III Interceptor and yet telling them nothing of yourself or your work, had proved difficult and incongruous. Other female agents, known in the Bureau as 'split-tails' or just plain 'skirts', had experienced similar problems. Dean Casey had been an infrequent visitor to her apartment, but a lodger in her affections. He had come, when his ego allowed, emotionally too close for comfort, making her flight to the Middle East a welcome escape. Kate had severed a string of failed relationships, the likes of which had left her often to question her own sexual orientation, not that she felt in any way attracted to other women. It was simply that a number of broken dreams had made her bereft of any rational reason as to why she moved from one man to another. It cast doubt on whether she might ever find, what the women's magazines crassly refer to as, 'a meaningful relationship'.

It is in the nature of us all to want everything. And there is also something intrinsic within each of us to question the value of that which we want, once it is obtained. To hold it at arm's length and, perhaps for the first time, ask the hard questions. Dean had been within reach. She had only to put out that small flame of doubt that lay within her for their association to grow into something she could accept as worth the sacrifice, for sacrifice there would be. But, after asking the questions of herself, the doubt remained.

She had first joined the FBI as a clerk, direct, like so many others, from the University of Maryland. At the time William H Webster was in his final years as Director and actively promoting the hiring of minorities and females. After a short spell behind a computer she had applied to become an agent. Agents who start as clerks are known within the Bureau as 'clagents', a derogative term but one with which she could live. To graduate from Quantico, Virginia, the FBI Academy, it is necessary, among other things, to qualify twice out of three attempts, with the Smith and Western Model 1076 semi-automatic ten-millimetre pistol as well as demonstrate proficiency with the Remington Model 870 shotgun and the nine-millimetre Carbine. Kate Cranley had never, until entering the FBI, become even remotely familiar with a firearm, of any description. Her 113 hours of firearms training had turned into something of a trial, the failure of which meant dismissal from Quantico. At the end of her training she had approached her test on the firing range with foreboding. To her surprise the first attempt had gone well and she had achieved the required cluster that constituted a pass. Her second attempt proved disastrous and it seemed that the previous months of arduous training were to come to nothing and that she was destined to return to a computer screen, complete with morning and afternoon coffee breaks. With everything riding on her final shoot, a situation that was the dread of all trainees, she attempted to remain calm and collected. Taking up the firing position for the third and final time, the noise around her faded into the voice of a Greek chorus. Her heart pounded so violently that she thought it would spoil her aim.

Later, along with other successful candidates, she celebrated. It was a night about which the memory cells were thankfully blank.

Her first posting had been to the field office in Denver, where she developed an interest in both skiing and the drug industry. Operation Polar Cap was winding down, having netted the US Government $1.2 billion in cocaine funds. It had been a joint FBI/DEA operation that had run for two years. This was followed by a move back east to the Washington Metropolitan Field Office, where she attended training courses and was admitted into the Bureau's drug section. A spell with the DEA, where she had excelled, confirmed her position as a drug agent, within the Bureau.

Shortly after taking up the post in Washington she had been invited to a party. It was the sort thrown for agents and their spouses in order that they might become better acquainted with one another away from the office and, since she had no one with whom she could attend, it had been with some reluctance that she rang the door bell at number 12 Franklin Drive. Although relatively new to the Agency she had attended a sufficient number of similar functions to know what a pain they could be, the wives complaining about the low salaries and the next posting, the men drinking too much and either ignoring or pawing any woman other than the one with whom they had arrived. It was February and Aldrich Ames of the CIA had recently been arrested for spying for the USSR. She later remembered how scathing they had all been towards both Ames and their sister organisation. There was no doubt that such a traitor could only have existed, undetected for such a long period, among the ranks of 'the arrogant, self-centred bastards' who inhabited the CIA.

She particularly remembered the behaviour of a tall physically awkward man, holding forth on the need for patriotism and integrity within the service, a man whose nebbish wife sat deep in a leather chair alone and, if not forgotten, ignored. Aided by drink, he had became quite agitated and suggested to all that with the CIA so heavily infiltrated, they alone stood between democracy and the pagan Soviet hordes. It was more the ranting of a Pentecostal minister than that of a red-neck loyal American and, although the subject may have been political, the delivery was religious. He was from Headquarters, the Office of the Assistant Director for the National Security Division. His name was Robert P Hanssen, who, on 6 July, 2001, pleaded guilty to espionage charges that spanned twenty-two years. She had been in the company of a master spy. Throughout that evening he had not spoken to her, or for that matter, any other woman there present and when introduced, had been less than perfunctory in his greeting. She had assumed that he was of the type that had little interest in women. A man's man, put on this earth if not to hunt and kill then at least to supervise those who did. After his arrest, at a drop site in a Fairfax park, rumours and counter rumours had rapidly circulated within the Agency. Not only had Hanssen hidden from the world the true nature of his being, he had done so with a libidinal energy, the strength of which was known only to his wife. It had been just a meeting, at a party, but it was one Kate would not forget.

As an FBI drug agent, her selection for the operation in the Middle East had been dependent upon acceptance by the DEA. Whenever the Bureau picked up a DEA slot they had the right of refusal. A woman working in the Middle East, even a few years into the new millennium, could be a problem. Throughout most of the Gulf there existed an enlightened attitude towards Western women, as long as they were suitably accompanied. But she would be working alone. The Bureau had, after a series of phone taps, confirmed that there existed within the DEA, a scheme for the eradication of a foreign national in Dubai. Such an undertaking was not beyond their brief, but it was unusual.

Normally they would attempt to extradite such a target or allow local authorities to carry out an arrest, on information received. During a routine cross-check of persons under international surveillance, something surfaced indicating that the CIA was interested in the same individual. However, discreet enquires among some of the other thirty-five US agencies tasked with fighting the drug menace, proved fruitless. The National Drug Intelligence Centre in Johnstown, Pennsylvania, were 'unable to assist'. Since the NDIC had no means of collecting its own intelligence, but relied upon the Bureau, CIA and the DEA, such a response came as no surprise. The Centre was more of a job creation programme than a serious narcotics fighter.

At a level high above the lowly status she inhabited within the Bureau, it was decided that an agent would be dispatched to Dubai. The relationship between the powerful intelligence community, White House directives notwithstanding, could be both anomic and dissonant. Events of September 2001 had left both the CIA and FBI floundering in a slough of mutual recrimination. No individual or authority was clear of suspicion. For the FBI, investigating the operation of another government agency, such as the DEA, had become routine. Within the Bureau such work was labelled 'auditing'. Her travelling companion aboard the special air force flight had been a bona fide DEA employee, the late Sam Dyson. They had met just before boarding when he had told her of his habit of taking a pill to sleep the flight away. His death had been unfortunate and for her a breach of cover, at least with the US Navy, a service not always noted for keeping secrets. She surmised that the six men from the CIA, spirited away in helicopters upon arrival, were those interested in Professor Batioushenkov, if not in his termination. In Dubai her cover, if one were needed, would be that of an escort, back to Washington, of an American woman wanted in a number of States for fraud and whose feculent behaviour had become an embarrassment to the UAR authorities, not to mention Uncle Sam. Meanwhile, the errant creature would be left to dwell on her lot from the questionable comfort of an Arab jail, until such a time as suited the FBI.

Only the constant hum of the air-conditioning unit remained relevant, as she dropped off to sleep.

Dubai

Captain Avraham Guriel, alias Gerald Lindsay, stepped out for a pre-breakfast walk but failed to notice the black Mercedes parked behind a FedEx truck, one block from his hotel. As he walked towards the Creek the following black Mercedes was careful to keep its presence undetected. It caught up with him just short of the dock. What happened next was observed only by a Pakistani street cleaner, who quickly turned away. The front passenger door opened, blocking his movement forward. He reached for the small pistol inside his shirt, but too late to stop a number of hands force a bag over his head at the same time pinning his arms to his side and pushing him into the car, which immediately accelerated away. His pistol was removed and handcuffs applied, preventing him from responding to the punches that were now being inflicted on his body. They were avoiding his face, aiming for his kidneys. He attempted to twist in the seat, to take the blows on his ribs or back. Eventually they contented themselves with kicking his ankles. Throughout they maintained the silence of trained killers, killers who were in no hurry to practise their trade. From the bag about his head the pungent odour of an exotic spice filled his nostrils. It was a smell like no other he had experienced. Possibly Indian in origin, but not a common spice, nor something you would immediately identify from a casual visit to an Asian restaurant.

They were now driving at a more sedate pace, heading eastward. The road was straight. He could hear the sound of shipping, close by. After approximately one hour they slowed and stopped. The car radio came alive, Arab music blared forth. He became aware of a face close to his own, with only the thin bag separating them. The voice spoke slowly, like that of an automated weather station.

'Jew, we have a message for you to take back to your people. The Voice of Gaza is holding two of your Zionist soldiers. They are alive, but for how long depends on you. Your leaders refuse to talk to us, so you will tell them that if they want their two soldiers to live they will deliver, to our agents in Larnaca, a number of our fighters held in your prisons. You have just twenty-four hours, that is all. The list is in your shirt pocket. Do not lose it, Jew or your soldiers will hang. You have no business here in Dubai. You are finished. Go back to your people if you want to live. Twenty-four hours.' A door opened and the heat from the desert invaded the car. He landed roughly, as they had intended, hitting the sharp stones, sending the message of pain deep into his body. Dust from the departing vehicle filled the bag and he began to choke. Scrambling to his feet his manacled hands tore the bag from his head. His weight on the damaged ankles almost made him crumble to the ground. It was with difficulty that he managed to remain standing and take in his position. They had dumped him beside the main eastbound highway. To his left a heavily laden super-tanker was heading through teal-coloured water for the open sea and, to his right, the desert, the view interrupted by yet another industrial site under construction. A truck roared by sending up yet more clouds of dust. In the distance, towards the city, a small red car was quickly approaching. He watched as it stopped and the driver got out. The young Indian of slight build grinned, as he took Guriel's hands in his own.

'Mr Lindsay, I am from the House of Patel. We are so sorry for your condition and the way you have been treated. It is not the way guests should be welcomed to Dubai. Let us return to town where we can remove these shackles from your wrists. May I help you walk?'

While returning to the city, the young driver explained how they had kept a watch on him since leaving the House of Patel, but had been unable to prevent his abduction. 'Such scum,' he protested, 'they are, I am afraid, far from rare in the Gulf.' They were and had been for a number of years, part of a much larger malodorous group the presence of which was an embarrassment to all in the region. They were a stain on Dubai but, even worse, they adversely affected trade, the free traffic of which was the lifeblood of the House of Patel.

The cityscape loomed up ahead. His body and ankles were screaming for relief from the pain inflicted on them and, as he left the car outside the House of Patel, it was necessary for the driver to help him to the office of the patriarch.

Iqbal Patel was beside himself with what seemed genuine sympathy and concern. 'Mr Lindsay, what can I say? Come, sit down. You will take tea? No, the situation calls for something much stronger. Where is that girl?' The sari entered and left with orders to bring whisky and some means by which the handcuffs might be removed.

'Please accept our most heartfelt apology for what has transpired. It was reprehensible of us to let such a thing occur. We were not sufficiently watchful I think... Such ruffians should be expelled from the Gulf, but only after they have been taught a severe lesson in good manners.'

The sari returned with whisky on a tray, two glasses and a middle-aged man clutching giant bolt-cutters. Once free Guriel took the malt whisky and downed it in one gulp. The liquid hit his empty stomach like a punch. He doubled over.

'Mr Lindsay, are you all right? Please, you are to take it easy. We will call the doctor.'

Once more the sari was summoned. Dr Ramdas Patel must come at once.

'My brother will give you a thorough examination to make sure there is nothing seriously wrong and then we shall eat. I do not suggest another glass of Glen Mhor, it may be deleterious to your health. Food is what you need and we shall send for some. Please excuse me, I have some matters to arrange, including our lunch.' As Patel left the office Guriel caught sight of the sari at her desk. A picture of serenity. There was an oriental inscrutability about her. His own sorry condition not withstanding, the happily married Captain Avraham Guriel felt unsettled by the serene woman in the outer office. The door remained ajar. Patel had moved to another room allowing him to view at some leisure the object of his attention and ruminate on his next move. He felt for the list in his pocket. The message from The Voice of Gaza would have to be relayed at the earliest opportunity and through a secure medium, which, given that he was under surveillance, would not be easy.

Following the decision to use the 'Indian Mafia' for activities in the Gulf, when appropriate, both AMAN and MOSSAD had withdrawn their respective resident officers. Both had kept a permanent presence in the region, AMAN through an agent in Dubai and MOSSAD in Bahrain. Technology now allowed for and economics dictated a change. Cell-phones and computer links had fallen out of favour, being open to interception, often with fatal results. Each operation now had a dedicated rescue contact, with sophisticated communications equipment, supposedly impervious to interception. For Guriel's 'Operation Deborah' it was a *sayan* wireless operator aboard a Panamanian container ship awaiting cargo off Dubai. The vessel was due to sail some three days following the commencement of the operation, time enough, but it had been delayed in the obtaining of a berth at the busy Jebel Ali terminal, a tax-free site and one popular with duty-free shoppers. He would extract himself from the solicitous hands of Patel, once he had seen the doctor and make his way to Jebel Ali. The lives of the two soldiers held by The Voice of Gaza, were of value, every Israeli life was a prize, but they were of secondary importance beside his own operation, which now appeared compromised. His body, however, had another plan. The beating he had taken at the hands of his abductors was worse than he had first thought. Large bruises were forming about his trunk and movement was both painful and difficult. His ankles were an unhealthy colour and swollen. The man upon whom the lives of two Israeli soldiers depended would be going nowhere for a while, without assistance. Unable to confide in Patel he would have to take a risk and use a taxi for the ride to Jebel Ali, trusting that those who were watching could be shaken off.

His prolonged subconscious staring at the sari had not gone unnoticed. She remained at her work, but now cognizant of his attention, her dark, deep-set eyes occasionally meeting his. Then he noticed that she had moved the computer screen so that he could read it and in bold print had written 'It is rude to stare'. As quickly as the message had appeared it was wiped. She resumed her work, but not before turning and smiling at him, a smile that was both pleasant and interesting. What was he to make of such an approach, if indeed that is what it was?

Moments later Iqbal Patel returned with an older man, who looked to be in his early sixties.

'This is Mr Lindsay, of whom I spoke. Mr Lindsay, this is my brother who is a medical doctor. Please use my office as you wish. I shall be along the corridor. After your examination perhaps you will take lunch with us, Ramdas?'

The reply was in Hindi. The invitation had been offered out of politeness, with no thought of acceptance. Left alone with the healer Guriel disrobed.

'You have sustained quite an attack, Mr Lindsay,' the doctor said, washing his hands in the small sink by the window. Unlike his brother he had a slight Canadian accent with flawless English. 'The effects of your attack could have been serious on an older man, but there doesn't seem to be any damage done beyond superficial bruising. Whoever did this to you knew what they were about. No facial damage, the sort of beating designed to leave a message. Wouldn't you agree, Mr Lindsay?'

'It is not the sort of thing I come into contact with on a regular basis, doctor.'

'Is that so? Well, I shall leave you to lunch with my brother. I find the lack of air-conditioning in his domain punishing. Why he prefers fans, I do not know. He insists that it is tradition. But whose tradition are we talking about? He is so Anglo, don't you think?'

As one Patel left so another entered. 'Now we shall take lunch, Mr Lindsay and then my staff will see you back to your hotel, where I shall keep you abreast of developments concerning our little business arrangement. May the rest of your stay be less eventful.'

It was sunset and the fourth call to prayer had gone out to the faithful. A gentle knock at the door made him struggle to his feet. Through the spy-hole he could see the black hair of a woman. Armed only with a small knife, he opened the door to 'the sari' who stood before him, not as she had been dressed at the House of Patel, in traditional costume, but in jeans and a yellow shirt. At first he didn't recognise her.

'May I come in?' She swept past him into the room. He closed the door and turned to face her. She was standing at the foot of the bed, her arms by her side. The sari had not done her justice. She was more round than he had imagined, yet athletic. It was the same person, but a complete transformation. No longer nebbish she exuded all the confidence of a thoroughly modern young woman. He thought her to be in the late twenties, yet in her sari she had seemed so much younger. But a greater surprise came when she spoke. Pure California. The obligatory spell as a junior military attaché in Washington had given him an ear for the regional dialects of the United States, even for those that were idiomatically weak.

'I hope you don't mind me calling on you like this, but when I saw you come into the office this morning you seemed in need of help.' Definitely California. Only then did he realise that he had heard her speak only once, when he had first walked into the office. The voice, like her smile, was pleasant and intelligent.

'Thanks for coming. I wasn't expecting visitors, at least not...' He felt foolish and disturbed at his reaction to her presence. Painfully he sat down on the side of the bed and looked up into her face.

'I am Iqbal Patel's niece, Mahashweta Patel, but I prefer to use my western name, Diana.'

'How do you get Diana out of Mahashweta?' he enquired.

'You don't. If you are a woman living in the House of Patel it's necessary to be someone else when free. And so I make my own world.' She turned away and moved to the window where she stood to one side, looking down at the hotel forecourt below.

'If you are to deal with my uncle there is something you should know. He has started to trade on both sides of the fence. Whatever business you have with him you should be very careful. On the one side he is a regular Indian Gulf trader, a pillar of what passes for society in Dubai. On the other he has started dealing with the trash that feeds the black side of the Emirate. This morning you met the trash. What I'm trying to say is that you must not trust him. I know why you're here and, if the price is right, my uncle will deliver on whatever deal he has struck with you. But these days I think he is running a Dutch auction.'

'I'm sorry. A Dutch auction?'

'He will go to the highest bidder. Your people should know this.' Her reference to his 'people' and not his firm or company, meant that she did indeed know more than was healthy or prudent.

'I'm not sure whether it has anything to do with your beating,' she continued, 'but, a couple of months ago we started getting visitors from Riyadh. People we had never traded with before. They had a lot of money to put about and my uncle was very interested. Since then I've been kept out of the loop. When they visit I'm excluded from the office, but I get to see some of what goes on. Don't ask me what it is they are doing with my uncle, but there are a chain of warehouses along the Gulf, owned or leased by the House Of Patel that have material harmful to, not only your country, but to the whole region.' There it was again, 'Your country.'

'What sort of material?' he enquired.

'That is not important, now. You need to be very careful.'

'Thanks for the warning. But what has all this to do with me?' He would continue the charade for a little longer. 'I came to do a little honest business with your uncle, on behalf of my company in the States, and I get followed, beaten up—' but she would not let him finish.

'A company whose address leads back to a box office in Washington, rented by the cultural minister of the Israeli Embassy, a poor front, Mr Lindsay. Not up to your usual standard, I think. No doubt your people felt that there was no need for a deeper cover, since your stay with us is brief, but you should not underestimate the eyes and ears of our people. There are over thirty million Indians living outside India, scattered clear across the world. Your people had their diaspora in the eighth and sixth century BC. Ours was in the nineteenth and twentieth century. Now our eyes can see all, our ears can hear the world and our noses are in everything.' Embarrassed by the intensity of her delivery she attempted a smile. 'Anyway, I just wanted you to know about Uncle Iqbal.'

He would not put his trust in a prince, but a princess, at least, this princess who was different.

'Thanks for the advice on your uncle. I'll bear it in mind. If you really want to help, I have to get to the Jebel Ali terminal.' It came tumbling out like a young boy telling a suppressed truth. 'Can you take me there?'

'You are being watched.'

'I know. But I have to go. It is, as we Americans say, a big ask, but if I use a taxi…?'

'Why do you have to go to Jebel Ali?'

He did not reply, but stood looking at her in the dim light of the room

After a moment's consideration, she replied, 'You really don't look up to going out on the town, but I will take you. We should leave the hotel separately. That way we stand a much better chance of losing them.' The woman became more interesting the longer he spent in her company.

'Them?' he enquired of her.

'You are a popular man. Not only does my uncle have you under surveillance, so do the local police and, I fear, your friends from this morning. All in all, quite a crowd.'

'How long is the drive to the terminal?' The simple act of looking at his watch sent a sharp pain from his recently manacled wrist.

'About thirty minutes. No more. This is what we'll do. I'll go out the front way. There is a service entrance that leads off the fire stairs, use that and meet me outside the café around the corner, by the photo shop, in five minutes.' She left, he had no time to agree or protest. His cover, perhaps the whole operation may be compromised. It was also evident that, once he had left the hotel he could not return. Stuffing what few things he required into his pockets he vacated the room.

All went as she had planned. Losing their trailers proved easier than expected. Her knowledge of the city's road system was equal to, if not better than those who attempted to follow. After backtracking a number of times and forcing their way through crowded traffic down narrow back streets they found themselves on the main coast road. She drove well with both confidence and style. Perhaps that was the attraction, style. This woman possessed chutzpah and style, the latter quality was one he found wanting in so many Israeli females. Ruth had style, it was something he first noticed about her when they met at university.

Ruth was a sabra with both attitude and style. Well dressed, but not ostentatiously, she had caught the attention of many on the campus, with her intellect and humour. Although they had not attended the same lectures, mutual friends had spoken of her sharp and responsive mind, one that was highly disciplined. Often, over the intervening years, he had thought that he should be teaching Israel's young and it should be Ruth who defended the State. She, however, suffered an endogenous conscience and abhorred violence. As father, he had not been allowed to lay a hand on either of the boys, even when he thought it was most necessary.

Off campus, they had come together on long walks under powder blue Levantine skies beside the beaches of the Ha-Tayalet and in the evening, in the cafés on Sheinken Street and Ibn Gvirol. From their first meeting he had been ineluctably drawn to her. Not shy to display an intellect equal, if not superior, to his own, she had discussed everything with him, from metaphysics to the art of good coffee making, from American films to Simone de Beauvoir. Prior to university, Ruth had elected to fulfil her obligation to the nation by serving, for two years, in a hospital rather than in the army, work that had bought her into contact with the results of terrorism and war and yet, when they did talk of the future, neither expressed a desire to abandon Israel, as so many of their friends had done. The insecurity of their nation had been something they had grown up with, something that was osmotic.

On their walks and over bottomless cups of coffee, they had explored each other's background, each learning more about the other, holding back only that which was not safe or prudent to divulge at that point in their relationship. They were not sparring so much as testing. He found himself wanting to know all there was to know about Ruth. Perhaps much more than he would admit, he needed to know if he would be the first man in her life? It had seemed so very important since he had first realised the depth of his feelings towards her. They were both from liberal Jewish homes, where contact with the opposite sex was considered less of a sin than the consumption of unclean meat, so why was it of such importance? While working in the hospital, she must have met many young men. Soldiers recovering from skirmishes with Israel's Arab neighbours, or airmen recovering from injuries sustained while ejecting from one of Israel's accident-prone fleet of new

French fighters. Had she given herself to one of them during some brief or extended relationship? In the twenty-first century, was not such a fear anachronistic? Was he a frightened boy that he could not accept the possibility? What right had he to ask for that which he could not give? He had not asked for nor expected it of the other women he had taken out, so why was it so important that Ruth be pure? But reason, like logic, was not part of the equation. And what if he were not her first? What then? What if she had been so attracted to another man? Had she not the right, the freedom to do as he had done? For Ruth such an intimacy would have been meaningful. There would have been little that was casual about such a relationship, no matter how brief. And, would the exposure of some past liaison derogate their relationship? He had felt shame at his need to know and at the unidentified underlying reason. As to whether it would make a difference between them, it was something he had, at the time, found impossible to answer.

'You haven't told me what you intend to do once we reach the terminal,' his driver enquired.

'I have to get on board a Panamanian container ship, the *Parthenon*,' he replied.

'Leaving us so soon?' Her response was playful.

'Don't ask. But if you can wait for me…?'

'This taxi goes off line at ten, OK?'

'Understood,' he replied.

'How do you intend to get through security? There are dock police at every entrance.'

'I have no idea. I don't even know if the ship has a berth. The last I heard it was still outside, waiting to come in.'

'So now we need a boat!' she turned and smiled at him.

He was losing control of events. First his abduction, Patel's duplicity and now he was unsure of the exact location of his emergency communication facility. Perhaps, after all, he would please Ruth by accepting retirement, or at least move to a desk in Jerusalem, but in so doing, would he not be engaging in moral flaccidity? Time and the events of the next twenty-four hours, might provide the answer.

The tall lights of the port came into view. Soon they were among floodlit warehouses and duty-free outlets. A three-metre high wire fence appeared ahead and beyond, ships, lined up alongside one of the Gulf's most vibrant windows of opportunity. Trucks of all sizes and shapes moved about, their headlights lost in the port's glare. Illuminated toplifters crabbed their way around with underslung containers. Paralleling the fence, they came to a gate that gave access onto the wharf. None of the ships in view were the *Parthenon*.

'Leave this to me.' She got out of the car and approached the gatehouse in which a number of dock policemen were resting. An Arab will rest whenever and wherever he can. He had always envied their ability to switch off, to relax and conserve both physical and mental energy. However, dock police the world over respond to an attractive woman and it was on that that she was trading. They gathered around her like bees around jam. She had produced from her pocket some form of ID and was gesturing towards the car. One of the men left the group and sauntered over towards him, his machine pistol slung around his chest. He came around the passenger side and stared through the window. What should he do? What could he do but stare back and smile. The policeman emptied the contents of one nostril in the manner of the east and returned to his colleagues. Erect and sure, she was surrounded by admirers whom she addressed in flawless Arabic. After a while she returned to the car, got in and, without speaking, started the engine. The gate opened and they drove onto the quay. Turning right they drove along inspecting the line of ships. Only then did she speak.

'Sometimes being of the House of Patel can be an asset. The *Parthenon* is last in the row. We are in luck, it berthed an hour ago and has just started unloading.'

'I'm impressed. What did you say to those men back there?'

'I told them you were an Israeli spy and that you were out to destroy the entire complex. Was that all right?'

They drove along the line of vessels in silence. The last ship on the wharf came into view, from which a tattered Panamanian flag flew at the stern. Giant container cranes were already at work. Agents and customs personnel were leaving the vessel as they arrived at the gangplank. A guard was mounted, checking the documents of those wishing to board the vessel.

'Here we go again. Follow me and say nothing. If they refuse to let us on board we will have to think of something else.' They both got out of the car and approached the guard. Although she spoke to him in fluent Arabic the guard was more interested in her, than anything she had to say. Why was such a creature entombed in the House of Patel?

The guard eyed her lecherously and Guriel with hostility. After a while the guard stood aside, she moved with him, still talking, at the same time ushering Guriel onto the gangplank. Once on board he made his way as swiftly as his swollen ankles would allow towards the stern and the ship's superstructure. Unchallenged he mounted the series of companionways that led up to the ship's nerve centre. His ankles revolting at the pressure being put on them with each run of the companionway. Since the ship had recently docked, the ship's officers were still at their stations and he quickly located the wireless room. Entering he found two men in uniform.

'I'm looking for Hans Scheuber,' he enquired.

'I am Hans,' replied a thickset man who had a more than passing resemblance to the late Abba Eban, Israel's most famous diplomat and one-time foreign minister. Heavy-jowled with large horn-rimmed spectacles he could, but for his height, have quite easily been mistaken for the eloquent statesman who helped persuade the world to approve the creation of the Jewish State.

For a second they eyed each other. Hans, one of the services many cut-outs, was like a stationmaster waiting for a train that came only once a year, such was his demeanour of expectation.

'Gerald Lindsay, from the States,' Guriel said.

Hans Scheuber addressed his fellow officer in Spanish, who promptly left. Guriel felt in his pocket for the list. He had looked at it upon returning to his hotel room. It carried twelve names, all Arab and none of them known to him. Twelve for two. A numerical distortion that had been a characteristic of all previous exchanges between Israel and her enemies.

Having completed his business with Scheuber he returned the way he had come. Moving along the main deck he saw her continuing to engage the guard in conversation. She was standing seductively close to him and he felt an anger rising from within.

Driving back towards the city he wanted to both take her in his arms and at the same time scold her for the ease with which she had flirted with the Arab guards. He wanted to know more about her, to learn of the two worlds she inhabited, to be better informed about the House of Patel. But they drove in silence.

It was she who first spoke. 'I don't think it would be a good idea to return to your hotel. Whoever was trailing you will be waiting.'

'Fine. I won't ask why you have helped me.'

'That's good because you wouldn't believe me. Will you be visiting my uncle tomorrow?'

'Maybe. It depends. Our business is not yet complete and, until it is I will be sticking very close to the House of Patel.' He found her company threateningly provocative. There had been many other women with whom he had come into contact during operations. None had primed the fire of desire like the one behind the wheel of the car in which he now found himself.

Giving him a card she said, 'That has my cell-phone number and another contact number if you need me again. Leave a message, if I'm not available. I'll drop you off on the next block. There is a small hotel on the corner, run by some friends of mine. Tell them I sent you. Do you have money?'

'Yes, thanks.'

Before he closed the door she added, 'This never happened, OK?'

Left standing on the sidewalk he could only watch her drive away, the rear lights of the car merging into the evening traffic.

...Dubai

George Dolby, of the recently combined security service of the United Kingdom, was used to change. He liked to think that he had adjusted well to the alterations and modifications inflicted on him over the years in both his private and professional life. Had he not reconciled himself to his wife's barrenness and lived with her drinking for all those years; the slow fall into the abyss of alcoholism and subsequent death? The loneliness that had descended on him as he had waited for Emma to reach the end, was that not change enough? As for his career, few were they, among his grade, who had experienced the changes within the service and remained to tell the tale. Change and adjusting had become a way of life throughout the cold war and many were the knives that had penetrated his back, though none fatally. Geography had, on more than one occasion, intervened fortuitously. Being in the right place, he had learnt, was less important than not being in the wrong place. The successive scandals that rocked MI6 throughout the years had failed to affect his position, save to help clear the way ahead of those less fortunate, most of whom were innocent of the spurious charges set beside their names. Seilschaft, although alive and well, had failed to protect many senior officers. By its very nature it had excluded more than it included. As an aside, he could say that he was not arriviste in his dealings with others. Indeed, his lack of ambition had been something upon which the service had often traded. George Dolby was the sure rock upon which the safety of the nation saw one climactic day through to the next. The end of the cold war had thrown his own service, MI6, into something bordering on stasis, relieved only by the international cause célèbre that was terrorism. In the darkness of his own being he would admit that there had been moments, when the symbiotic relationship between the two services had become serried, he had found the alterations and mergers bewildering. Long established branches had swiftly and quietly ceased to exist. Names disappeared off personnel lists. New internal telephone directories were issued, only to be replaced the next day and the ephemerality of most promotions became a characteristic of the time. For some, long nurtured pension schemes were arbitrarily and summarily severed. The house in the sun, near some continental beach, so long desired, would become a 'semi' in Dorset. Somehow, through it all, he had emerged in one aging piece, saved by a lack of ambition. Now he was charged with the recruitment or the removal from service of one Professor Batioushenkov, a man who would have to make his own adjustments to change or die.

He was woken from his reverie by the thud of the high-pressure tyres of his British Airways A360 landing at Dubai International Airport. As he walked along the airbridge the smell of a past long remembered returned. The Middle East had provided some of the golden days of his career, with many friends. The game, to quote Summers, had seemed more interesting, particularly in the Lebanon. Beirut's Corniche, the Tartan Club, the Caves du Roy at the Excelsior had all provided a welcome backdrop for a young operative in search of adventure and excitement.

Muhammad Ibadis stood beyond the barrier, his frame now stooped, the hair grey, but the distinguée remained. Decades rather than years had intervened since they last met, yet his greeting was casual. The nod and an outstretched hand were sufficient acknowledgement of a past spent together. Muhammad was not a devout Muslim. But the pride he exhibited in his faith was that of one who viewed a *giaour* as a lost soul, someone upon whom it was only a matter of time before the light of revelation would shine. Evangelising the lost, however, he would leave to the clerics. They had talked of faith on a number of occasions, the Muslim with the agnostic, an antonyms discourse the dialectics of which had invariably favoured Muhammad.

Emma had been a lapsed Catholic. Meeting her had been his first encounter with that peculiar phenomenon, the English papist. His own religious education, of meagre proportions, he had acquired from compulsory attendance at the Anglican

Church, while at prep school and then later at college, but it had failed to light a spiritual fire within. In the classroom, divinity had been studied alongside metal work and Latin, but with less commitment. Neither of his parents exhibited a spiritual awareness, secure in their belief that the Anglican Church, like the Bank of England and the National Gallery, represented their class and station in life, rather than some spiritual home in which eternal salvation may be found. Marriage to Emma, in the sight of God and Monsignor Clarence Montague, since defrocked, had caused few ripples among his friends, but such could not be said of her family, even though he had undergone the mandatory church's indoctrination prior to the event. Their exogamous coupling had been greeted coolly, no matter that few within her family ever took the blessed sacrament or saw the need, from time to time, for a priestly interlocutor with Christ, an act they viewed as both sacerdotal and jejune. Before her death he had often speculated on a hypothetical dialogue between Emma, the lapsed Catholic and Muhammad the believer. Now Emma was in the unassailable position of being able to confute the belief of one or the other.

Dubai was not Muhammad's usual stomping ground, any more so than other parts of the Gulf. He was a modern nomad, one who had forsaken the cantankerous yet reliable camel of his forebears for a series of comfortable but insensate American sedans. The black Buick, the latest in a long line of similar conveyances, parked illegally among the hotel courtesy coaches and to which Dolby was led, bore strong witness to a car salesman's skill and to the truth that Detroit had not always been at the forefront of automotive design.

'You are looking older, Mr Dolby,' were his first words since they had met at the barrier.

'Thank you. So also are you, Muhammad.'

They were negotiating one of the numerous roundabouts between the airport and the city, the car slewing from side to side, throwing its occupants about. Out of habit he had sat in the back. Muhammad would not have expected or wished that he join him in the front.

'It is good to see you. I was in Qatar when you asked for my services. The Qataris are my friends. A cousin of mine married an al Thani and no longer works. He lives well.'

'He is a lucky man, Muhammad. Not so you and I who must continue to make our way in the world.' The pleasantries were coming to an end and Muhammad would soon ask the reason for his visit to the Gulf.

'We should not be idle. It is best that we are busy. *Inshallah.* Your visit to the Emirate is brief?'

Dolby was now at liberty to explain his need for the man who had once been among the most competent of fixers in the region.

'A few days. But I need your help in a little matter.' To appeal on anything other than a personal basis would have offended a man who knew that he would be well rewarded, but would deny all material ambition.

'There is a man flying into Dubai, from Kazakhstan, that I hope to persuade to come back to London with me.' It seemed an easy task, but one the speciousness of which would become self-evident.

Muhammad denied him that luxury. 'What if he does not see the wisdom of your words, Mr Dolby?'

'Then, Muhammad, we have a problem. In the past we have solved similar ones. What is important is that this person does not continue his journey to Baghdad.'

It was a few moments before Muhammad spoke again.

'Everything has changed in Dubai. New roads are made between calls to prayer. A new building appears over a meal. Each time I come here it is a new place. It is all the same, from Oman to Kuwait. Without oil there would be only desert. Will the desert return when the oil is gone?'

Muhammad half turned to view his passenger: 'This person, when is he arriving in Dubai?'

'Maybe tomorrow.' Prior to leaving the airport Dolby checked on the flights or lack of same, from Almaty. There would be time enough for preparations. Uppermost in his mind now was a shower and a bed.

'I will call for you at eight o'clock tomorrow morning,' Muhammad said, 'there are things I must arrange. Matters you do not need to know.' They drove onto the forecourt of the St George Hotel, the doorman less than impressed with the black Buick that appeared before him.

...Dubai

Having allowed himself the modest luxury of a shower and a brief rest, Guriel stepped out into the evening air. From a hurried call he had learnt that Kahzak Air was still on the ground at Almaty. Whether the target had left Astana or not was academic. Professor Batioushenkov, he mused, might die of old age before he could leave Kazakhstan.

The three-storied hotel into which Diana had delivered him was run, like so many other enterprises in Dubai, by Gulf Indians, the front for whom was a Yemeni businessman from Khanfar. On entering he had only to mention her name for the Arab youth behind the desk to hurriedly disappear into a back room, returning with a portly middle-aged Indian male who smiled and, perfunctorily dismissed the youth upstairs to prepare a room. Having been invited into a rear salon for tea, Guriel explained that his luggage would arrive later and that he needed a room for just one or two nights. Offering his American passport, by way of identity, he also proffered payment in US dollars, only to have both waived dismissively aside.

'The name of our mutual acquaintance suffices. You may pay at the desk as you leave our humble establishment.' His voice was unusually high and he spoke in the sing-song manner of many Indians, his head nodding from side to side. A red velvet curtain parted and an elderly sari-clad woman entered carrying a tray of tea. She was older, leaving Guriel unsure as to their relationship. Deferential yet proud, she might be an older sister or a dependent aunt? Having poured the tea she left as she had arrived, through the red velvet curtains.

'We serve Ceylonese, I hope you like it?' the man enquired.

The coded message he had passed to Jerusalem from the container ship, informed his superiors of Patel's possible duplicity and the need for a closer investigation into the House of Patel, as well as those with whom they had recently exercised their commercial expertise. Anticipating an early response, he had arranged to meet Hans, the 'cut-out' off the *Parthenon*, in a coffee shop, close to the Al-Musalla Post Office, on the Bur Dubai side of the Creek.

Bereft of a change of clothing he slipped into a department store and purchased a few items, after which he sought out the nearest restaurant toilet in which to change. Resuming his journey he dumped the soiled garments he had taken off into the first bin he found. His ankles remained swollen and sore, but walking became easier when he put his weight on the ball rather than the heal of his feet. Stopping several times to check that he was not being followed, Guriel, upon reaching the Creek stood in the doorway of a glass-fronted bank building, one of a number that front the waterway. Waiting until an *abra* was about to depart, he quickly crossed the wharf and jumped aboard just as the taxi driver pushed the small craft from its mooring. A slight breeze, along with the setting sun, made the journey more bearable. As they approached the Bur Dubai *abra* dock, Guriel observed, through the glare, a number of uniformed men assembled on the wharf. Gradually the silhouettes crystallised into policemen, some of whom carried M16s. Their attention was centred on the *abra* in which he sat, exposed, unable to do anything other than await events. As the craft came closer to the landing so the more agitated the waiting policemen became. Around him his fellow travellers sat in silence, as if awaiting sentence, each avoiding the gaze of others. Concomitant with the boat touching the side of the wharf two of the waiting constabulary rushed aboard, almost capsizing the vessel. Guriel watched as they grabbed a small palsied Arab, seated to his right and, ignoring all others, escorted him ashore. An unmarked white van drew up, into which the prisoner was unceremoniously dispatched. As it drove away the remaining policemen dispersed and Guriel, his heart thumping against his chest, mounted the steps that led to his rendezvous.

Selecting a corner table, adjacent to a side door that led into an alleyway, he ordered a coffee and sat back, seemingly engrossed in the Middle Eastern edition of the *Herald Tribune*. An hour passed before the *Parthenon*'s wireless operator, no longer in uniform, entered the café and sat opposite him, simultaneously sliding a small grey pack beside Guriel's shopping bag. Only when the waiter had withdrawn, having delivered a cup of flat white coffee, did he remove from his pocket a single sheet of paper.

'This is for you, I received it just an hour ago. I was instructed to deliver it immediately. Also I put together some items for you in the pack. They include a satellite phone for emergencies, and a mini Uzi, which I hope you will not use until we have left port.'

'Thanks. They think of everything. When do you sail?' Guriel opened the message and, having read its contents relegated it to his trouser pocket.

'We'll leave within twenty-four hours for Aden and then Rotterdam.'

Guriel eyed the Abba Eban incarnate before him. Sweating profusely and out of breath, how such a person would physically perform in an emergency was open to speculation and yet he appeared to move with the ease of a man half his size. Beneath the mid-European accented English, Guriel detected the clipped vowels of South Africa. All of Israel's intelligence community, MOSSAD, AMAN, SHABAK and LAKAM had, over many years, built up an army of *sayanim* or volunteers, only some of whom received a retainer. They might be the head waiter of an international hotel in Geneva, a police sergeant in Paris, a bargee on the Danube, or a wireless operator on a container vessel. The success of Israel's intelligence community could not rest on the personality and genius of a few outstanding individuals in Jerusalem, assisted by a small *camarilla* of professional operatives. Rather, if the nation was to survive, it would do so as a result of the quality of the intelligence gathered and the help given, by a highly diverse group of dedicated individuals, some of whom were 'helpers' in waiting for an indeterminate time, when they may be called upon to perform some seemingly innocuous task, ignorant of its value and outcome.

'I think that completes our business, Mr Lindsay. If I can be of further service, before we sail, you can reach me through the *Parthenon*.' Adding with a hint of black humour, 'I don't use a cell phone, they have a habit of exploding in this part of the world, which doesn't improve the health. I hope your trip is a success.'

Guriel watched him leave, a peripheral player departing the field, his part done, but one with whom he would have preferred to spend more time. To harbour such a sybaritic feeling was not uncommon among operatives alone in the field. A friendly contact, albeit with a peripatetic sayan, was a link with one's own kind, but every contact constituted a threat; it was a route, no matter how circuitous, back to its origin. He had experienced similar sentiments, of varying intensity, with every external operation. And yet, the contact between agent and 'cut-out' were perforce of a transient nature. Once he had discussed the matter with the services psychologist, a disciple of Schopenhauer, who had viewed it as inimical and a weakness, something that if pampered, compromised operations.

Later, after returning to his small room, he recovered from the slick or hiding place, Karl Baedeker's percipient guide to the Hellenic capital and sat on his bed to decode the message. The pocket guide had been one of the few items he had taken, before hurriedly departing for the shipping terminal. It was the two-part codebook for the operation. Using a one-off text, rather than set codes, limited the fallout, following a hostile interception. Any system, whether code or cipher, has a short shelf life, as security at best is of short duration. Because of the limited nature of the operation Jerusalem had gone for codes rather than ciphers, a message being more rapidly encoded and decoded than it is enciphered and deciphered. Also, ciphers are more prone to serious error, unless painstaking care is taken when enciphering and deciphering.

With each word that fell from his pencil it was evident that Jerusalem's interest now embraced not only the traveller from Kazakhstan, but also the contents of the warehouses, mentioned by Diana, contents which were 'harmful to not only your country but to the entire region.' His original operation had been to ensure that the House of Patel prevented 'the traveller' from reaching Baghdad. It remained of the highest priority. Although the assassination was a weapon Israel had placed in the hands of others, his duty was to ensure success. Now they had instructed him to carry out a further task. It was time, he reasoned, for another visit to the House of Patel.

Diana was seated behind her desk as he appeared, unannounced. At first she seemed flustered, but quickly regaining her ice-like composure, she informed him, formally, that Iqbal Patel was out. Her manner gave no hint of their earlier collaboration, or of the intimacy he had experienced in her company. Junior members of the trading house busied themselves behind computer screens in adjacent offices, sometimes leaving the confines of their small working area to deposit messages or papers on her desk. A middle-aged man, in a blue linen suit, emerged from an inner office and was introduced as yet another Patel, one of Iqbal's many cousins. Having ascertained that he could be of no help to the visiting American businessman, he scooped up a number of discs from the desk and, smiling weakly, returned to his office.

'How many Patels are there?' Guriel enquired.

'More than you can imagine, Mr Lindsay. If you have come to call on Mr Iqbal Patel you may have to wait some time, he is away at a meeting. Perhaps your company's interest would be better served if you were to phone him later in the day.'

Guriel was being given a message, but it was one he did not understand. Was it a warning to leave or something concerning the activity of Patel?

'Yes, perhaps I will. If you would tell him that I called. You know where I can be contacted.'

'Thank you for calling,' she replied, in the imitative manner of a Bell Telephone receptionist.

As he left the building, within the confines of the small foyer at the bottom of the stairs, an area devoid of furniture, he smelt the same odour he had encountered from the bag that had been placed over his head, during the abduction and subsequent beating. He was alone and had passed nobody on the stairs. Beyond the glass doors that lead out onto a small parking area a white Mercedes was being driven away from the building down the narrow street.

Without delay he found a telephone in a bank close by, and dialled the House of Patel. His call was instantly answered.

'Ms Patel, Gerald Lindsay here. Could I ask you who just drove away in the white Mercedes?'

'I am sorry, I can't help you. I am sorry you missed Mr Patel. The House of Patel values your business, Mr Lindsay. Please call back later.'

'How much later and when can I see your employer?'

'You can't. Not today. I hope you are comfortable in your new hotel, Mr Lindsay?'

'Yes thank you. If I can't see your boss, perhaps we could meet?' The invitation had been spontaneous. It was something he would square with his conscience later, when he would reason, from hindsight, that their association was necessary for the success of the operation. Would she accept?

'That might be a little difficult. If you would like to return to your hotel I will try and contact you there, later today. In the meantime you should ring the airport about your shipment.'

Back at his hotel he found a fresh bowl of fruit in his room and his suitcase, along with all his effects, from the Metropolitan Hotel. He had opened the suitcase only after a careful and thorough external examination. He meticulously checked every item, but found nothing amiss. The shirts had been neatly folded, along with his socks in such a way as to suggest that a female had packed the case. Upon enquiring, he was informed that it had been delivered just an hour earlier, by a person unknown. Had she been responsible for its retrieval? If not, who? It was safe to assume that if he was not once more under surveillance it was only a matter of time. But why return his belongings? Perhaps it was a reminder to him that there were those in Dubai who did not welcome his presence?

A call to the airport confirmed that Kazakh Air were again operational and that domestic flights between Astana and Almaty had been resumed, along with the airline's operation to the Gulf. Barely had he put down the receiver when his phone rang. It was the House of Patel.

'Mr Lindsay, it's Mahashweta Patel. You mentioned a meeting?'

'Yes. Where and when?'

'I am not free until later in the afternoon. Why don't I pick you up about 5 p.m., at your hotel. What did you have in mind?'

'I'll explain it all when we meet.'

'OK. By the way, it seems your consignment is at last on its way.'

'So I understand. I will see you later.'

'Till then.'

She arrived on time, at 5 p.m., dressed in black slacks with matching sweater. Together they drove to a yacht marina where, in a restaurant devoid of atmosphere, the staff deferred to her as a woman of influence. The House Of Patel owned a yacht moored at the marina and were regular customers at the expensive establishment. Their yacht, incongruously named *Chatham*, seldom left its dock, but was, like so many of the other social trappings belonging to the family business, a statement to the world and more particularly, to the other Indian trading companies of the Gulf, that the Patels were a necessary and inherent part of the commercial fabric that made up one of the most vibrant trading areas on earth.

To Guriel, a morally committed socialist and servant of the state, social influence was a tool of his trade, something to be used. For an agent, access to the best establishments means access to influential people and, *ipso facto*, the information they hold. Some of Israel's top agents have, at one time or another, belonged to the most influential clubs and restaurants throughout the Middle East, rubbing shoulders with leaders whose sworn aim was the destruction of the Israeli state.

Beyond the large window beside which they sat, lights of the yachts moved up and down with incoming swells. A full moon filled the sky dimming the reflection of lights on the polluted waters of the Arabian Gulf. Far out to sea, an illuminated super-tanker glided by with its golden cargo from the oil fields of Kuwait, bound for who knows where. Within the vast room only a few people were dining, it being too early in the evening for most. Among the few who had chosen such an unfashionable hour at which to dine, were three family groups, scattered about the large room like tribes in a desert. The Dubai male is seldom seen in public with his family. When he allows them the privilege of his company it is usually in a restaurant, where he is surrounded by wives and children and pampered by all. Waiters, Filipinos mostly, in starched white uniforms, were positioned at strategic points around the room, over eager to serve lest they be replaced by one of the waiting army of migrant workers in search of employment. A wine waiter offered a list to Guriel, who waved him away.

'Mr Lindsay, after having been a slave to commerce all day, this lady would like a drink.'

'I'm sorry. What would you like?'

'Perhaps we could have a California wine,' she replied, extravagantly. 'White Pinot? This evening we are the guests of the House of Patel. Feel free to choose the most expensive items on the menu.' Mischievously, she continued, 'After all, you have gone through a lot in order to trade with our company. We wouldn't want you returning home complaining about our hospitality.'

'It never crossed my mind.' What had crossed his mind, but something he would prefer had not, was the attraction he held for the dark-skinned Indian lady seated opposite. That he would now be able to extend his time in Dubai both pleased and disturbed him, putting at risk the one truth in his life. His marriage to Ruth was a thread of reality in a garment of lies wrapped around a life over which he had little control. Would he now give it up in exchange for another lie?

'You wanted to talk.' The incongruity of her North American accent struck him for the first time. Her face was classic Indian, fine, with deep black eyes, her ebony hair tied back to hang at shoulder length. She could have walked directly out of a Bombay film set.

'You mentioned the existence of certain warehouses my company may be interested in visiting,' he began.

She looked up from her menu to fix him with a penetrating stare. 'I thought that you might want to talk about that.'

'Is it safe to do so here?' he enquired.

'Oh yes. I doubt very much if there are any listening devices. This is somewhere to show off, to be seen, not heard.'

'Can you help me visit one of these warehouses? I don't expect you to come along. Just point me in the right direction.'

'I could, but before doing so I would prefer we were honest with each other.'

He met her request with a silence that hung in the air-conditioned environment for what seemed like hours.

Eventually she said, 'Let's order some food, shall we? I understand that Moslems and Jews do not eat pork, we Hindus do not eat beef or veal, so that only leaves sheep, goat and chicken, if you are carnivorous. The chef here is Punjabi, so may I recommend the tandoori chicken. He does it in a clay oven, baked very quickly and served with a nice naan, bread made with yeast.'

'That sounds fine.'

After the many dishes of the meal had been squeezed onto the table and the waiters had retired, she continued.

'Gerald,' her use of his name, albeit one given to him for the duration of the operation, was an act of intimacy that sent a warm glow through his body, 'we are not as different as you may think. My work at the House of Patel gives me access to information that's of interest, not only to your company, but also to, shall we say, another. This other identity has entrusted in me a duty. Just as you serve your masters, so I serve mine. To the folks at Patel I'm nothing other than an overeducated secretary, trained in foreign ways, waiting for my family to find the right Hindu male to marry. Male supremacy is enshrined in the Vedas, you know, the ancient Hindu scriptures.'

'Do I detect a clash of cultures?' he enquired.

'Let's just say, I would have trouble fitting into the traditional Indian role of a wife. Paradoxically there's also a strong matriarchal bias within the Hindu faith, which means that women can be both goddesses and slaves, matriarch and chattel. In the nineteenth century the Hindu cultural renaissance decided that, if Hinduism were going to survive, it must cleanse itself of the oppression of women and caste prejudice. It worked well for some women, depending on how traditional their families were, but the caste system still needs a bit more work done on it.'

'How did you end up in California?' he enquired.

'Indian nationalism, unlike Arab nationalism, has modernised its country through education. That I come from a Gulf family is irrelevant. The family, for all its Anglo-affectation, remains Indian and, for Indians, education is the key into the first world. They wanted me to go to the LSE, the London School of Economics, but I dug my heels in and went to America. Things happened there, so that when I came back from California it was to take up employment, specifically to report about what goes on in Dubai and throughout the Gulf. Now you know more than anybody else and I might have to kill you,' she smiled politely.

'Why are you telling me this?'

'Because unless we are honest with each other there is no trust and trust may be something we'll need, if we're to work together.' For the next few moments she engrossed herself in her meal, eating from each of the vibrant coloured dishes, enjoying the subtle and not so subtle tastes of India. He watched, waiting for her to continue. The admission that she was more than she seemed, was something that had been bothering him since they first met. There was an intelligence, a competence about her that alerted him to the possibility she was more than an office employee. Then there was her composure throughout their visit to the *Parthenon*. It had been impressive. The explication of what she had revealed and its impact on his work, would take time. Meanwhile he would attempt to find out more, to flush out the truth, while he lied both to himself and the person who now solicited his trust.

'You're not eating? Don't you like Indian cuisine?'

'Yes, it's very nice,' he replied.

'I specifically selected dishes without pork.'

'That was very considerate. But there is nothing I like more than a bacon sandwich.'

'I'll try to remember.'

'About these warehouses,' he pressed, 'what makes them of so much interest to my company?'

She was at the point of putting some rice into her mouth, but returned the fork to her plate.

'The warehouses are a fact. It's their contents that are of interest. As I mentioned, my uncle has been dealing with some new customers from Saudi Arabia. They are not very nice people. They are the bad guys in the play. I don't know a lot. Normally I'm able to keep a check on what passes through the office, but, where these guys are concerned, my uncle is very discreet. I do know that whatever is in those warehouses has the potential to cause a lot of headaches for a lot of people, throughout this entire area. And that includes a certain state to the west that shall remain nameless. Perhaps, Gerald, if we work together, we might find out a whole lot more.' She resumed eating.

'I hope we can, Diana. Would I be right in thinking that you know a little more than you're telling me? After all, it could be milk powder for the starving masses.'

'I can assure you that, whatever is in those buildings, whether in Kuwait or Qatar, it's not milk powder. You'll have to trust me, won't you?' The edge that had crept into her voice belied the smile she affected.

'Then there is the little matter of the consignment from Kazakhstan.'

'Oh yes. We shouldn't forget the consignment from Kazakhstan. My uncle has contacts among the Indian Mafia who are to take care of your consignment. Not really my scene. But, I suppose you have your reasons. Or are you just obeying orders?'

'Just obeying orders.'

'You don't strike me as the sort who blindly obeys orders.'

She had taken the conversation into the realm of the personal. It was an area that for Guriel was not open for discussion.

'Perhaps we should talk about the warehouse,' he suggested.

'Perhaps we should. But I am thinking, can I trust this man? Who is he? We both know what you are, but who you are is another matter,' she answered reflectively.

'Can't we work together without all this analysis? We seem to have an equal interest in what is in those warehouses. So why don't I check on a little matter and then we leave here and go and find out?'

'The airport lighting is out at Almaty, again. I guess they couldn't pay the bill. So, even if your consignment makes it that far, he won't leave for Dubai until tomorrow. At least, when the Soviets ran things they worked, to a fashion. Not that I was a fan of theirs, you understand.'

'If you knew that why didn't you tell me? About the lighting, I mean.'

'Mr Lindsay, do you not think that you are asking for more than you are prepared to give? It's not a good basis for our working relationship.'

'What do you mean?'

'Trust. You want me to be open with you, while you persist with this ridiculous pretence of being an American business man.'

'If you know so much about me, what does it matter what I say?'

'OK. Have it your way. You have barely touched your food,' she observed.

'It was very nice. I wasn't hungry. Shall we leave?'

As they drove away from the marina, past high-rise apartments clustered along the shoreline and lit up like so many enormous blocks of Christmas trees, the moon went into hiding behind a thin sliver of cloud. The blinds were drawn on most of the windows of the concrete towers they passed, but in one he saw an ex-patriot woman, standing before a mirror, combing her hair. It was a private and singular act, one no Arab woman would allow a male, other than her husband, to observe. Within such a simple thing lay the conflict, between his world and Israel's neighbours.

Just over thirty minutes later they were among commercial buildings and castles of empty containers. The area was well lit and patrolled by private security firms, a fact she included in her briefing only as an afterthought.

'This particular building has received a consignment in the last month, like others in the Gulf, that are under surveillance. The major shipments, until recently, have been going into Bahrain, from where they have been distributed to other states.'

It was on his tongue to ask, 'under surveillance by whom?' but he kept silent.

'There are security guards in the building, Pakistani employees. I am not supposed to know about the place, let alone the existence of the security guards, so we can't just front up and bluff our way past them, like we did at the docks. Any suggestions?'

'Let's look around first and maybe we will have to come back another night,' he suggested.

By the time they had parked the car a discreet distance from the warehouse, the moon had chosen to return to its illuminated state in the heavens. It was not a night one would have selected for covert activities. Such areas that were not lit up by strong street and security lights, were illuminated by moonlight. The smallest of mammals could not have moved without being observed. Leading the way, she walked quickly and purposefully along the deserted wide street, keeping to one side, in the shadows. At one point they had to hide among empty oil drums on a building site, as a security vehicle drove past, shining its roof light. Suddenly, without warning, she turned right into a narrow street that was wide enough for only one vehicle. After passing two tall warehouses on their right she stopped again and gestured to him to follow her into a lane that went between the steel walls of smaller storage buildings, at the end of which rose a new brick warehouse, with security lights strung out along its roof, illuminating everything beneath. Moving forward they were confronted by a loading door that gave all the appearance of being impregnable. Walls both to the left and the right blocked off any thought of moving around the outside.

A gentle breeze came in from the shore, sending a shiver through his body, beneath his sweat-saturated shirt. They were standing close to one another and he could smell her and found himself aroused. She seemed impervious to their physical proximity as she lent closer still to converse.

'This is the side entrance. The front of the building is on the wide street we have just left. We wouldn't have a chance of getting in from the front. The security guards are in an office that opens onto that street. They patrol inside. The outside they leave to the goons in the cars. What do you think?'

'If you are asking me, "how do we get in", I haven't any ideas. What about the back end of the building? Can we have a look at that?'

'There is a tall wall with wire and floodlights, at the back end. You can only get to it through one of the adjacent buildings.'

'You may not know what is inside, but you know a lot about what is outside.'

'Is that a problem?' she replied.

'Just an observation.'

A few minutes later they were walking along a narrow passage between a security fence and a tin wall that still gave off heat from the day. The smell of stale urine and faeces was evident.

'Be careful where you walk,' she advised.

The passage gave on to the rear wall of the warehouse that was the object of their attention. They had secured access to the passage through another warehouse, the security of which had been left to chance. Passing through, in search of a side exit, Guriel could again smell the spice he had first encountered from the bag that had been earlier forced over his head.

'What is that smell?' he enquired.

'It's a spice of some sort,' she replied, eagerly leading the way among the burlap bails.

The high metal fence, separating them from the rear wall, was unlit but too high to climb, and by way of further discouragement, razor wire had been strung along the top. But, closer inspection revealed a small hole cut into the wire at ground level, about half way along.

'Do you think an animal made the hole?' she suggested.

'I doubt it. More likely it was made for a child to get through. Do you think you could squeeze through?'

'I can try. Is this where we part company?'

'I'm afraid so. If you're not out in ten minutes I'll call for help,' he offered.

'Thanks a lot. You might at least lift up the wire.'

As she slithered under, on her back, he was struck by how athletically she moved, for one so sedentarily employed.

'If you knew how much I paid for this top I'm wearing you wouldn't have suggested this.'

Before he could reply she was on her feet exploring the wall for some means of access. He could just make her out against the wall, moving slowly away. Moments later she was standing in front of him, separated only by the wire fence.

'There's a back door. I'm not sure how secure it is. I'm going to try and get into the building.'

'I think it unlikely they have left it unlocked,' he suggested.

Suddenly she was jingling a bunch of keys in front of him.

'You are full of surprises.'

'Mr Lindsay, you ain't seen nothin' yet,' her voice trailed off as she returned to the wall.

As he waited for her to return a large cargo plane flew overhead on its approach, its tailplane illuminated, showing the flag for UPS. Away to his left, beyond the buildings, beyond the shore, a ship heralded its departure from the Emirate, having disgorged its cargo, not of spices and silks as in the past, but shiny new automobiles for Dubai's fashion conscious. Once the sound of the four Pratt and Whitney engines, that powered the parcels for UPS through the air, had faded, he could hear the faint sounds of her activity. A sharp crack gave notice of something breaking, and then silence.

After a few minutes, he was about to force his way under the wire when she appeared as quietly as she had left. Lying on her back with arms outstretched, she allowed him to pull her through the hole. As they retraced their steps back to the car, through the warehouse by which they had come, she held back from telling him of her findings. Several times he attempted to prise from her an answer to their evening's labour, but she kept silent until they were entering the city.

'Empty,' she confided. 'Nothing. The place was empty. Everything gone.'

'In that case it is just as well we are both paid by the hour,' he replied.

'Speak for yourself. I'm moonlighting.'

'How did you get in? It didn't sound as though you had the right key.'

'Now isn't that something else. The door at the back had only a simple lock, but two bolts on the inside. One was only partly in place, the other had been drawn. I forced it. Luckily the guards were busy in the front office watching television.'

'Why bother bolting an empty building?'

'When was it emptied?' she asked, more to herself than her travel companion.

'If we knew what had been in there, we might have some idea why it was moved and where it has gone.'

Suddenly she came to life, as if from a dream. 'Well, that was a waste of time,' she stated.

'Where do we go from here?' he enquired.

'I'll drop you off near your hotel. I'll ring in the morning.'

'Don't leave it too late. I have a date with a Russian.'

He put down the phone and went into the pocket-sized bathroom, the slick, for the items from the *Parthenon*. A hard knock on the door set him about recovering the mini Uzi, secreted behind the shower cabinet. It was the latest model from Israel's Government arms factory, with threaded barrel. Its firepower and manoeuvrability made it an ideal weapon for use in aircraft and houses. Returning to the bedroom he crossed to the door. There was another knock followed by a concerted attempt at forced entry. The door was stout enough to retard the progress of whoever was trying to enter just long enough for him to bring the mini Uzi to bear on the would-be invader. The door sprung open, slamming against the wall as two robed figures, both armed, rushed in, the first rolling forward into a ball, the other wildly swinging a High Standard 22 silenced automatic. Guriel fired a short burst, hitting the standing assailant before he could fire. As he swung around to face the other a thunderous roar exploded in his left ear and his vision blurred, followed by a sharp jolt to his right shoulder that sent him spinning like a top. He had been shot and yet felt no pain. Then blackness.

He was in a bus, the front of which was on fire. Waves of heat washed over him, as the flames advanced from the front of the vehicle. He was alone in the inferno, but there were inimical voices about him, calling out in a language he did not understand. Beyond the shattered window to his left, Ruth was looking into the burning vehicle, her distraught misshapen face mutely pleading with him to escape the oncoming flames. Beside her, Aarran and Moshe looked on insouciantly, oblivious to their mother's distress. It was a scene that had been played out before, but without his family as spectators, aboard a bus in Tel Aviv in which he had been travelling, along with a suicide bomber, some years earlier. Then as now, both the heat and the flames grew in intensity. As they enveloped him darkness descended, yet again. A nothingness in which he seemed to hang, as if suspended in mid-air, but without pain.

Pain came, along with light and a face he vaguely recognised only to disappear again, but the pain remained, a cauterising sensation of excruciating intensity in his head and right shoulder. When he eventually reached consciousness it was to discover the hotel manager and another man of Indian extraction, looking down on him in bed. The mouth of the manager was moving in a manner that begged a response and yet he could not hear. Or rather, what he heard made no sense, just a buzzing. Gradually the sounds took on a shape within his mind, the visual manifestation of which was a script he had seen in an office, just a short time previously. They were speaking Hindi. The pain seemed to grow ever stronger and he felt sick and wanted to vomit, but within him there was nothing to emit.

'Mr Lindsay, we are so pleased to see that you have returned to us. We were very concerned as to your health. Please do not move. The doctor will come again and check your wounds shortly. Ms Patel was asking after you and we shall now be able to tell her you are awake. Also, your colleague will want to know that you are better. But we do not know how to contact him.'

Guriel attempted to speak, but the effort intensified the pain and he desisted. Swiftly sleep overcame him and he drifted away, into the turbulent chaotic arms of Morpheus.

He awoke to look into the face of an angel. Seated beside him was Diana and standing behind her Dr Ramdas Patel. The room had the smell of a hospital ward that had recently been cleaned.

'Mr Lindsay,' she said, her voice was soft and concerned. 'How are you feeling?'

It was the look of incomprehension on her face that made him realise his error. He had replied in Hebrew.

'Since I can now hear and see you I must be better,' he corrected, in English.

'A relative condition, Mr Lindsay,' added Dr Ramdas Patel.

'What happened?'

'You have been shot with small calibre ammunition. Twice to be exact. In the left side of the head and in the right shoulder. Fortunately, neither wound is life threatening, at least, I don't think so, but I'm afraid you will be out of action for a while. May I suggest that you change your line of endeavour, before you do yourself permanent injury. You seem particularly prone to upsetting people.' Dr Patel had a bedside manner that would have been acceptable in a corrections hospital.

'How long have I been out?' he enquired.

'About six hours. I was on my way to meet you when I heard what had happened. They must have followed you back here,' she said.

'What happened to the...?'

'The men who attacked you?' It was left to Dr Patel to enlighten him. 'Somehow your attackers got into the hotel without being seen. When the hotel manager arrived he found you sprawled on the floor, along with two dead men and the man who saved your life, who left without leaving his name. You killed one of your attackers and your friend got the other. Both bodies have been disposed of, the manager was very thorough. There was no need to involve the local authorities. But it might be best if you leave Dubai as soon as you feel well enough.'

'When will that be?' she enquired.

'A few days, no more. Meanwhile you should take care. Whoever is trying to kill you will no doubt try again. I will look in tomorrow. Mahashweta will get whatever you need.'

Alone with her there was much that he needed to know, but not even the identity of his 'friend' was worth disturbing the peace that existed between them.

...Dubai

Allen Bobrowski and Paul McCone, assisted by three locally recruited office staff, constituted the US Gulf Office of the US Drug Enforcement Administration, the lead Federal agency charged with enforcing narcotics and controlled substances laws and regulations. Both Bobrowski and McCone were career officers who, unable to gain selection for either the FBI or the CIA, had opted for a life as drug busters, with a government agency that offered a career structure that culminated in the collection of a pension that few in the United States would choose yet many around the world might envy. Whatever initially motivated the two in their respective careers, it was, after seven and eight years' service respectively, something that was now peripheral to their existence, a card that admitted them to a world ripe for exploitation. A gravy train of their own design and manufacture which, if skilfully manipulated, would provide for their increasingly lavish earthly needs until each was no longer capable of enjoying the sins of their ill-gotten wealth. Avarice was the enemy within, an excessive display of which, in material possessions or a pretentious lifestyle, would bring the world falling down around their rapacious necks. With greed in check, such was the administrative oversight of the DEA that, they could rest in the belief that their misdemeanours would remain undiscovered. Each had become aware of the other's fallen nature when their paths had first crossed, during a mopping up operation in Bolivia's Chapare province, since when they had collaborated at every opportunity, working the system for all it was worth. An adulterous administration clerk, in the Human Resource Department of the Agency, compromised and open to blackmail, made sure that, whenever possible, Bobrowski and McCone went out as a team.

Now, not only was their gravy train under threat of derailment but also at stake was the future of the entire agency. In one year the DEA spends $20 billion in its fight against drugs. During one fifteen-year period it managed to rid itself of $300 billion fighting the menace, three times what it then cost to put a man on the moon. Such largesse attracts the unscrupulous and corrupts those who might otherwise lead a blameless life. Fighting the drug trade was an industry itself, one that provided work for thousands and wealth for many.

That an aging Russian biochemist should threaten the very existence of the DEA, *ipso facto* the lucrative endeavours of Messrs Bobrowski and McCone, was beyond acceptance. The exact nature of the threat, known only to a very few at 600–700 Army Navy Drive, Arlington, VA, was not the concern of either man. Informed only that the Agency had an enemy far greater than any Latin American drug baron, was sufficient for both to do whatever was required of them in the execution of their duty. DEA directors of middle rank had long suspected the corrupt pair, preferring to put their names, along with others, in a drawer marked, 'when needed'. Now was such a time. Professor Batioushenkov would have to be eliminated, in the course of which, should it become public knowledge, all was deniable, since the personnel records of Bobrowski and McCone were marked, showing them to be unscrupulous and corrupt agents, rogue elements in an otherwise spotless agency.

Kate Cranley, an FBI operative with special knowledge of the DEA and its modus operandi, aware that an aberrant operation was under way against a foreign national by the DEA, was in search of Bobrowski and McCone, absent from their Bahrain office. Having escaped the clutches of the US Navy, in Bahrain, she had journeyed to Dubai in the belief that there she would find those of whom she was in pursuit, along with the reason behind the highly questionable attempt on the life of a foreign national, by officers of the US Government. Dubai was becoming a vortex of conspiracy into which she, along with the CIA had been drawn. Both the CIA and the FBI are independent of each other and neither may access the files of the other, intelligence being shared on a mutually agreeable basis, a point not lost on the critics of the US intelligence community. Not allowing the right arm to know what the left arm knows, as an enemy aims for the heart of America, a nation both agencies are sworn to protect, will seem, to the casual observer, absurd. But that is the way of it. From her meeting on board the military aircraft that had brought her to the Gulf, Cranley deduced that she was involved in something beyond that for which she had been briefed. It was one thing to travel half way around the world, to uncover an assassination plot, against a person unknown, by two errant agents of the DEA, quite another to do so with a SWAT team from the CIA breathing down your neck. With little time in which to assess the situation, she would need to use her not inconsiderable initiative and act boldly. Being bereft of backup support in Dubai, it seemed prudent to go against explicit procedure and inveigle or cajole the assistance of Mr Alex Kelday and his CIA team. She was, after all, a DEA agent, an American citizen on her own in a foreign country. Whatever the solution, she would find it by the end of breakfast.

Wearing carefully selected clothes that would attract the least attention from the local populous, she set off in search of Mr Alex Kelday. A taxi deposited her at the US Consulate, a fortress-like structure, just as the staff were preparing for another working day. An indolent young fresh-faced official, from Arkansas, greeted her with indifference, until she produced her bogus DEA ID, after which his behaviour became that of one friendly government employee to another, the kindred victim of a vast bureaucratic machine.

Breakfast had produced but one idea as to how she might recruit the assistance of her agency's sworn rival, the CIA. Finding a CIA SWAT team in a foreign city, against the inexorable ticking of the clock, wouldn't be easy, how much better, then, for the fox to come to the hound. For that she must first plant a scent. The US Consulate, although in all probability ignorant of the operation under way in their territory, might be capable of creating the vibrations that would bring her the genus Vulpes from its hole.

'The Consul will see you now, Ms Cranley,' the official from Arkansas said.

The Consul was your average well presented ascetic State Department officer, complete with button down shirt and conservative tie, with a demeanour that screamed Ivy League. His short cropped hair hid premature balding on top of a scull that could have been carved from stone. The nameplate on the door read Melvin Thorvald and Kate Cranley fought hard to imagine this urbane official leaping ashore, a Viking in Vinland, bent on exploring the New World. In all likelihood his forebears, like her own, had arrived in America crammed into steerage aboard a malodorous immigrant vessel, at the turn of the last century. If the name was Viking his speech was East Coast and soft.

'Ms Cranley, take a seat. I wasn't told that your agency was sending out someone from head office, or have you come down from Bahrain? We're normally kept well informed about such visits. We try to keep our eye on the ball. Would you like a Coke or something, coffee perhaps?'

'Coffee would do just fine,' she replied.

Having summoned refreshments he sat back, flanked by the star-spangled banner and the State Department pennant, to examine the woman with the short red hair and ankle length cotton dress. In her he immediately detected a keen intelligence, a quality found lacking among the women that frequented Dubai's American Club. Her face, almost void of make-up, was alive and confident.

The visit of an official, no matter from which segment of government, was never something he took lightly. Respect for the system, a reverence for the wheels of government were the tenets by which he tried to live his expatriate existence, a philosophy easy to expound yet often hard to live by. He had served around the world under a number of different Administrations, not all of which had upheld the best interests of the American people and mankind. The policies advanced by some had been incompatible with American interests and values, policies that he had sworn to uphold. Domestic politics and Bureaucratic self-interest, although not unique to the United States, had, on a number of occasions, made for sleepless nights. In serving errant Administrations he had been able to partially reconcile his conscience with the belief that the American democratic process was self-correcting and that he had only to do his duty and all would come right.

At another, more personal level, he had often found himself enviously comparing the State Department with the diplomatic services of other nations, services that allowed and encouraged professional career officers to reach ambassadorial rank, rather than the US payola system to which he was bound, where an individual so often purchased their ambassadorship with lavish electoral campaign contributions. Administrations notwithstanding, as a professional diplomat whose career had stalled, he had, from time to time, caught himself harbouring contumacious thoughts towards the system he tried so hard to respect and revere, particularly while serving under individuals who knew nothing of the art of diplomacy and even less about the country to which they had been appointed, an appointment purchased much as they would a vacation cruise. Such crass opportunism had filled him with indignation. For a while he had even kept a dossier of certain happenings, the diplomatic faux pas of the politically appointed parvenu, in the mistaken belief that one day he might effect a change by exposing their ignorance. However, others before him had gone public, to the eternal detriment of their careers and so his dossiers would serve only one purpose, to ruin his own. He had burnt them, one rain-soaked evening, in the chancery's incinerator, in Manila. But his thoughts were not of such insubordinate matters or of morally bankrupt Administrations, while observing his visitor. She was fresh air to an office and to a life in need of ventilation.

'How can we be of help to the DEA, Ms Cranley?'

'Ordinarily I would not bother you and I am not asking you not to report my visit, but your discretion would be most appreciated.'

'You understand that I can't make any promises until I know what it is that you want,' he replied.

'I need help in passing a message on to a federal employee, an Alex Kelday. He flew into Dubai yesterday.' She had hoped that the mention of his name might prompt a response or a reaction of sorts. But none was forthcoming.

'And you don't know where he is staying.'

'That is correct. I need to be in touch with him as soon as possible. If you could put it about that I was asking after him, that would be great. It's a professional matter, if you see what I mean. I'm staying at Le Meridian, by the airport.'

'I know it. And what brings Alex Kelday to this part of the world?'

'That question would be best answered by Mr Kelday.'

'I see. We'll do what can be done. Have you been to the Gulf before?' he enquired.

'No, this is my first visit.'

'The US had good relations with the UAE, Ms Cranley. It is my job to see that things stay that way.' The innocuity of the warning did little to mask its meaning. This territory was his responsibility and nothing would be allowed to disturb the status quo.

'Thanks for your help, Mr Thorvald. The DEA appreciates your assistance.'

'It's a pleasure, Ms Cranley. I'll be in touch. If my office can be of any further help, just let us know.'

The combination of her intelligence and physical allure, in spite of her clothes, was overwhelming. Assisting an official of the DEA would, he thought, be a pleasure.

Barely had she returned to the air-conditioned comfort of her hotel, when the phone beside her bed rang.

'Ms Cranley?' It was a voice she had last heard aboard the aging air force plane that had dropped her into the less than welcoming arms of the US Navy.

'Speaking.'

How had Thorvald located him so soon, unless he had known all along of Kelday's whereabouts? Was the CIA using the Consulate as their base of operations? A CIA SWAT team would normally operate independent of the local diplomatic service, through the local station chief, preferring not to directly implicate the US government. Perhaps Thorvald had struck lucky, which, she had to admit, was an unlikely occurrence.

'You were making enquiries about me at the Consulate.' The voice was formal, but not unfriendly.

'Thanks for getting in touch. Could we meet? I need your help.' A woman, she reasoned, should use whatever nature gave her to achieve her aim? A perceived helplessness had never failed her in the past and Alex Kelday was not immune to such a wile.

'Intergovernmental agency cooperation is something I specialise in. Just as long as there are no more corpses lying around. I hope the Navy was not too hard on you?'

'We got it sorted out in the end. Are you free today?' she enquired.

'I can get away. How well do you know the area?'

'Not at all.'

'In that case I'll come to you.' Did she detect an eagerness in his reply?

'When do you think that will be?'

'By the time you take the elevator down to the foyer I'll be there. Is there somewhere we can take coffee?'

'Yes. There's a small place just inside the main door, on the right. But where are you?'

'Not too far off. See you in five.' The line went dead.

Upon exiting the elevator she found the foyer empty, save for an SAS crew booking in for their stopover. The light blue uniforms of the hostesses set off their coveted golden tans as they pulled their bags towards the waiting reception clerks. Ahead of them the flight crew were completing registration formalities.

Entering the café she ordered a coffee and sat at a table that looked into the foyer. The SAS crew were still filling out forms at the desk as a relaxed Alex Kelday entered the hotel.

'Thanks for coming so quickly,' she demurred.

'I was just passing.'

'How fortunate,' she replied, but how unlikely, she thought.

'And what brings you to Dubai, Ms Cranley?'

'I am trying to locate two of our citizens, missing from Bahrain.'

'Missing persons, is that normally the job of the DEA?'

'Our brief is wide. It's important that I find them as soon as possible and I thought I might ask you for your help.'

As he drank his coffee he eyed her over the top of a garishly coloured mug. She seemed younger than he had remembered and taller. Twenty-four hours or so, had failed to improve her taste in clothes. Did all female agents, he wondered, dress so frumpishly or was the young-grandmother-look something the Government promoted among their employees who travelled?

'Well, we're really not into the people finding business, just now. What made you think I might be able to help?'

There was a dissemblance in the question that disarmed her. His eyes did not leave her and she felt foolish continuing with, what was rapidly becoming, a farce.

'Mr Kelday…' she attempted.

'Don't you think it would help if you called me Alex?'

'Alex, I don't know what you are doing in Dubai, but—'

He interrupted, 'I have already asked the same of you, since I thought you were heading for Bahrain.'

'If you would let me finish. Two American citizens have gone missing from Bahrain, and—'

He again interjected, 'You would like me to find your two guys from the Bahrain DEA office.'

'I didn't say they were DEA personnel.'

'You didn't need to. Also, if I am to help you find these two clowns, don't you think I should know who I'm working for?' he suggested.

'You would be doing it for me. As a favour. And, who knows, perhaps I will be able to help you out one day.' She attempted a smile, but an adjuration, even one so lightly given, was a humiliation, putting her in his debt before he had even agreed to help.

'Ms Cranley. Kate. After arriving here, yesterday, I made a few phone calls. One was to 5th Fleet HQ, in Bahrain. The Provost Marshall was very helpful. Now he may not cut the mustard when it comes to intelligence, but he knows the difference between the DEA and the FBI.'

'You have been busy. I still need your help or do you have instructions not to assist Bureau personnel in need and far away from home?'

'I have to admit, knowing who you are doesn't make helping you any easier. I don't think J Edgar would approve. But, since we are both on the same side, what the hell. Perhaps a little interdepartmental cooperation might work for us both. I won't tell if you don't. Tell me what you are trying to do and then I might be able to help.'

It fell just short of being patronising, but near enough for her to feel challenged. Alex Kelday was not the tractable individual she had perceived him to be, rather it was she who was being managed.

There seemed no point in holding back the little that she knew. If the CIA were after the same target as Bobrowski and McCone then they would at least know who the target was. Find the target and she would locate the two errant agents.

'Through "an audit" we found out, from various sources, that Bobrowski and McCone, our two employees from the Bahrain office, were taking an unhealthy interest in a foreign national that was due to pass through Dubai.' She paused. 'That you were also interested added to our concern. They are running a little operation of their own, one that does not have the official backing of the DEA, but seems to have come from somewhere within its middle management, well, maybe. I'm here to find out what these guys are planning to do.'

'I'm sure you are a very competent agent, Kate. But is the Bureau in the habit of sending a women out to do a man's job?' he replied in jest.

'Frankly, Mr Kelday, I didn't think the CIA was in the habit of employing agents with palaeolithic views on women in the workplace.'

'OK. Point taken. I'll see what can be done. Just for you. Though we wouldn't like the Bureau getting any ideas that we are a soft touch. Meanwhile, I think you would be wise to keep a low profile. Whatever is going down here might become quite noisy.'

'I can look after myself,' she replied defiantly.

'I'm sure you can. Suppose we locate your two guys, what then?'

'I find out what they are planning and inform Washington.'

'And you have no idea who it is that they're after?'

'The Bureau is interested in Bobrowski and McCone. Naturally we also have an interest in knowing the who and the why,' she replied defensively. Confessing her ignorance continued to weaken her position with Kelday. She had nothing with which to bargain.

If she was any judge of age, they both post-dated the stormy days of CIA–FBI rivalry, which had come to a head in the 1970s with the establishment by the CIA of the Domestic Operations Division

(DOD), a special component of the Clandestine Services. Until then, internal security had been the sole responsibility of the Bureau. It was the establishment of the DOD that, in return, allowed the Bureau to operate abroad, when circumstances dictated. But the relationship remained distrustful and competitive. Cooperation, particularly after the events of 2001, although high on the official list of priorities, for both the CIA and the FBI, was low in its quotidian application. For an agent of the Bureau to wantonly solicit the assistance of the CIA would take some explaining at field level. It was doubtful that the inter-service cooperation she had initiated, when laid on the block for examination, would receive anything other than disapprobation. A successful outcome of the operation, would be ameliorative, but complete redemption unlikely. This she had known when the idea had first presented itself. However, to succeed in her allotted task seemed infinitely preferable to failure. She would face the inquisition when it came.

'Whatever your two guys are in the frame for, is your concern. If I've got it right, your brief is simply to find them before the object of their interest arrives in Dubai.'

'Right,' she confirmed.

'Then we will see what can be done, but whether or not we find your two missing people, I would prefer you didn't get in our way.'

'Since I don't know what it is you're doing in Dubai, if I get in your way it will be an accident. Can I take it you are issuing me with a warning?' she coquettishly enquired.

'A preference, that's all. As you say, you can look after your-self.'

'Thank you. Where will you start looking?'

'My guess is they aren't too far away. If they're interested in meeting up with someone flying into Dubai they will be out here, at the airport or not far off. Can you give us a description?'

She pulled from her bag two small photos, surreptitiously gleaned from the Human Resource division of the DEA, with the help of an all too compliant staff member.

'They look like a couple of linebackers. Why don't you sit back and relax. Go for a swim or something. I'll contact you.' Before she could reply he had gone.

...*Dubai*

The boiled egg that confronted George Dolby, on the first morning of his return to the Gulf, did not receive his approval. There is no other gastronomic treat quite as idiosyncratic as the boiled egg. Its preparation, although simplistic, presents the practician with an exercise in physics. For there to be a successful outcome it is necessary for both producer and consumer to be of like mind. That they were not, on this occasion, may be traced back, through the Palestinian waiter who took the order for a lightly boiled egg, to the Bangladeshi cook, who, just a few hours previously, had been thrust into the position of breakfast chef, forsaking the pots and pans that required his cleaning, to practise a vocation about which he knew little. The interaction between egg and water had not been a success because the Filipino, who normally passed as the St George's *chef de petit déjeuner*, had, that very morning, been deported from Dubai for actions unbecoming of an illegal migrant, having failed to meet the monthly bribe demanded by a local official. Dolby, no stranger to the culinary art, viewed the ovoid stone on his plate and was tempted to carry out an invasion of the kitchen to demand satisfaction of the perpetrator, but instead, satisfied himself with another slice of cold toast, before going in search of Muhammad Ibadis and his black Buick.

Their relationship had resumed where it had left off. The intervening years were as days, between the proud Arab fixer, ensconced behind the wheel of his aging American automobile and the Crown's most loyal servant, seated imperially in the rear. Not that Dolby would ever have described himself as an imperialist, having an abhorrence for the trappings of power. Their relationship was not one of master and servant, they were not partners, nor were they friends and yet that which existed between them could be construed as possessing elements of all three, arrayed in a manner of mutual acceptability born from shared experience and respect.

'You are rested, Mr Dolby?' Muhammad enquired.

'Thank you, yes. And you?'

'Dubai has too many motor vehicles for there to be sufficient peace for sleeping.'

Dolby awaited patiently Muhammad's report. To have launched into matters of importance, without the grace of time, would have been anomic. The intervening years had seen much waiting, it had come with the job and now age provided the weapon with which to combat the frustration of time. Before, when every youthful day had produced an adventure, he had found such restraint exasperating. Now he could relax and allow events to take their prescribed course.

'There was little time to prepare for the arrival of your friend. A cousin, Ali Hassan, works at the airport. He has the honour to be among the aircraft as they come in and can easily approach your friend.' Muhammad had acquired more cousins in his life than most, drawing on the relationship at will and whenever the need arose.

'He will need to do so before others have the opportunity, Muhammad.'

'We will be the first to meet him when he arrives,' Muhammad was looking at him in the rear view mirror.

'Does he have access to the airbridge?' Dolby enquired.

'Yes. My cousin will take him from the airbridge, through a door used by engineers and down onto the ground. There will be a security van, which will be driven by another cousin, whose name you do not need to know. He will then be taken to a safe place where you will be able to talk to him.'

'Your Ali Hassan will need to look official if he is to take our friend off the airbridge.'

'That has been arranged. Both my cousins will be dressed as airport policemen. Who would stop a security van with two policemen in it?' Muhammad delivered his plan of operation with the confidence of one who had never been a victim of fate's fickle nature.

'Thank you, Muhammad. You have been busy. Your cousins will be properly rewarded for their trouble.'

'That is very generous, Mr Dolby. What would you like to do now?'

They were approaching the airport.

'We'll take a look at the layout of the terminal and see who else is interested in the upcoming event. Are you armed?'

'You are sitting on an AK47, there is also a pistol on my person. But it would not be wise to enter an airport building carrying a weapon. There are too many cameras and detecting machines, as well as a lot of policemen.'

'And your cousins. Will they be armed?' It seemed a facile question, but one that required an answer.

'All airport security officers are armed. It is part of the uniform,' Muhammad replied glibly.

Parking the conspicuous old Buick among the shining Japanese and European cars that filled the airport terminal car park, they walked, unsheltered from the burgeoning heat of the sun, towards the mirrored building that was the gateway to the emirate. The take-off of a Lufthansa Boeing 747–400 made communication between them impossible until they were inside the main concourse.

'I want to look over the ground, Muhammad.'

'Then I will meet you back at the car, Mr Dolby,' he murmured, disappearing into the crowd.

As a prop, Dolby carried an empty travel bag and a briefcase. To a casual observer he was just another Western businessman, plying his trade among the descendants of Ishmael. Above him large flight notice machines clicked away incessantly, one announcing departures the other arrivals. The growth of Dubai as an international flight terminal, eclipsing all the other states of the UAR, has made the emirate the hub of the Gulf. Thousands of international travellers daily transit through its large well-appointed modern terminal, but, on the day in question, it was the expected arrival of just one old man, a scientist from Kazakhstan, en route to a new master, that absorbed the attention of George Dolby. That he was not alone in his absorption, that there were others to whom the arrival of the man from Kazakhstan was of supreme importance, was a known and accepted fact. They were there, somewhere within the terminal complex, bent on the same task as himself, eager to gain the anticipated prize of acceptance or its elimination.

It was as he passed one of the many souvenir shops, the kind that sold poor quality brass work and Arab head-wear, that he noticed two thickset Caucasians exiting a security door that led into the operational area of the terminal. Quite why they should have attracted his attention he could not have said, but years of surveillance work had taught him to accept the validity of such intuitive feelings. If their clothes and deportment labelled them North American, the assurance with which they behaved made it possible that they were CIA. Lost momentarily from view, behind a line of pastel-shaded Taiwanese tourists in search of golf clubs, they reappeared meandering towards that point in every terminal where bleary-eyed, baggage-encumbered passengers emerge from the hiatus between plane and nation.

Keeping his distance, Dolby watched the two men circum-navigate the arrival hall, after a thorough inspection of which they returned to the main concourse, only to disappear past two heavily armed security guards into that area denied to the travelling public. The fact that they had free run of the security classified areas of the terminal was, to Dolby, proof sufficient of their pedigree. Their intent, however, had yet to be confirmed.

Through the large windows that looked out onto the tarmac an animated scene was in view. Aircraft were departing and arriving, the latter of which, upon coming to a halt, were immedi-ately surrounded by ground engineers and an army of baggage handlers. It was a scene that to him was redolent of a racing car pit-stop. As a youth, an indulgent uncle, tired from army service, had taken him to a formula one race meeting at Silverstone, where he had watched the legendary Fangio race against such luminaries as Moss and Kling. They had, through the influence of his father, been admitted to the stands that overlooked the pits. The ease, the celerity of a well-trained pit crew at work is something that impresses all those fortunate enough to have witnessed the display. It was an image that remained with him and awakened each time he travelled.

Most of the baggage handlers were of Indian origin, the physical nature and social standing of the position being beneath the native sons of the UAE. Their lethargic labours were attenuated by a pitiless sun, as trains of shimmering baggage trolleys pulled by small diesel belching tractors, careered among the stationary aircraft, coming to rest beside the cavernous holes that appeared in the side of fuselages. Fork-lift trucks removed containers, as a number of other purpose built vehicles took up position beside and under each arriving aircraft. It was a scene filled with activity and anticipation. As to how many, if any, of those reduced figures he viewed, labouring below in the polluted heat, were considering a crime against the personage of Professor Vasily Batioushenkov, it was something time would reveal.

A group of Yorkshire trainspotters noisily passed by, en route to the Himalayas, the comfort of their strong North Country dialect momentarily replacing the linguistic cacophony that echoed throughout that temple of travel. Ahead of him, two loudly attired Max-Factored American matrons in spotless white sneakers, far from their orderly mid-Western homes, went vainly hunting a bar, their bulbous bodies being quickly swallowed up by a fresh wave of Bangladeshi migrants. Everyone was going somewhere.

Alex Kelday and John Mitchell parked the unmarked air-conditioned van, in a space adjacent to the main entrance of Dubai's international airport terminal, in an area reserved for US Consulate vehicles. Other members of the team had already taken up their positions within the terminal. The strategy for the snatch they had prepared the previous day, following a reconnaissance of the area. It left little to chance and much to timing. Both men were of the opinion that success rested not in persuasion, but in the removal of all choice. If the Professor was to become a permanent guest of the US Government then the matter in hand would best be served with force and alacrity. Once the target had been apprehended, two helicopters, on standby, would whisk them off to Bahrain and an awaiting military transport aircraft. The local CIA Station Head would be left to clean up any fallout from the abduction and flight. Assuming the hit was surgically carried out, Dubai would look the other way, in preference to an embarrassing incident involving the US Government.

With plans in place and little to do but wait for the arrival of the Professor, there was time enough to locate and perhaps deal with the two DEA agents. Their removal from the equation would only improve the odds, not that they were anything more than nuisance value. Such mountebanks were apt to disrupt the synergy of an otherwise professional engagement. There was, however, the problem of legality. The arrest and detention of American nationals not engaged in acts of terrorism, even outside the United States, was the prerogative of the FBI. That they had requested the assistance of their sister organisation, albeit in an informal manner, could be construed as providing sufficient latitude in which to operate. It was a legal nicety but one Kelday was willing to exploit.

The coolness of the terminal hit both men as they entered. There was nothing to be seen of the other members of the CIA team, nor would either of them have welcomed such a revelation. Making their way to the main arrival concourse, they inspected the assembled greeters and arriving passengers. Even among such a cosmopolitan gathering it would be relatively easy to locate two Americans, the likes of Bobrowski and McCone.

Rolando Alegria, a Puerto Rican and the youngest member of Kelday's team, was the first to spot the two DEA officers. Rolando, with his Latin skin and mop of thick black hair, had, on various occasions, passed himself off as an Arab in London, a Greek in Japan and as a Filipino while assigned to the US Embassy in Canberra. That he was fluent in four languages assisted in the deception. Whatever the environment he was one of those whom you saw but did not notice. The two agents of the DEA had passed the two heavily armed security guards and gone through a door marked Restricted Entry. Taking up a position of surveillance within a shop that sold to the travel weary, books the like of which are never read beyond the confines of intercontinental aluminium tubes, he waited. His reward came when, after a short period, the two emerged again. Rolando Alegria, the chameleon, tracked the two along the concourse. Sighting Kelday he signalled unobtrusively. Within seconds three local policemen, led by a portly superintendent in starched khaki, confronted the two agents of the DEA. Kelday and Mitchell watched as they mimed their affront, protesting their innocence, only to be led away. The relationship between the CIA and the local authorities was cordial, but had undergone an improvement with the recent American assisted extirpation, from Dubai, of a virulent terrorist cell, the payment for which would be extracted as and when Langley desired. There would, of course, be the usual protests from Washington, concerning the arrest of two American nationals, which would be followed by their extradition. Of interest to Kelday was that they would be off the streets for a number of days, after which, they could be, for all he cared, buried in the desert or given twenty-four hours to disappear for ever, but not before he had questioned them on their interest in Professor Batioushenkov.

From his position in the concourse, George Dolby had also witnessed the arrest of the two DEA agents. He had also observed the arrival of Kelday and Mitchell. Recently he had noted a level of sophistication creeping into the manner in which the Americans worked. There was speciation within the intelligence community brought about by the new world order, with younger, brighter agents better able to blend into the new environment, including the extensive inclusion of ethnics and women in the field, all of which had given the agency a new and sharper cutting edge. These two, however, were, if not of his vintage, close enough to be familiar. His own fractured organisation, emerging from a forced merger and tired at birth, had yet to realise the potential that lay within Britain's ethnic minorities. Women had long been accepted within Britain's intelligence service. Britain had further led the way with the appointment, in 1991, of Stella Rimington as Director-General of MI5, the first woman to head such an organisation in a Western liberal democracy. But suspicion was held within the service, towards those of ethnic origin, resting on the, as yet unproven possibility, of divided loyalty. Would an agent of, say, Pakistan origin, an Islamist from the depth of Bradford, to whom the Indian subcontinent was foreign, would they, when push came to shove, side with London or Rawalpindi? With democracy or Islam? Such went the thinking.

Dolby watched as the two DEA agents were escorted out of sight. Whatever the reason behind that which he had just witnessed, there existed within him a surety that, in some way, it was connected to the anticipated arrival from Almaty of Professor Batioushenkov. Before his departure from London, he had anticipated rivalry for the hand of the bride from 'Hell's Kitchen'. That it had made its appearance in one guise did not negate the possibility of others eager to woo the keeper of so many evil recipes. The two men he had seen removed by the local police were American. It was a puzzle Dolby felt compelled to shelve for the moment. The Israelis had yet to put in an appearance, one that would no doubt be less obvious. The Iraqis too would be there to escort their prize. Unaware of the 'accident' in the Satawa district that had befallen the gentlemen from Beirut, about whom the Lebanese consul was unconcerned, Dolby was reliant upon Muhammad Ibadis to ferret out the Mukhabarat operatives. To Baghdad, the Professor, although an important catch, was nothing more than another ex-Soviet biochemist, another commodity Iraq would add to its existing stock. Certainly he did not qualify, as others had before him, for his own private jet, sent personally by Saddam. Batioushenkov had left his run a little late to be considered anything more than an addition to Iraq's arsenal of evil. His work on the mould, Aspergillus, was unique, as were some of his contributions in the advance of anthrax. He would be an asset, but one that only qualified for a tourist class ticket on a normal commercial flight, thus making any approach that much easier.

Dolby's plan to abduct the Professor prior to his leaving the airbridge, would, if successful, pre-empt that of his competitors, who, it was anticipated, would make their move on the Professor as he entered the main public area. Due to security considerations, passengers transferring in Dubai, for seats to Baghdad, were forced to re-register for their flight in the main departure area. Those other passengers transiting the emirate were able to avoid such inconvenience by using the transit lounge. Exiting through the main arrival area and then making his way to the departure counters would leave the aging Russian exposed to a number of possibilities.

As Dolby ruminated on the Professor's arrival, he felt suddenly detached. The frisson induced by other operations had failed to materialise, to be replaced by indifference and fatigue.

Summers had selected him for the operation out of loyalty and trust, at a time when, within the service, both commodities were rare. In Britain's newly constituted security apparatus, fractured from a previous life, Summers and Dolby were history, as were so many others who had managed to survive the redundancy purges that had preceded the merger. It was a given that their usefulness to the service would expire when it could be wheeled out of the maternity ward, a new child of the intelligence community over which the politicos would in future exercise complete control. There would be no mandarins, no established procedures or practices from the past. A new life had come into the world.

As Emma Dolby had sunk into alcoholic oblivion, the service had replaced her totally, giving a complete and explicative meaning to the world of mirrors in which he laboured. It had always been there, between them, taking him away, depriving their relationship of any continuity. The abjuration of the vow, taken before God, was not something he would have accepted as fact. In sickness and in health it had simply become a duty, one among many. If there was a divorce, it was between the practical and the emotional. Going home meant returning to the office, where support and depuration were to be found and the whole damn thing was something he would live through. Looking after Emma had become something mechanical, much of which, particularly towards the end, he had been pleased to delegate.

But, standing alone, in a foreign airport terminal, observing the unfolding of a game from which he felt removed, there now seemed little in his life of value. His lack of ambition had allowed him to complete a career, when many others, having strived for better things, had found the ground removed from under them. Now, that same insouciance had exposed a future as barren as his wife, a wife who had drunk herself to a premature death.

Above him the arrival display informed all those who were interested that Kazakh Flight 550, from Almaty, would arrive at gate 8 in just forty minutes. In a shop to his left a small crowd was gathering around a television set, slung from a wall. CNN had a message for the world that seemed to be of intense interest to those watching. Before he could move closer Muhammad appeared beside him.

'Have you been watching the television?' he enquired.

'No. Should I have?'

'There has been an uprising in Baghdad. Of more interest, bandits of the Mukhabarat, sent to bring your friend to Baghdad, were killed by a car bomb, here in Dubai. The Israelis.' He spat the last words out, as if ridding his mouth of something unpleasant. Muhammad's attitude towards Israel was no less tolerant than that of the rest of the Arab world. To him the Zionist nation was a malignant tumour on the body of the Middle East, a tumour that would one day be removed. Being a man of peace, however, it was something he would leave to others.

There had been several attempts to remove Saddam. There was no reason to suppose that this particular one would be any more successful than those previously attempted. If he had been overthrown the Professor might be forced to change his travel plans. Dolby tried to bring his mind to bear on what effect events in Baghdad might have on his rivals. The Americans would already be informed, as would the Israelis. But how would an aging Russian scientist, having turned his back on all that he had known, react to the news that his benefactor, the Butcher of Baghdad might have hung up his apron and that the services of an aging biochemist, would, in all likelihood, no longer be required?

As he looked at the small television screen over the heads of a crowd that was becoming increasingly restive, there appeared a senior Iraqi officer, flanked by two other officers, reading from a prepared text, into a battery of microphones. Martial music completed the scene. The senior officer looked serious and determined. To his left an unidentified colonel faced the world expressionlessly. On the other side a more junior officer looked about in bewilderment, seemingly confused by the events that had put him in front of the world.

Benjamin Disraeli's dictum, 'Assassination has never changed the history of the world,' is a message that has gone unheeded among the military of Iraq. Since World War II there have been a number of coups, including that of Abdul-Karim Qassem who, along with other 'Free Officers' killed the young King Feisal II and the Crown Prince. Qassem was himself overthrown, as were others who followed until the arrival on stage of Saddam Hussein.

The plots were similar, only the actors gave it a contemporary appearance.

Dolby again glanced at the flight information screen. Kazakh Flight 550 was no longer showing. The rotating indicators fluttered then came to rest. Still no indication of Kazakh Flight 550, its place on the screen having been taken by an EVA flight from Singapore. Across the hall the two Americans he had earlier observed had also noted the disappearance of Kazakh Flight 550 and were heading towards a flight information desk.

Dubai International Airport Police Station

Alex Kelday and John Mitchell had quickly assembled their team, with time to spare, before a US government chartered helicopter would fly them to Bahrain, where Kazakh Flight 550 now sat with a major malfunction in one of its two Soviet built engines. Such was the financial situation within Kazakhstan's national airline that few expected the grounded aircraft to fly again. Its passengers would remain stranded in Bahrain, until a carrier could be found that was willing to take on the debt for onward passage, there being little hope that they would ever receive payment for providing such a service.

The removal of the two delinquent DEA agents to the holding cells of the airport's new police station, pending the purported arrival of the US Consul, afforded the opportunity for Kelday, along with Kate Cranley, to briefly question both men. She had been quickly summoned to the airport, having sat in her hotel, waiting for Kelday to make contact.

Bobrowski sat across the table with the confidence of innocence. He had, he explained, been on a mission fully sanctioned by his superiors, the nature of which he would not divulge without their explicit instruction, in writing. With no time to confer, Kelday and Cranley were impelled to extemporise.

'I'm not concerned with your future,' Kelday said, 'or that of your buddy, Bobrowski. To be frank, your so-called "mission" is not strictly kosher. Whatever is going on here, you two are out on a limb and you've got both the CIA and your own agency on your butts. I don't have time to spend playing games. You can rot in an Arab jail for eternity as far as I'm concerned. On the other hand you can both walk out that door and take your chances on the street. Just tell us, why the interest in Vasily Batioushenkov?'

'You can't hold US Government officials without proper authority. I have the right to see the US Consul.' Bobrowski's voice was relaxed and confident. It was a protestation the words of which reminded Kate Cranley of her own incarceration at the hands of the US Navy.

'The US Consul has been delayed. In fact he's delayed until we're finished with you. I wouldn't be surprised if he doesn't wash his hands of you two.' Kelday rose from his chair to stand behind Bobrowski, his head level with that of the seated man. 'Whatever it was you two were going to do to the good Professor, it's over. And I'm picking that so is your time with Uncle Sam. You're on your own.'

The vehemence with which he pursued Bobrowski came as a surprise to Kate Cranley. He had approached the interview like a sprinter leaves the blocks. Kelday was either bluffing, or he knew as much about their activities as herself. Possibly more.

'We were just doing what we were told to do,' Bobrowski protested.

'Told by whom?' Cranley asked.

'Our boss, in Washington. You can check, if you like.'

'I already have and the news is not good. You two have been hung out to dry. Nobody at the agency wants to know, so whoever you thought you were working for has dealt you a dud. You have both just become fall guys,' she replied.

'I'm running out of time, Bobrowski. Perhaps your buddy, McCone, can tell us what we want to know. If he does he walks and you stay.' Kelday returned to his seat.

Bobrowski reached into his pocket.

Kelday waved a finger in the air. 'No smoking. It's bad for the health.'

After a pause Bobrowski sat back in his chair and laid both hands on the table. 'We were told to make sure this professor guy didn't make it beyond Dubai, that's all.'

'That's all,' repeated Cranley. 'Since when did the DEA engage in assassination?'

'Lady, where have you been?' he replied.

'On whose orders, Bobrowski?' Kelday enquired.

'I told you. Our boss.'

Kelday slid across the table a small piece of paper and a pen. 'Write down his name and anybody else that comes to mind.'

Bobrowski wrote down one name and returned the paper to Kelday.

'Why did your boss want the Professor removed?' she asked.

'I don't know. Ask him yourself.'

'I have a helicopter waiting for me, Bobrowski. If you want to leave here without an escort, talk.'

Beyond the slab concrete of the police station, a Boeing 777 was winding up for take-off.

Bobrowski looked about him as one who had only recently become aware of his surroundings.

After a pause, he spoke. 'OK. McCone and I, well, let's say we enjoy our job, if you know what I mean. We have our own way of doing things, but on this one we were just following orders. Make sure that this guy doesn't get to Baghdad, that is what they said.'

'They?' Kelday repeated. 'You gave us only one name.'

'After some talk with Washington, McCone and I were finally briefed for this job in Bahrain. The boss came out personally for the briefing. That was different. There was another guy, neither of us had ever seen him before. He was also DEA, or so he said, but we weren't told his name. He seemed to be higher up the chain. It was his operation.'

'And you have no idea why they put out a contract on the Professor?' Kelday asked.

'Something to do with his work?' he suggested.

'Now we are getting somewhere. Why didn't you say so?'

'I don't think they wanted him eliminated because he drank too much, do you? It had to be his work, didn't it?' Bobrowski was beginning to sweat. Although air-conditioned, the room was hot and smelt of paint. The builders had only recently vacated and small piles of sawdust lay on the floor. The ceiling had yet to be painted and the one window still had builders' tape across the glass.

A cell phone rang.

'Your time is up, Bobrowski, I have to leave. They're all yours Ms Cranley. I'll send in a guard.' He made to leave.

'So we can go?' Bobrowski asked.

'That's up to Ms Cranley.' Kelday held out his hand to her.

'Nice working with you, Kate. Perhaps we can do it again some time.' And he was gone. An Arab policeman, with a side arm, entered and stood by the door.

Kate Cranley sat in her chair and examined the prisoner. He was large, with a bull neck around which hung an immodest gold medallion, that sat on a pillow of greying hair spilling from his shirt front. It was the sort of neck that, in collar and tie, would always look too big for the shirt. Small beads of sweat collected on his upper lip. From what little she knew of the man, the swiftness of his cooperation had come as a surprise. Perhaps, knowing that both he and McCone were expendable, he had only been waiting for such a day. He must have known that the game in which they were engaged was being played out on several layers and that theirs was not at the top. His hands, the backs of which were covered in black hair, were still spread out on the table. Large gold rings adorned three of his fingers. Two on his left hand and one on his right.

'You're not DEA, are you?' he said, reclaiming some of his confidence.

'Who I am is not your biggest worry. If there is nothing more you want to tell me I'll see what your friend McCone has to say.'

'When will the Consul be here?' he enquired.

'Couldn't say.' As she made towards the door Bobrowski rose from his chair, the bulkiness of his body having been hidden while seated and his physical presence now seeming to fill the room. The guard moved as if to draw his weapon. Cranley paused.

'Yes?' she turned to face Bobrowski.

'Let me get this right. I tell you what I know and I walk. Is that the deal?'

'Let's see what it is that you know and then we can decide.'

'No walk, no deal,' he said, slumping back in the chair.

Knowing that, in all probability, she lacked the legitimate right to hold him in custody, she made as if to resume her seat, but then remained by the door. She could feel the lecherous eyes of the policeman exploring her.

Prior to entering the room, Kelday had quickly informed her of the fate of Flight 550, news that was of limited importance to her, now that both Bobrowski and McCone were out of circulation. However, it begged the question of what she should do next. Attempt to have them deported? Sit tight until help arrived with an arrest warrant? Her brief had simply been to find out what business they had with the man from Kazakhstan.

'You are in no position to say what is and what is not a deal, Mr Bobrowski. Don't you understand, your boss has pulled up the drawbridge on you. The DEA doesn't want to know. The best on offer might be that you and McCone tell all and then, as the man said, "You take your chances on the street." You've probably both got some money hidden away for your retirement. Now might be a good time to start using it.'

'How about some coffee?' he enquired.

'That might be arranged. Think about what I said, while I see how your friend is getting on.' She was pleased to leave the room and its smell, pleased to be free, if only for a minute, from the policeman's eyes.

Through a small aperture she could see McCone laying on a bench, gazing at an unpainted ceiling. She would probably get no more information from him than she had from Bobrowski. Having requested some coffee, she was about to return to the interview room when her way was blocked by an Arab police officer, wearing an immaculate uniform. He was tall, in his late thirties and exuded an air of authority.

'You are here to interview the two American prisoners? Could we speak in my office, please,' he said, gesturing towards an open door.

'Please excuse the mess. We are still moving into the building as you can see.'

'Thank you for your cooperation, officer.' She would like to have addressed him by his rank, but the pips on his epaulettes meant nothing to her. She supposed that he might be an inspector of some kind.

'Our arrangement with Mr Kelday was of a temporary nature. Your fellow countrymen have not, as far as I am aware, committed a crime in Dubai. An intention to do so would, I think, be hard to prove. Don't you agree?' His speech was measured and friendly.

'I would like just a few more minutes with them, if that's OK?'

'After which I must release them or your Consul will start to complain,' he replied.

'I doubt that. Thank you. Your English is very good. Have you spent some time in London?'

'I lived in England as a child and went through the police college at Hendon. My wife is English.'

'And now you are a policeman in Dubai.' She could think of nothing else to say.

'As you see. For the moment we will make sure your friends don't leave the Emirate, that is, unless you would like them expelled. But on what basis?'

'I have to get in touch with Washington. If they can't leave town, then I guess there's no rush.'

'You will find coffee waiting for you in the interview room. I hope it meets with your approval, I know how much you Americans like your coffee.'

'Coffee drinking, along with a number of other things, is a national sin.'

'Something of which we are all guilty, Ms Cranley.'

Bobrowski was drinking his second cup as she entered.

She poured her own and settled into a chair before speaking. The eyes of the policeman were again viewing her with undisguised pleasure.

'Your friend McCone wants to speak,' she lied.

'What about? He doesn't know any more than I do. Look, this Russian is passing through Dubai on his way to Baghdad. We get told to do the business on him. To make sure he doesn't leave Dubai. Why, we don't know. Perhaps he's upset someone in Washington. Who knows?' He sat looking at her.

She let a moment pass before replying. 'Why don't you speculate a little? I mean, why you? Why the DEA? You said yourself, it must be to do with his work. What was he doing in Kazakhstan?'

'He was a biochemist. What do Russian biochemists do? Particularly the kind who go for a career change in Baghdad? Maybe he was making crap stuff. You know, the kind that wipes out thousands.'

'Except that biological warfare is not normally the business of the DEA. Is it?'

'So maybe the agency is branching out,' he replied. 'Look, if you worked for the DEA, which I don't think for one damn minute you do, then you would know that you don't go asking questions. Like "why" is something you don't ask. Maybe he was making crack, on the side. Who knows?'

Bobrowski was a man with few illusions. His time as a rogue agent within the DEA had exposed him to all manner of corruption, some of which was at his own instigation, the rest he was only too willing to succumb to and be part of. That it reached right to the top of the totem pole was a given.

Dubai

Mahashweta Patel was startled by the phone that rang on her desk. It had invaded her consciousness, evicting the puzzle to which she sought an answer, namely the identification and whereabouts of goods, taken from a guarded empty warehouse. This puzzle along with concern for the health of a man to whom she was increasingly attracted, had dominated her thinking since leaving his bedside.

'Miss Mahashweta?'

'Speaking.'

'We have a mutual friend who has met with an accident. I believe you are helping to nurse him to better health.'

'Who is speaking?' She did not recognise the voice, but detected, beneath the accented English, a European, although he had addressed her, as would an Arab, using her first name after the title.

'Please, I am a friend. We need to meet?'

'We do?'

'Yes. I will be in a blue SAAB, at the *abras* terminal, Al-Sabkha and Beniyas. 5 p.m.' Giving her no time to refuse, he rang off.

She sat staring at the phone. Quickly, but methodically, she worked through the list of those who knew of the shooting in the hotel. There were a number of possibilities.

It was 4 p.m. Whenever the partners were absent from the building, family members tended to drift off early, leaving the office to those unfortunate enough not to have been born into the House of Patel. Their lot in life was to serve the family business, but was it not verity, that they had a better life than that which they would have been subject to in Calcutta or Madras? It was true that most non-family employees were second-generation Gulf residents and thankful to be part of the economic miracle that was Dubai, grateful also to, if not envious of, the family that had helped to make it all possible. She would need all of the hour, if she was to complete the report in front of her, return to her apartment, shower, change and be at the Creek by 5 p.m.

As she hurried through the evening crowd, the quayside lights were illuminated, casting a multitude of weak shadows on the polluted water of the Creek and reflecting off the paint on the blue SAAB that waited innocently beside the quay. Inside sat the hunched figure of a man who looked to be in his late twenties. The mop of greasy black curls that sat under a blue denim cap, stopped just short of the soiled collar of a shirt that stuck to him, a patchwork of sweat. She had barely entered the car before he drove off, without speaking.

'Who are you?' she enquired, looking at the profile of the stranger. He did not reply. The car's air-conditioning unit, she could not fail but notice, was in conflict with the body odour of its driver. It was a victory of man over machine. Having got her into his car he was now happy to ignore her.

She drew comfort from her left hand that gripped the friendly small stock of a Browning hammerless .25 automatic, in the pocket of her trousers. It was a weapon with limited range, being utterly useless beyond three metres, but deadly in the confines of a car.

Just five minutes later they drove into the almost empty car park of a tall glass-fronted office building, where they parked between two identical tall white commercial vans.

'It is good that you came. We need to talk. Before I tell you who I am, let me tell you who you are.'

'I already know that,' she replied.

'You are Mahashweta Patel, niece of Iqbal Patel, head of the House of Patel. He's also your employer. You were educated first in India and then in California where you were recruited by Dharma, part of Indian's intelligence community. What does Dharma mean? Is it an acronym?'

Now it was her turn not to reply.

'Never mind. It is of little importance. You are here protecting the interests of mother India. Their woman in the Gulf, we might say. Am I right so far?' His tone was sardonic.

'I don't know what you're talking about. But if I was who you seem to think I am, would I admit it to you?' Her dislike of the stranger was both immediate and professionally egregious.

'That too is of little importance, although it would help us in our mutual interests.'

'Which are?'

'The contents of certain warehouses along this coast, where the consignments have been moved to and, of course, let us not forget the health of Gerald Lindsay.'

'And what is your interest in Gerald Lindsay? No, don't tell me. It was you who killed the other man in the hotel.'

He shrugged.

'Gerald, Mr Lindsay, does he work for the Israeli Government?' she asked.

'If he did, would you expect me to confirm it?' She was witness to a rare smile.

'Mr Lindsay came to Dubai to carry out some business. He is no longer able to complete that business. Now we are more interested in another matter. That is why you and I are sitting here. We should work together.'

She was finding the smell within the car suffocating. It was the odour of a man not recently acquainted with the benefits of either soap or water and which, in the heat of the Gulf, can become, objectionable in the extreme. Forsaking the questionable effect of the air conditioning, she opened the window, allowing in a light evening breeze that blew in off the Creek. He was, she observed, so unlike Gerald. They could have been from different planets, rather than, what she assumed to be, the same country. The one disciplined and groomed, almost military in his behaviour. The other putrescent, the sort of ex-patriot to be found among the brothels and illicit drinking establishments of the Gulf, waiting for the chance to secure a small piece of the immense wealth that sloshed around that small area of the globe.

It would not be easy to work with such a repulsive man. 'What proof do I have that we are on the same side?' The naivety of what she had said struck her before the words were all out. Of course there would be no proof. Proof, like truth, did not exist within the world they shared.

'I don't have a CV to show you. It doesn't exist in our line of business, as I am sure you are aware. You may not trust me, but you do, I think, trust our mutual acquaintance, Mr Lindsay. Am I right?'

'What if I do?' It was true, she had trusted him, even if that trust had not been fully reciprocated.

'We will go to the hotel and I will give you a word. He will verify it for you and then we can stop wasting time. India is too far away to feel the need for urgency, but for us each day is a threat.'

'For us?' Was she near to hearing a confession? 'Who is "us"? You said you were going to tell me who you were.'

'Did I?' Starting the car, he reversed from between the two white vans. As he stopped to move into forward gear, she caught a glimpse of the right-hand rear door of one of the vans slowly closing.

They drove in silence through the busy evening streets, she with her window down, taking in the smell of the streets and exhaust fumes, preferring both to that of her driving companion and he, slumped in his seat but alert, like a cat. She had not had to tell him the way. He was as familiar as herself with the roads of the emirate. A small diversion was explained upon their arrival. There, sitting by the curb, across the road, was a white van. Their escort had been allowed to precede them, the appearance of which was confirmation of Israel's concern with the contents of the warehouses. He did not stop in front of the hotel, but drove around the corner, coming to rest outside a small bakery. One of two men, clad in the traditional dish-dasha and seated at a small sidewalk table in front of the shop, looked up from under his gutra and then resumed his conversation. Although her driver ignored them, as he left the vehicle, she knew that their presence begged no explanation. They were part of a protective shield that would not allow their enemy a second attempt at killing Mr Lindsay.

She left the stranger in the blue denim cap, at the bottom of the stairs, within the hotel. Two Indian youths now stood sentinel outside the door of their injured guest. Gerald Lindsay had again been moved, this time to a room that overlooked a small inner courtyard. As she unlocked the door and entered, his hand had moved swiftly beneath the sheets and she found herself looking into the barrel of a machine pistol. He was sitting up in bed, his head and shoulder swathed in bandages. He looked drawn and pale.

'Diana,' he greeted her with more enthusiasm than intended.

'And how is the patient today? Ready to blow my head off?'

'He just got a lot better,' he replied, sliding the gun out of sight.

'I'm glad to hear it,' she said, sitting down beside him. 'They are certainly protecting you. There are two young men outside your door and two of your own people on the street, around the corner, along with two small trucks full of who knows what.'

'What do you mean?'

Quickly she explained her meeting with the man in the blue SAAB, at the same time, giving him the validating word, 'Shamor'.

'What does it mean?' she asked.

'Observe, it means observe.'

'So?'

'It also means you can trust the man who gave it to you.'

'That's comforting. Even if he doesn't wash. I think it's the same man who killed the other—'

'Possibly,' he interjected. 'Will you keep me informed about what you are doing?'

'Is that allowed? I mean, if this man is taking over your job, won't he want my total loyalty?' she said with a smile.

'He might want it, but I'm sure he won't get it. After all, there's the House of Patel and then there is…' he paused.

'What?'

'A sick man has time to think. How is it, I asked myself, that a humble secretary knows so much? Invites me to go snooping around empty warehouses in the night? And why is she so sure that I am not who I say I am? Also, why is she so interested in the secret affairs of her employer? Which brought me around to asking, who she really is and who is she working for?'

'And what conclusion did you come to?' she asked.

'That will have to wait. You should leave now, otherwise people will begin to talk.'

'In Dubai people are always talking. It is what they do best. Talk and make money—'

'Diana, I am a married man.' It sounded ridiculous, but he had, for a number of days, wanted to tell her. To be honest about it, whatever she may think. Why, in such a fallen world, did it matter? Would she even care? Why had he, a trained operative of one of the most efficient intelligence services in the world, found it necessary to tell her? It wasn't as if there hadn't been other women in the course of his work. It was part of the job. It was also, however, something he and Ruth shut out. Their marriage was secure within the rules they themselves had created and any intimacies with other women had taken place in the name and for the protection of Israel and as such were no threat to their family. Being faithful to his country did not mean he was unfaithful to either Ruth or the boys.

She stared back at him. Sweat began to form on his forehead. A broad grin spread across her pleasing face. 'I know,' she said, releasing him from his discomfort.

'How?' he enquired.

'Whatever I am, I am still a woman and a woman can tell, especially when the man is a good one. I would also say that your marriage is a happy one. Correct?'

'Yes. Yes, it is.'

'Which is saying a lot, considering your line of work.'

'I—' he attempted to speak, but she interrupted him.

'Please, I don't need to know any more.' She gently touched his hand. 'I must go. Has the doctor been today?' Suddenly she might have been a nurse on a crowded ward, asking after the health of a favoured patient.

As she made to leave he said, 'Diana, the man who brought you here. You can trust him, but be careful. You might say that he and I are both of the same desert, but different tents.'

Descending the stairs she could smell the man who waited for her at the bottom. What did Gerald mean by different tents? Had she moved seamlessly from working with one part of the Israeli intelligence community to working with another? And if so, what difference did it make?

Dharma means righteousness or duty and to contravene dharma is to invite disaster. It was not an intelligence service that attracted the attention of the world, but its main adversary, Pakistan, knew well how deadly it could be. Unlike most intelligence organisations, it relies upon a loose cooperative arrangement with its agents. Initiative and enterprise along with a loose administrative structure, characterise Dharma. It is extremely flexible and operates wherever there exists an Indian community, which gives it global coverage. Dharma has broken the world down into various groups, the individual administration of which is left to a regional controller, who reports to a Director-General in Delhi. At one stage in its development, the British had been requested to submit a tender for the training of agents. But after some consideration they had declined, as it did not conform to any existing intelligence institution with which they were familiar. They were unable to understand the framework within which they or Dharma were expected to operate. A similar request to the United States had been withdrawn, following the transfer of sensitive intelligence material from Washington to Rawalpindi, after which it was decided that India would find its own way within the mirrored world of the international intelligence community. This was the inscrutable organization for which Mahashweta Patel worked.

'I assume you are satisfied?' he asked.

Since first hearing him over the phone, she had attempted to identify the moderate European accent behind his English. Now she knew. Russian Jew. It had come to her out of the past. While studying in California she and some classmates had driven out to hear a world famous pianist at the famed Hollywood Bowl. The man who now stood in front of her and the pianist she had listened to enraptured, all those year before, were almost one and the same, save for their attire.

'You don't, by any chance, play the piano, do you?' she enquired, as they left the hotel.

'Why do you ask?'

'No reason. Gerald, Mr Lindsay, says I can trust you. The question is, should I?'

'It would help us both, if you did. Either way I intend to find out where the material from the warehouse has gone, along with the other consignments. And your Mr Lindsay has given me his seal of approval, which should be enough.'

The suggestion that she had some sort of proprietorial rights on 'her Mr Lindsay,' was not an unpleasant one. She had found herself looking forward to her brief visits to the hotel, where she would dress his wounds and serve him tea. There had been no one in her life for some time. Her uncle had seen to that. Dubai was too small and his influence too wide.

They were now driving back towards the Creek. In the mirror and keeping a discreet distance behind, she could see a white van.

'Do you know what my uncle had, in the warehouse?'

'We have an idea about what it was. There are similar consignments stored around the Gulf.'

'If you think we can work together, without your telling me what you know, you should think again. Sharing is a two-way street where I come from.' Gerald Lindsay had been equally as reticent. It was, however, a disposition she would not accept from this stranger.

'What do you want to know?' They were back at the Creek. She looked out at the various vessels navigating their nocturnal way between Deira and Bur Dubai. Water taxis darted about, like intermittent sea-born fireflies, alight for seconds in the floodlight of the quay, only to become small shadows in wet relief. The white van that had followed them was no longer in sight. She had little doubt however, that it would not be far away.

'Let's start with the easy one,' she commenced. 'Who are you? After all, you claim to know who I am. If you want us to work together I think I should know who I am dealing with.'

'You have not chosen well. Try again.' His hands rested on the steering wheel. They were strong, with short fat fingers, the nails of which harboured filth accumulated over many days. She could never imagine allowing such hands to touch her, not that he had shown any interest in her as a woman. Rather she felt that he was as likely to snap her neck as caress it. His languor masked a violence equal to any she had imagined possible. Any comfort this man sought from the female sex would be paid for from the contents of his wallet.

'OK,' she said. 'Let's try this one. What do you think was in the warehouse?'

'That specific warehouse, the one you and your Mr Lindsay

visited?' Was he playing with her or engaged in some verbal exploration. She could feel anger mounting within her.

'Yes. That specific one,' she replied decisively.

'I think I can answer that one.'

He turned to look at her, before speaking. 'Patchouli.'

'Patchouli?' So that was the smell they had experienced in the warehouse. 'Gerald said he had smelt it in the bag they put over his head, when he was attacked.'

'Thanks to you, your Mr Lindsay stumbled on something that we were already aware of, but could not locate. With your help he merely pointed us in the right direction.'

'You mean my uncle had a warehouse guarded for sacks of patchouli?'

'Let's not denigrate a very rich smelling plant. One that comes from your own country. It's normally used in the manufacture of perfume. But in this case it had another use.'

'What?'

'We think it was to cover a consignment of Iranian Shahab–350 short to medium-range rockets. A number of these missiles have been positioned along the coast, in Dubai, Qatar, Bahrain and Kuwait ready to be fired, simultaneously, at ships in the Gulf.'

'You mean oil tankers?'

'We believe the targets to be American warships of the 5th Fleet. You would agree that it is not in the interest of anyone, except the fanatics, that these ships be attacked?'

'So why aren't the Americans searching for these things?'

'We believe our methods to be more successful than theirs,' he replied sardonically.

'And your country gets to earn some much needed brownie points with Washington.'

'I leave politics to others.'

'These missiles must be large. Even if you can hide their parts in bales of patchouli until its use date, how do you put together such a weapon and fire it undetected?'

'The Shahab–350 is one of a new breed of covert rockets. The technology is Chinese. They come together like a child's building set. A half competent engineer would be able to assemble it in less than two days. The missile probably has a single warhead with conventional explosive. But then, maybe not. Maybe there is something more threatening on the end. We cannot wait to find out. You are in a good position to help us locate the other consignments quickly and before they are moved. The House of Patel does business in all the places that are of interest to us and your uncle is at the centre of it all. It would be easy for you to help us find out what we want to know.'

'Not as easy as you think. My uncle has been very secretive about his dealings with the Saudis. But if these missiles have come from Iran, why are the Saudis involved and why position them in the Gulf States?' She already knew the answers to the questions she had asked. What she needed was time to think. It would not be possible to contact her regional controller, or solicit from Delhi their analysis of the situation, as it might affect India. And even if she could, there would be little time for them to reply. If the consignment in Dubai was on the move, just as the stranger feared, then so also might the others.

The stranger removed his cap and ran his fingers through a thick mat of unwashed hair. Replacing his hat he said, 'It works like this. The Saudis pick up the tab, Iran supplies the missiles and Islamic Jihad, The Voice of Gaza, Hizbollah, whoever, delivers it. Riyadh and Tehran can deny all involvement and the Gulf States are drawn into a war they have, until now, managed to stay out of. All very simple.' After a short pause, he added, steely, 'We don't have the benefit of time, Ms Mahashweta. What we want you to do is help us gain access to your uncle's office. After that we will do the rest. It is best that our visit to the House of Patel goes unnoticed. Only the night watchman will be there at this time. We know that all of the partners are away, including your uncle. What could be more normal than your returning to your office to pick up something you forgot. You can help us get into the building and keep the watchman occupied while we find out where the other missiles are located.'

'You seem well informed. But then, you have been dealing with my uncle for some time.'

'You disapprove? I am sure your boss in New Delhi would want you to work with us, if only for world peace. Something your government is keen to promote. We are on the same side.

I'm only asking you to help supply some information. What we do with it need not concern you.'

'Why do you need me? Why not just use your goons to storm the place and take what you want?' Her reference to 'goons' failed to rile him.

'We could do that. But, as I have already said, we want the visit to go unnoticed.'

He was running out of patience with the woman who asked too many questions when time was what mattered most.

'What about the consignment here in Dubai? Don't you need to find out where that has been moved to?' she asked.

'We are working on that. We haven't located it yet, but we will and you will help us. What we want to know is where the others are stored.'

'Are you sure that the information you want is in my uncle's office?'

'Where else would it be? Anyway, it is a good place to start looking. And you will help us.' There was a suggestion in his voice that any choice she may have had in the matter was quickly evaporating.

'What about Gerald? Mr Lindsay?'

'What about him?' he asked quizzically.

'What are you going to do with him? He is too sick to move. Have you thought about that?'

She reasoned that, if they were to find the missile and strike at the terrorists in Dubai, Gerald's life would be in even more danger.

'Your concern for him is commendable, if misplaced. We are all expendable in this line of business. Or haven't you worked that out yet?'

'That is not how I see it. If you want me to help you there has to be some guarantee that you get him safely out of Dubai. You have saved his life once, now do it again.' As she spoke the stranger moved in his seat to face her and she was suddenly assailed again by his odour.

'You said yourself, he is too sick to move. We are not here as some Red Cross evacuation service. For that you should phone Geneva. After we have dispensed with the missiles we'll look after your Mr Lindsay. Meanwhile he is safe enough.'

'I don't think that is good enough.' From every viewpoint her stand was an abjuration of professionalism, the defence of which would be hard to justify. What was the value of one man? A week ago she had not known he even existed, yet here she was bargaining for his life.

'We will take your Mr Lindsay with us when we leave, sick or not.' Chillingly, he added, 'We don't leave our people behind.'

'Do you want to go now?' Her acceptance had relieved what was becoming, an increasingly hostile atmosphere.

Arriving at her office, she had seen both white vans in the short street that led to the House of Patel. They were parked 300 metres apart on different sides of the otherwise deserted street. The security guard, a retainer of many years' standing, had admitted her to the building without question, securing the large ornate doors behind her. He did not question her arrival, at such an hour. To have laid doubt on the veracity of her visit would have been to challenge the very structure upon which the House was built. Family members enjoyed immunity from suspicion, except among themselves.

Once behind her desk she had summoned the guard to help her move some computer equipment from one office to another, the location of which would keep them well away from her uncle's domain. For a family member to be moving furniture around and outside of office hours, not to mention soliciting the assistance of the guard, who regarded his position to be superior to that of the office janitor, would set tongues wagging among the staff. After which it would only be a matter of time before her uncle became aware of what had taken place. As well as having to answer to her regional controller and Delhi for the evening's activities she would have to front up to her autocratic employer. These three impending confrontations sat in the back of her mind as she manipulated the servile servant in the arranging and rearranging of the furniture. Unable to sustain the charade any longer, she had, in aberration, sat and engaged the man in conversation, solicitously asking after the welfare of his extended family. Such familiarity should have alerted the guard, instead he bathed in the attention being extended to one so humble by an exulted personage, albeit a junior member of the family. As she listened to him there came from the direction of her uncle's office a sharp crack, after which, silence. Clearly they had gained access to the building. Had the guard heard what she had heard? If so, he gave no indication of it, but continued to regale her on the convoluted machinations of his large and seemingly, dysfunctional Bengali family, the size and adventures of which grew with the telling. After what seemed like hours, but in reality was less than twenty minutes, she heard the prearranged signal, two short blasts on the horn of one of the vans, indicating that the team were clear of the building. After hearing both vehicles drive away, she tactfully attempted to conclude her conversation with the guard, but the man had warmed to the occasion and was oblivious of her desire to terminate, what had become for her, an irritating background noise. Abruptly she stood to leave. To her utter shock and surprise, the elderly guard, instead of standing deferentially aside, grabbed her arm and pushed her against the wall, where he rubbed himself against her. It took a number of seconds for her to realise what had happened. An attack on a member of the family, by an Indian staff member, by any staff member, was as unlikely as the sun rising in the west. It had been unplanned, a moment when the man had allowed his fading lust to take control and, in so doing, put into danger the livelihood and well-being of all those reliant upon him. Such was the influence and power of the House that they had only to mention a name to the Dubai authorities for the miscreant to be on the next dhow leaving port.

The shock and surprise she felt were quickly replaced, first by repugnance and then by relief, as she pushed him clear. It was the first time he had seen her in Western dress, was it this that had inflamed the man?

He staggered back, knocking a number of files from a desk top, their contents spilling across the floor. She looked him in the eyes and saw both lust and fear. He had grasped the gravity of his situation almost as quickly as she had seen the advantage. For a brief second she could see his mind turning over the possibilities, one of which would have been to kill her and pretend there had been a break-in, but only after he had violated her further. Or he would back off and possibly pretend it had all been a mistake.

Before he had arrived at a conclusion she had moved away to gain authority, to confront him as niece of the head of the House of Patel. She ordered him to stay where he was, as a lion tamer would address a large cat in the ring. Within him a lifetime of docility and servitude hung in the balance, as lust and fear struggled for supremacy. He froze.

'Are you mad?' she screamed. 'Do you realise who I am? Do you want to be sent back to India along with your entire pestilent family? How dare you attack me.' There comes a time, in every similar confrontation, when all is lost or gained, on a word or a deed. Would he back down or, feeling that all was already lost, continue the assault?

He remained frozen. Seizing the moment she continued to harangue him.

'You'll pay for this. Attacking me is the most stupid thing you have ever done in your meaningless life. I will make sure that you are finished with the House of Patel. You can start packing your bags!'

Slowly the man sank to his knees, all the lust and aggression now drained into a pool of despair and contrition.

'I am so sorry. Please, I didn't intend to hurt you. It was a mistake, I—'

'It was that, all right. Who do you think I am? Surely you didn't think I would let you touch me?'

'No, Miss. No. I am unworthy. Please forgive me. I will do anything, but you must not tell the master.'

'You don't tell me what I can and what I cannot do. Do you hear me?' Her voice rose to a level the like of which neither he, nor any of the others who worked in the House of Patel, would have heard before. Suddenly, she felt free. The graceful sari-clad secretary, in the leather sandals, who had glided so serenely through the commercial rooms of her uncle's firm, had emerged into a screaming banshee and she found the experience exhilarating.

The security guard now cowed and still on his knees, begged for both his family and forgiveness.

'You are a stupid man. Do you hear?'

'Yes, Miss.'

'You are responsible for the lives of your family, yet you act like an animal. If I were to tell my uncle what has happened, you would be out of here and out of Dubai so fast there wouldn't even be time for you to get out of the uniform you have just disgraced.'

Sensing that all may not yet be lost, the man now lay prostrate on the floor, affecting the most sympathetic whimper.

'If you want to keep your miserable position with this family you will say nothing about what has happened here this evening. You will pretend that I was never here. Do you understand?'

'Yes, Miss.' His eyes narrowed as he tried to think how he might best turn events to his advantage. This woman had something to hide, why else would she engage in such a subterfuge, and the humiliation he had just been subjected to would have to be avenged. He would continue to grovel at her feet until the time was right for him to use the knowledge he was now party to.

'Now get up and go back to your duties. If I hear that you have talked about your attack on me to anyone, you are finished.'

'Yes, Miss.' So saying he slunk from her presence.

As she left the building she felt the eyes of the guard stabbing her in the back. Looking around she saw a shadow move swiftly from one of the windows.

Bahrain International Airport

Bahrain International Airport is on the island of Muharraq, just ten minutes from central Manama, the new capital of the monarchy. Although home to one of the region's largest carriers it is now second both in size and prestige to its sister airport at Dubai, none of which was of interest to those on board the chartered helicopter that touched down in that part of the airport leased by the US Defence Department. As they came into land Alex Kelday and his reduced CIA team had seen Kazakh Flight 550 on the ground, parked away from the main terminal. Efforts were being made to tow the broken aircraft to an even more remote part of the airport complex. Whoever, whatever had been on board the aging Tupolev 134B, had long been offloaded, following the premature termination of its flight.

One of 850 produced in Russia, it had been built at the Kharkov factory and had once been part of the STIGL fleet based in Grozni, Chechnia, most of which were destroyed in the battles that enveloped that unfortunate republic. Having escaped to Almaty, along with thirty flight crew and their families, it had been requisitioned by the government of Kazakhstan and pressed into service for the national airline, only to die now on the apron at Bahrain. Although on the ground but a few hours, this once proud workhorse of Soviet aviation already looked derelict. The cowlings of both Soloviev D303 rear-mounted engines were covered in oil, the tyres worn through to the canvas save for those on the outer wheels. The paintwork was peeling from the fuselage, revealing evidence of its previous owner. The tail fin and rudder swung free, stark evidence of a crew having failed to complete their shutdown checks. A forward passenger exit had been left open and a number of items lay scattered about the apron. Tupolev, production number 66191, built in 1983, would join a number of other aircraft for which Bahrain had become the final resting place.

Although the US Navy had only a short time in which to prepare, they had met Kelday's return from Dubai with the information and equipment requested. Having left half his team behind and all but the most essential pieces of equipment, Alex Kelday had been forced to call on the assistance of the Navy, through the local CIA agent. The news that now greeted him was not that which he wanted to hear.

Passengers from Kazakh Flight 550 had been allowed, through an error that no one could explain, to pass through customs and were now scattered around the terminal, awaiting onward passage to Dubai that would never come.

As the military jeep swung out of the Navy compound towards the international terminal, the black Navy driver described to Kelday the dramatic arrival of Kazakh Flight 550. Having declared an emergency it had been given priority in the approach sequence. Believing that he also had priority in the landing sequence, the pilot had come barrelling in on one engine, landing down wind, forcing a Gulf Air flight to overshoot and an Air France B747–400 to abort its approach. Once on the ground, the airport authority had made sure that the miscreant flying machine was marshalled to an area away from more respectable aircraft.

In the terminal Kelday and Mitchell approached the service counter for Gulf Air, the reluctant agent for Kazakh Air. The attractive woman behind the counter, wearing the trademark headscarf of her company, could only tell them of the chaotic arrival of Flight 550 and the adventitious dispersal of its human cargo. A passenger list, if one existed, could only be obtained, she informed them, upon request to the local police authority.

Not two metres away Madhev Ramdas was in pursuit of the same information, having received a fax and phone call from Dubai with instructions to locate and eliminate a Professor Batioushenkov, a passenger aboard Flight 550. If Alex Kelday had been able, at the last minute, to call upon the resources, if not the alacrity, of the US Navy to effect that for which he had been sent to the Middle East, Madhev Ramdas was equally blessed, being a resourceful and ambitious soldier of the India Mafia of the Gulf, a far more effective instrument for the task at hand. Iqbal Patel, head of the House of Patel, having entered into a contract with

Dubai's infamous branch of that criminal group, could rest easy in the knowledge that it would be honoured, whether in Dubai or Bahrain. The life, or to be more precise, the termination of Professor Batioushenkov had cost him US $50,000. As such events went it was an extraordinary amount, but, as the middleman, he had to satisfy both ends of the candle. He would still make a small profit on the transaction. Jerusalem had always been generous and prompt in paying their debt and a satisfied customer was one who would call upon his services again. In his iniquitous dealings with the Mafia of the Gulf he had always been scrupulously clean. To have been otherwise would have been both foolish and counter-productive. Face and honour were not the exclusive property of Palermo or New York.

Madhev Ramdas had overheard the fruitless conversation between Kelday and Gulf Air. He would find his own way around officialdom, in order to secure the whereabouts of the Russian from Almaty and where better to start than with the baggage boys and loaders, most of whom were either Indian or Yemeni. But first he would dispatch his two compatriots, who, like he, wore false ID cards, permitting access to the most secure areas within the airport. They would search the terminal, questioning his fellow passengers, interrogating frightened staff members. Throughout the region, it is not necessary for a uniform to be worn in order to identify those who prey on the exploited immigrant community. The poor and vulnerable in any society are able to recognise those who live off their vulnerability. It helped that the Gulf Arab, socially, does not see the Indian. Although Indians outnumber the indigenous Arabs, they are simply part of the infrastructure that allows one group to live well and avoid those unpleasant but necessary jobs that are part of a functioning society. Whenever their paths cross the Indian can grovel, deal or bribe with the best. As in feudal Europe, so in the Gulf, each has his place in the scheme of things.

It was the bad luck of grandfather Andrei Maisky, left to look after the bags while the rest of the family went to window-shop at the duty-free stores, that he looked similar to a certain Russian professor of biochemistry. En route to Israel, where the entire family would start a new life, after many years of saving and acquiring the necessary permission to immigrate, Andrei Maisky felt tired. The flight from Almaty had not been without incident. Now he wanted only to sit and watch the well-dressed and exotic travellers parade before him. Soon his family would return and they would find a way to fly on to Dubai and from there to Cyprus, for the final stage of their journey to Tel Aviv.

When the attention of Madhev Ramdas was first drawn to the old man in the ill-fitting Russian suit, sitting on a cardboard suitcase, leaning back on a guard rail, he was unsure of his target. The faxed photo he had received earlier of Professor Batioushenkov, was not clear. But the more he studied the man the more he was convinced as to the identity of the weary transient. Taking the small pistol from his trousers he walked up to the target who started to rise, pressed the short barrel into his chest and fired twice. The life of Andrei Maisky came to an end through shock rather than as a result of the intrusion of the two small calibre rounds that penetrated his fragile body. Ramdas let the body fall back onto the suitcase, propped up by the guard rail and walked away.

When Kelday and Mitchell arrived at the scene of the crime it was to find police and airport staff busily trying to remove the body of an old man amid the wailing of grief-stricken relatives. It took a few minutes to ascertain, from a reluctant and irritated policeman, the cause of death. Pushing forward, Kelday spoke to the senior police officer, after which he returned to Mitchell.

'Are you sure it's not Batioushenkov?' Mitchell enquired.

'There's a similarity, but that's all. His name was Mansky, or something like that. He was on his way to Israel,' Kelday replied.

'Obviously someone else thought he looked like our man. So where is the good Professor?'

'I have no idea. How long before the assassin realises he made the wrong hit?' Kelday was reasonably sure that whoever had carried out the attack on the hapless stranger would be keen to report their success and would, in all probability, be out of the picture for a while, at least until the real target surfaced and they realised their error. All he and his team could do was to continue searching the terminal. It didn't help that it was a busy time of day and that a number of aircraft had recently landed. A terminal that had seemed only relatively full when they arrived now teemed with humanity. The enquiry counter, check in desks and departure gates offered the most hope. Batioushenkov would be attempting to secure onward passage to Dubai, unaware that his Iraqi reception committee would not be there to meet him, or that his would-be employer had been removed by his own military command.

Some time later, as Kelday was supervising the positioning of a member of his team, at a departure gate, he caught a glimpse through a glass partition, of an elderly man, accompanied by a young clean-cut person, leaving the security check and heading towards the departure lounges. It was only a glimpse, nothing more, and yet he knew. Somehow the Professor had evaded them and found passage onto Dubai. Checking the clattering departure board he saw that there was a flight shortly to depart for the Emirate, as well as others to Athens and London. Only a boarding pass now separated them from their target. Dispatching Mitchell to purchase a ticket Kelday questioned the gate attendant. Had he seen an elderly person pass through the gate? Could he show him a list of the passengers bound for Dubai? The attendant, a Palestinian, would rather have breathed his last breath than help the American. Feigning first to not understand and then appearing too busy, he brushed the questions aside. Passengers pushed passed Kelday, handing their boarding passes to the uncooperative attendant, as he anxiously awaited the return of Mitchell. It was only then that he noticed that there was not one but two flights bound for Dubai and both shortly to depart. One of the two was a shuttle, the other, the one he had missed on the departure board, was an onward flight from Damascus. Fortuitously the shuttle was scheduled to depart as number two. There might just be time enough to check its passengers. However, both would leave within ten minutes. Even if Mitchell was able to return with a ticket, which flight would he board, assuming loading had commenced and the Professor had already vacated the departure lounge? If he had not, then Mitchell would have to do his best, in the less than private environs of an airport departure lounge, to persuade one of the world's most experienced BW chemists to throw away his, now worthless, Iraqi pension plan and join Uncle

Sam in the land of the free. There was no time to secure another seat on the other flight. By the time Mitchell returned and his flight was identified it would be too late.

Kelday was about to give up on Mitchell arriving in time and was considering the instigation of a more forceful approach, when he saw him struggling towards the gate, through a crowd of Japanese, each pushing a trolley loaded with luggage.

'I'm on the shuttle,' he panted.

'Get in there and if he hasn't already boarded you know what to do. If you can't find him on board your aircraft we will know that he must be on the other flight. Use your cell phone. We'll arrange a reception committee the other end. If you are carrying, you had better give it to me. You don't want to be held up at security.'

Kelday watched Mitchell pass through the gate and disappear from view.

Ten minutes after the departure of both flights to Dubai, Kelday was on the phone organising the remnants of his team into a reception committee for the professor, after which he returned to the US Navy compound, to await developments. Having relocated from Dubai to Bahrain he was reluctant to return to Dubai until the Professor had been located and pinned to the wall.

It was almost dark by the time Mitchell called. Kelday stood at the window looking across the parallel runways, with their array of multi-coloured illuminations and beyond, at the lights of the airport terminal, along with the reflection in the sky of an adjacent oil refinery.

'Give that to me again,' he barked.

Mitchell repeated his message. 'Batioushenkov was not on either flight. Our aircraft got away first so we were on the ground when the other arrived, and I can tell you that he was not on either. I managed to sweet-talk a young woman who works for Gulf Air and she confirms that the passenger manifest for both aircraft shows no one by the name of Batioushenkov. But there was a man by that name on Kazakh Flight 550 out of Almaty, transiting through Dubai for Baghdad.'

'So where the hell is he?' Kelday enquired.

'Maybe it wasn't him you saw, after all. Maybe he's still in Bahrain?'

'It was definitely him, I know it.'

'What do you want me to do?'

Kelday gave himself a moment before replying. 'Stay in Dubai. I will contact you when we find out where the SOB has gone.'

Dubai

Iqbal Patel, patriarch and emblem of success to all the Indians of the Gulf, was pleased that the matter had been successfully dealt with. He had received the call during a moment of reflection in his office, when everything about him spoke of his legacy to the world. There was still much to be done but, the House of Patel would last for centuries and it would grow even stronger, before the baton would be passed to another. Through the scholarships he had established at St. Paul's, his old school, in Darjeeling, there would flow a succession of pupils who would know of his generosity and commitment to learning. Such largesse would also be the subject for discussion on the balcony of the *Darjeeling Planters' Club*, an establishment to which he paid an extortionate annual membership fee and from which he derived little benefit, save the privilege of leading the Club's First Eleven onto a bone dry pitch once a year. Because of the myopic vision of his father, an ignorant but shrewd businessman, he had not been sent to England for his education, unlike his worthless brothers. That they had amounted to nothing was testimony to his father's lack of intelligence and discernment. How he would have loved to confront the man with his success, but an early death in the bed of an Armenian whore had robbed him of the pleasure.

The caller had simply informed him that the contract had been fulfilled, in Bahrain. A life had been extinguished, but what was that to the House of Patel? All that remained was to secure payment for services rendered from Jerusalem. Their emissary, having met with an unfortunate accident, would now either be eliminated or recalled and his niece would pine. Yes, he had seen how she looked at the alias Mr Gerald Lindsay, when he had visited the office. He knew also of the assistance she had given him and of their nocturnal visit to the empty warehouse. Perhaps it had been a mistake to employ her, but she was family. His own absence from the office did not mean, as others thought, that he was unaware of what went on. There were always ears to hear and eyes to see from those most eager to please. That amateurs, sent by the Voice of Gaza, had given the Israeli agent a warning and not killed him, had created an opportunity open to exploitation. The promise, by him, of a substantial payment in US dollars, made it easy to conflate their agenda with that of the House of Patel and to be rid of the meddlesome Jew. That they had failed meant that he would not be paying them or calling upon their services in the future. The closure of the contract, in Bahrain, confirmed for him, as if any confirmation were needed, that in such matters, he could rely only on the Indian.

This new venture with the Saudis, upon which the House of Patel had only recently embarked, was not without its problems. Although extremely lucrative the outcome was at best dubious. The inward shipment and dispersal of the product were not his concern. The House of Patel was simply the legal conduit through which importation and storage would be effected. But the men from Riyadh had left him with little choice and life for Iqbal Patel was all about choice. In the end it came down to power and wealth, something he understood and appreciated better than any other man in the Gulf. Compared with that of the Saudis, who had arrogantly summoned him like an office boy to their hotel, his empire was a minnow and for a minnow to swim among such big fish and survive required guile. He could only hope that the final use to which the merchandise would be put would not have too adverse an effect on business. Meanwhile he would concentrate on the speech he was to deliver that evening to a gathering of visiting Brussels businessmen, in the Jumeirah. A good malt and flattering conversation were the perfect antidote to the bile he had been forced to swallow at the hands of the Saudi Arabians. He would wear his new dinner jacket, tailored in London, complete with a set of dress medals purchased at Sandfords. That he had never been in the military, not even in the armed services of mother India, was of little importance. If asked, he would merely reply that they were obtained in the service of Her Majesty.

Mahashweta Patel closed the door of her car and walked the short distance to the blue sedan, parked in the same spot as before, flanked by the two white vans.

'Thank you for coming, Miss Mahashweta.' His greeting was formal but not unfriendly. She had prepared herself for the odour that permeated the interior of the vehicle, but still she gagged upon entering. Sitting beside him, she left the door open to allow in the zephyr from the Creek.

'The air conditioning will not be so effective if you leave the door open.'

Only once before had she suffered from claustrophobia and that had been in the packed elevator of the Eiffel Tower, on a hot June day, while visiting Paris as a teenager. Then as now, fear grew within her. Although she could see through the tinted windows of the car, the interior bore down on her, a feeling made more intense by the close proximity of the vans and the wall directly in front. Her breathing became spasmodic and the urge to open the door and flee was almost overpowering.

'Could we walk?' she pleaded.

'I don't think so. Our visit to your uncle's office was very productive. We found more than we expected.' His voice resonated within her brain. She tried to concentrate on the likely importance of what they may have found within her uncle's inner sanctum.

He continued, 'Thanks to your assistance, by the end of today we hope to have neutralised all of the consignments including, with your continued help, the one here in Dubai. It is very important that it be located before it can be used and we think you can help. Do you know a Ramdas Valrani?'

'No. I don't think so.' Valrani was not an uncommon name among the 3.5 million Indians of the Gulf. But she could not recall having heard anyone of that name in connection with the House of Patel.

'Maybe your uncle mentioned him?' There was more than an air of impatience in his question. A note of desperation had entered his fractured English.

'What about Farhan?'

'That name is known to all in the Gulf,' she replied scornfully.

'But not to us, Miss Mahashweta. Please, who is he?' More pragmatic than proud, he humoured her as he would a child.

'He is part of the Indian underworld. Our Mafia, but my uncle doesn't deal with such people.'

'I would like to agree with you, but I cannot. Your Uncle is, as the Americans say, in it up to his ears. But then, who isn't in Dubai? Where are we likely to find this Farhan?'

'He has his base in Abu Dhabi, along the coast, but he is deeply involved in the "Festival City", a resort development here in Dubai. What sort of business would my uncle do with Farhan?' Her Uncle had spoons of every length, so as to sup with those at various levels of morality. It would come as no surprise to her to find that he had been dining with the Gulf's most notorious gangster.

'It was Ramdas Valrani, along with some friends, who picked up the consignment from your uncle's warehouse, before you and your Mr Lindsay, decided to take a look. The guards confirmed that it was Valrani from a photograph we showed them of his body. He was found this morning floating in the water at Port Rachid. In his pocket was the address of the warehouse. After a little persuasion they also gave us the name Farhan, but that was all and it was not enough.'

How much she could believe of this unlikely tale was open to question, but she was in little doubt that, if true, the failure of the guards to offer more information would have come from ignorance rather than from want of prompting. Maybe they too were now dead.

'You think that Farhan has this consignment?'

'Maybe. If not he will know who has.'

'You might find him at the Al-Rashid Hotel, on the Bur Dubai. They keep a suite for him all year round, but he is always protected. You will have to be very careful.'

'Thank you, I knew you would help us, but it is you who will need to take care. You will go to the hotel and flush out for us this Farhan.'

It was an order, rather than a request, one delivered in a manner that left no room for dissent.

She bristled at his arrogance. How could anyone find such an anomic individual remotely attractive? Why should she put herself at risk for this filthy man and his cause? What did they share that he would expect her to do as he wished?

'Give me one good reason why?'

'Because if you don't a Shahab-350 short, to medium, range rocket is going to slam into a warship of the American Navy and that would not be good news for you or us. There will be those who would call for retaliation. This place you call home would then be a place to leave. Is that what you want? I do not think you are so stupid.'

'There is no guarantee that he will be at the hotel.' In so saying, she felt that she had accepted the order. Was she now under the command of this odorous Jew? If by finding Farhan she would be rid of him then surely it would be worth the effort.

'Go to the hotel and see. If you do find him at home we will do the rest.' It was the second time she had heard him use the phrase. It sounded no less sinister.

The Al-Rashid Hotel is situated on the Bur Dubai side of the Creek, five minutes from the World Trade Centre and ten minutes from the airport. It was one of the first hotels in the emirate catering to visiting American businessmen. Once part of an international chain, it was now locally owned. Having seen better days and after several facelifts the old lady had settled down to being host to middle of the market tour groups from Eastern Europe and Asia. That Farhan had found a retreat within its concrete walls spoke more for its anonymity than its faded luxury.

As she entered the stale air-conditioned environment, pleased only to be free of the car's stifling odour, she caught the eye of the head clerk, an Indian for whom the House of Patel held particular respect. His youngest son was a junior in the London office. A son who every month dutifully sent home a proper and fitting sum of English pounds to his family.

'You are most welcome to the Al-Rashid, Miss Patel. Have you come to dine or are you here on business?'

'Sadar Nagpal. Nice to see you again. How is your son?'

'It is so good of you to remember him, Miss Patel. He is well, but he is finding London very cold. His mother is missing him.'

'I am sure she is. I am here on business, Nagpal.'

'Whatever it is I will personally see that it is done,' he replied enthusiastically.

'It concerns a permanent guest of yours.' Their eyes met in mutual understanding.

'Is he at home?'

'Miss Patel, it is a lot that you are asking. A little if it were for any of our other guests, but for him…' His voiced trailed away as if lost in thought. Oblique though her reference to Farhan had been, it was sufficient to reduce the confident desk manager of the Al-Rashid to a cowering wretch.

'I am aware that such a request may cause you some difficulty, Mr Nagpal. But my uncle would be most appreciative, should you be able to supply the information he desires.'

To ask such a man to turn *delator* on one of the Gulf's most notorious crooks was to put his neck in a noose. But to reject a request from the House Patel, in Dubai, particularly when your son is a junior employee of the company in London, would be an act of extreme foolishness. Caught between the two he elected to run with the latter.

The Hindu believes that we have come into this world because we wanted to. On that point and at that time, Nagpal questioned his original decision. In death, the law of karma meant that he would be reborn. But it was the parting and the manner in which he might be forced to leave that concerned him. It is a widely accepted principle of Indian thought that anything which changes cannot, in an ultimate and final sense, be real. The indignities to which his body would be subjected by Farhan and his men would be real enough. He could only trust in the protection of the House of Patel, in whom he was about to put his future, no matter how limited it might be.

'The person you seek is in residence, but he is never alone. His suite is on the sixth floor, east wing.'

'And is he at home today?' she pressed.

Before he could reply their attention was drawn to the main entrance through which swept a tall middle-aged well-dressed Indian, closely followed by a retinue of four. She instantly recognised him from a photo that had appeared in a dossier of prominent Indian underworld figures in the Gulf, given to her by her regional controller, but a dossier bereft of detail. The two groups faced each other across the small hall. The cringing head clerk and the niece of Iqbal Patel, by the check-in desk and the five arrivals standing centre stage in the hotel's otherwise deserted lobby.

'Mr Farhan. I am Mahashweta Patel,' she said without moving.

'Mahashweta Patel, do I know you?' he enquired without interest.

'I am the niece of Iqbal Patel.'

'The House of Patel. Are you now running messages for your uncle, or is this a friendly call?' Farhan's voice betrayed his humble origins. Little was known about his family and how they eventually came to be in the Gulf. It was sufficient that he was a powerful leader within the underworld. What else could possibly be of more importance?

'It was you I came to see, but this sniffling clerk tells me you do not live here.' She could feel the relief come over the man standing beside her. It was a favour he would remember and repay.

'Now you have seen me. Is that enough?' The group moved off towards the elevator.

'There is something we need to talk about,' she offered.

'If your uncle wants to talk to me he knows where I am.' He talked not in the idiosyncratic manner of a Gulf Indian, but rather as one who had learnt to speak English from the cinema.

She could hear the poorly serviced elevator grinding its way towards the ground floor.

'He doesn't know I am here. This is between you and me.'

'Then you are a stupid bitch to come here.' He was about to step into the elevator when he turned and said, 'What do you want?'

'It is about a consignment that has recently gone from one of the company's warehouses.'

'There are many consignments and many warehouses in Dubai. Can you be more precise?'

She became aware that a number of other guests had entered the hotel and were standing close to her, waiting to be checked in, oblivious to the drama unfolding before them.

Raising her voice she continued, 'A container of patchouli. Maybe you remember it?'

'Patchouli? What is that?'

'You should know, you took delivery of some very recently.'

Her boldness surprised even herself. She was talking to one of the most cruel of men as if he were hired help.

'Maybe I did. I have many business interests. Like your uncle.' He smirked.

'I want to know where it went.'

Along with his retinue he had entered the elevator, the door held open with a foot. She had only to stay silent for the door to close. She would then return for her meeting with the Jew and it would be done.

Instead she added, 'It may be in your interest to tell me.'

'Miss. Patel. For an Indian woman you have a big mouth. If you want to talk, OK. Come for a ride.' So saying, he ordered his escort out of the elevator.

Never had she been this close to the infamous Farhan. Once, before moving to America, he had been pointed out to her by a relative. Farhan had been leaving a nightclub as they drove past. The relative, a cousin, had told her of some of the crimes committed by the man who now stood beside her and of the many women he had enjoyed throughout the Gulf. Since returning to Dubai, to work for her uncle, she had known him only as someone about whom others spoke in whispered tones. There was always gossip within the so-called legitimate business community, about the parallel economy operated by the Indian Mafia. In truth, men like Farhan were, probably, more wealthy than many of her uncle's respectable business acquaintances.

He did not speak but stood silent beside her as the aged elevator slowly climbed between floors. He was clean and smelt fresh, in marked contrast to the individual with whom she had been forced to spend the earlier part of her day. His clothes were expensive and well tailored. And, unusual for an Indian male, the hands were free of jewels. The right wrist carried a Rolex, which she assumed was genuine. A man like Farhan could afford such a trinket. She had observed by the way he had moved when entering the hotel that, somewhere in Dubai or Abu Dhabi, there existed a gym at which he worked out, regularly. A mental note was placed in her mind to, at some later date, locate its where-abouts. Such information could be useful.

At the sixth floor he stepped out of the elevator and walked at a fast pace down the corridor to the right. To her left a door leading to a fire exit opened through which came four puffing men, forced to run up the fire escape by their employer. With Farhan in front and his escort behind she entered a world from which respectable people were normally excluded. The first room she entered was a windowless hall, the walls of which were covered by enormous mirrors. Beyond she could hear the rattle of glasses. One of Farhan's men barred her from joining his employer.

'Bring her in,' Farhan called.

On entering a richly furnished room she found him sitting in a large leather chair, which, in spite of his height, made the occupant look short. In his left hand was a glass. His legs were stretched out in front of him. Around the room were a number of bronze and marble statues of naked women. One was life size. They were not the kind that you might find for sale in some cheap shop on the waterfront, rather they were the sort that might be purchased, by a discerning collector, at an auction.

One of his men had followed her into the room and now stood behind her. She could feel his still panting breath on her neck.

'Do we need to search you?' Farhan enquired.

'I am not armed, if that is what you mean.' She had foolishly left the Browning .25 automatic at her apartment.

'That is exactly what I mean. I didn't think you were. Perhaps I should search you, anyway. It might be pleasurable. Would you like that? Would you like me to search you? What do you think your uncle would say if he knew you were here?'

'I haven't come here to talk about my uncle. What did you do with the consignment you took from the warehouse?'

'I won't ask you if you want a drink. A good Hindu woman doesn't drink. Or aren't you a good woman?'

She did not reply. If he so chose he could do whatever he wished with her and there would be nobody to hear her screams. Not for the first time had she acted in such an imprudent and headstrong manner. Farhan was different to those she had fled from in the past. This was not some fired up suitor whose ardour had got out of control. There would be no point in appealing to his better side, if it existed. If she was lucky she would simply be raped and then thrown into the street.

'You said it would be in my interest to tell you where this consignment was taken. Why are you so interested?'

'That's not important. Do you know what was in that consignment?'

'You told me, patchouli.'

'I'll assume you do. The people you gave it to, whoever they are, intend to use it against the American Navy. Did they tell you that? Or did they tell you they were going to use it against their fellow Arab or even the Jews?'

'Politics. I don't take part in politics. There is no money in it.'

'If they use that thing, there may be no business for anyone in the Gulf, except for gunrunners. But you're already into that, I suppose?'

'Since when did the House of Patel become guardians of us all? Oh, I forgot, your uncle doesn't know you are here. Maybe you should be talking to him and not to me. He imported the consignment.' It was a line of argument the logic of which was inescapable. But Farhan, for all his power, was vulnerable. He needed the Gulf, it did not need him.

'If it is fired against an American warship, from Dubai, the Americans will retaliate. It could lead to the Emirate being drawn into a war that's not in our interest and I mean the interest of the Indian community. If the Arabs want to kick sand in the eyes of the Jews that is not our business, and if the Jews want to kick the hell out of the Arabs, that too is not our business. But war is something we would not be able to escape.' She paused to collect her thoughts. 'With the world's police forces all connected up to the same computers, there can't be many places in the world willing to accept Farhan, even with a forged passport.'

'I don't know whether you are just stupid or very brave. Do you know how many women have walked out of here still wearing their knickers? None.' He poured another drink before continuing. 'What makes you think I care what happens to you or Dubai. You are wrong about there being no place to run to. If you have enough money there is always someone who is interested.

And who needs forged ones when states sell their precious passports on the open market.'

'OK, how about this. If that thing does what it has been imported to do you will find that there are a number of organizations, who will come down on you so hard that you will be out of business by tomorrow, from one end of the Gulf to the other and I am not talking about what passes for security services in the Gulf. You will be playing in a different league.'

'I suppose you're talking about the CIA or MOSSAD. But you still haven't told me why *you* are so interested in all this. You don't expect me to believe that a Patel has the interest of the Indian community at heart, do you?'

'Who has the consignment?'

'You have a one-track mind. Are there any men in your life, or are you interested in other women?'

'It is not me who has a one-track mind! Perhaps you should start thinking about tomorrow, instead of what is between your legs.'

'And perhaps you wouldn't be much fun, after all.' He looked into his glass, as if to read some message from the melting ice cubes. 'Supposing I did tell you where it went. What compensation would there be for me?'

'Compensation? You have been paid for it once! Do you think you should be paid again?'

'The business of business is business, someone once said. Do you want to know or not?'

'You will be paid thirty per cent of what the consignment was worth. And I am not talking about the patchouli. That is, once the consignment has been recovered.'

It was a figure plucked out of thin air. She had no idea how much a Shahab–350 cost on the open market. It might be worth a million dollars. Quite where the money would come from was something to be sorted out later. The thought crossed her mind that, what passed for a government in the Emirate might be persuaded to stump up with the cash. After all, had she not saved their nation from possible war? On the other hand, maybe the Israelis would pay?

'Fifty per cent,' came his reply.

'I accept.' Were they playing a game? What was she doing dealing with such a man? And why was he bothering to treat with her? It was surreal.

'We have not done business together before. How do I know I can trust you?'

His question was not one she could answer readily. Where was she to find the money? Her Uncle was most unlikely to pay twice for such a consignment. Her regional controller would not support any payment from Delhi. She would first talk to Gerald about the possibility of Jerusalem picking up the tab.

'I wouldn't have thought trust was part of your vocabulary Anyway, we don't have an agreement until you tell me where it is,' she replied.

...Dubai

Muhammad Ibadis, the itinerant, had many cousins, some of whom he would call on frequently. Others he would see only occasionally, when the need arose. Ali, the eighth child of his mother's third brother, belonged to the latter, a travel agent, whose office was in an industrial area close to the refinery. He could not boast of managing a successful business. The location alone was sufficient to deter all but the most desperate of travellers. Most found their way to his modest establishment in search of documentation and subsequent onward passage to colder climes, such as Berlin or London. That most of them ended up in the refugee and asylum centres of France or Italy was not his concern. With Ali there was no after-sales service.

Three hours later and after copious cups of green tea, Ali's weakness, Muhammad had that which he sought, the possible whereabouts of Professor Batioushenkov. His cousin, through hacking into various airline computer reservation systems, assisted by yet another cousin employed by the Bahrain Airport Authority, had succeeded where the intelligence community of the major powers had failed. For those whose public persona was such that passage to Europe, in anything other than a packing case, was impossible, his cousin had provided an invaluable service and now he had delivered confirmation of the movements of the old Russian through Bahrain International Airport and beyond.

Dolby sat back into the worn leather of the black Buick behind an unusually animated friend and associate. He had retired to his hotel to contact Summers in London and ruminate on the events of the day. With the Professor unlikely to arrive in Dubai it was necessary to consider the next course of action, this being best achieved in an air-conditioned room, with his shoes off and a strong drink. He had dispatched Muhammad to find out what he could, from his myriad contacts. The reception desk had woken him to say that his driver was waiting for him in the car, a driver who, it transpired, was clearly pleased with himself.

'You are rested, Mr Dolby?'

'Thank you, Muhammad. You have something to tell me?'

'I went to see a cousin of mine who has a travel business. It is not a big business and he is not a rich man.'

'And?'

'The person you seek will not now be coming to Dubai. He has left Bahrain and has gone to Athens.'

'Athens? Is he to fly onto Baghdad from there?'

'No. He is going to America and he is not alone. He is travelling with another, much younger man.'

Dolby was not a competitive person, a shortcoming that had manifested itself early in his days at public school, an institution founded on the principle that to compete, in all things, was the duty of every pupil. It was a condition that remained with him throughout his career, one that had worked as much for him as against. He had seen others for whom competition was a life force, something that drove them on, often to destruction. Now, from his employer's perspective, to have been bettered by his colleagues in the CIA should have left him feeling less than pleased. But he felt indifferent to the Professor's fate. It seems unlikely that the Americans would have anticipated the failure of Kazakh Flight 550 to reach Dubai. It was more likely that they had gained control of the Professor's movements before he had reached the Gulf and had spirited him off to a life of fast food and equally unsatisfying television. All that remained was for him to again contact Summers, inform him of the latest developments and return home.

His second call to London did not go as he had anticipated. First there was the line, a connection of poor quality making reception difficult. Not, however, that difficult that he was unable to hear his superior.

'Are you saying that we still have a game?' Dolby queried.

Summers reply was faint but instant. 'Yes.'

'But surely...' an echo retuned to him, as if he was conversing in a large hall. Summers sounded even further away.

'Whoever his travelling companion is,' Summers continued, 'he is not one of our friends. I think you should return for a chat, don't you?'

Dolby put down the phone and started to pack.

Bahrain

Kelday, after receiving the call from John Mitchell in Dubai, sat down to a Navy meal and the thought that he had screwed up the operation. A more thorough search of the international terminal had failed to produce any sign of the Professor. Explaining away the loss of his target as 'bad luck' would not suffice. Although he could not have foreseen the failure of Kazakh Flight 550 to arrive at its scheduled destination, he had, nevertheless, failed to cover that eventuality. Wherever the Professor was, he was not under the protection of the US Government and it was that which 'the Greek' had sent him to effect. Just as he was sure that the man who he had caught a glimpse of entering the departure area had been the target, so now was he equally sure that the target had left the Gulf. One of the two flights that Kelday had seen departing Bahrain, at around the same time as the two flights to Dubai, one to London, the other to Athens, had been the Professor's ticket out of Bahrain. Subsequent enquiries into the passenger listing for both flights had turned up nothing. His quarry had assumed a new identity, which meant that he had received help from another quarter. Logic dictated that the Professor had flown to London assisted by British Intelligence and that he had been under their control from the time he had left Stepnogorsk. In all probability the old Russian had never intended to go to Baghdad at all; all along his destination had been London. Had not the original information concerning his departure for Iraq, come from the Brits? The Agency's attitude towards their British counterpart was, if not one of contempt, something closely related. It would be better had the Professor been taken out by the folks from MOSSAD, than escorted into genteel retirement in the United Kingdom.

His team had been beaten to the draw and it hurt. How 'the Greek', his boss, Paul Damaskinos, in Washington, would take the slight was predictable. There would be an explosion followed by an analysis, not on why or how the operation had failed, but how best it might be presented, for the record. With the freedom of information bill currently on everybody's lips, life was all about covering your back. For him and his team there remained nothing more to do than to bring them together and return to the States. If there was one thing good about the operation it had been his meeting Kate Cranley. It was a bonus, one that would not be lost. Meeting her again was made easier since they were both based in Washington. There was, after all, a case to be made for inter-agency cooperation.

Jerusalem, Israel

In a small office, not far from Yad Vashem, behind a door marked 'Statistics' Colonel Yaacov Levin, of the Military Intelligence Bureau, closed the file on Professor Vasily Batioushenkov. Although there had been no confirmation of the success of the operation, he had received a direct report from their intermediary in Dubai, Iqbal Patel. The failure of Avraham Guriel to confirm the death of the Professor and so complete his mission, had been unfortunate. That he had uncovered the shipment of Shahab–350 missiles had become an embarrassment, to AMAN. Operating within a greatly reduced budget had meant many operational cut-backs. Nobody within the service was happy employing foreign nationals, be they Indian or Australian. But the time had gone when they and other units of Israel's intelligence organisation could mount simultaneous operations, around the world. Withdrawing from the Gulf had been an executive decision taken at the highest level. Their sister organization, MOSSAD, was operating under similar restraints but, unlike AMAN, had learnt of the possible shipments of the Shahab–350s, from Iran into Kuwait, Qatar, Bahrain and Dubai. Without agents on the ground, deep cover operatives in all four states, it had been impossible to quickly confirm and locate their whereabouts. Guriel had stumbled onto them through the niece of Iqbal Patel and almost got himself killed in the process. It was thanks to the niece that MOSSAD were now in close pursuit of the missiles. Whenever AMAN and the Central Institute for Intelligence and Special Missions were forced to work together relationships were strained, often to breaking point. Although Guriel had uncovered the existence of the missiles in Dubai, finding them remained a MOSSAD operation. Recovering Guriel had also fallen to MOSSAD, something that, in the past, would have been unheard of. AMAN had looked after its own. In this, as in other operations, the service had been reduced to that of spectator. Perhaps the elimination of Batioushenkov, one of the world's most knowledgeable BW experts, was of some value, something AMAN could write up as a victory, albeit a rather small one.

...Dubai

In the years that were to follow, Mahashweta Patel would ask herself time and again, why she had not left the search for the Iranian made Shahab–350 missile to the Israelis. It would have changed nothing, but had she immediately left the hotel and simply reported the whereabouts of Farhan to the man in the cap, her part in the subsequent events would have carried less guilt.

One of Farhan's goons had escorted her to the cage and watched as she struggled with the door. Only when his feet disappeared from view did she relax. The elevator stopped at the next floor and a thin Indian migrant worker from Mangalore entered, balancing a pile of towels, behind which she stared at Mahashweta Patel. At the next floor she got out. A knowing smile appeared on her emaciated face. For the staff of the Al-Rashid the niece of Iqbal Patel had become another of Farhan's women, something that would provide endless hours of coffee gossip, not only among the hotel's staff, but in a very short time, throughout the Emirate's Indian community. To the woman who had been erroneously stripped of her virtue it would, under other circumstances, have been inconceivable that she would be seen in the company of such a man. To now be labelled as one of his conquests could only harm her uncle's name, as well as her own. She knew, as did most others in the world of Indian Gulf traders, that her uncle had, for years, dealt with the Mafia, although his dealing with Farhan had come as a surprise. But face was all. In the Salic environment of Gulf commerce, she had removed the myth of moral exactitude longingly cultivated by her uncle. Few had tried to be as pukka and corrupt at one and the same time.

The value of her own name and that of her uncle's, the exaction extracted from her by Farhan, all were of secondary importance as she descended in the creaking elevator. He had given her the location to which the consignment had been taken, from the warehouse. It was what Gerald would have wanted, but was unable to receive. Whether it had been relocated was something they would have to discover. Farhan would only receive his 'compensation' if the missile was recovered, therefore it was unlikely he had lied. But if it had been moved again they might not find it in time to prevent its firing.

As she exited into the foyer she was met by the man in the cap, who quickly ushered her out of the hotel and into the blue car. As they drove off, followed by one of the arcane white vans the muffled sound of gunfire could be heard, behind them.

'Well?' he asked, impatiently.

'He told me where it is. What is happening?' She twisted in her seat to look back at the Al-Rashid hotel.

'You were only supposed to find out if he was inside the hotel and then come out. What kept you?'

'I went up to his apartment.'

'In the circumstances that was an extremely stupid thing to do. When you didn't show we decided to find out what you were doing. The manager was very helpful when we mentioned your name.'

'So you…?' She let the question hang in the air that was thick with his smell.

'Your friend Farhan seems to have resisted our coming into his small world. He was an amateur. Gangsters should stick to what they know best. Where is the consignment located?'

'Umm Suqeim. It was delivered to a place between Al-Jumeirah and Al-Wasl Roads.'

'Umm Suqeim? That's to the south, along the coast, past Jumeirah?'

'You know Dubai well,' she observed.

'I can read a map.'

Now that they were on their way, she could put her visit to the hotel to the back of her mind and concentrate on finding the missile. But the gunfire required answers. Had they been waiting to enter the apartment, as she left, and then killed Farhan? If he was dead the Gulf would be a better and safer place for all. But safer still for the many women upon whom he preyed. Whether the many prostitutes he ran, from one end of the Gulf to the other, would now be free was something upon which she preferred not to speculate. As always, the desperation of many opened the way for exploitation by the few. Russian and East European women were finding their way in increasing numbers to the Gulf. One entrepreneur, originally from Madras, had even started a language school, so that his girls would be better equipped in the bedroom. Any space left by Farhan would be quickly filled by someone equally as ruthless, though possibly not as urbane or as sophisticated. Within her there stirred something she would not at first acknowledge. The feeling she had for Gerald, who now lay helpless and injured in a hotel, was different to the naked attraction she reluctantly felt for Farhan. There was something about the individual that was disturbing, an attraction that had stupidly taken her alone into his apartment. How could she find such an anomic man remotely appealing? Was it power? It was a known fact that women were attracted to power. While at university in California some of her female friends had gone, not to hear President Clinton speak, but just to be near him. Power was an aphrodisiac like no other. There had not been a moment in Farhan's company when she had lost control or had she been fooling herself? How fiercely would she have fought him, had he attempted to take that which he thought was his right? She would never know. Now that the temptation had been permanently removed, it would be something that she could bring out later and examine, alone, without fear of making a fool of herself.

The traffic had been heavy leaving the city. But once the call to prayer had gone out cars began pulling over to the side of the road, after which they were able to make better time. For most of the journey he remained silent, constantly checking to see that the van was still following.

The traffic temporarily increased once prayer time had passed, at which point they were passing Safa Park, on their left, noted for its small-scale models of famous landmarks from around the world. Although open most evenings until 10.30 p.m., it was the time of day when many locals were leaving to return home. Expats too were heading back to the city and its many restaurants.

The ramifications of failure were immeasurable. Destruction of one or more American warships by a missile fired from any of the Gulf States, would bring immediate reprisal. It would not be enough to claim ignorance. The world's mightiest power had lost patience with that argument. Drawing the Gulf States into the endless war between Arab and Jew had long been the aim of various terror groups. Until now the Emirates had paid them off, giving generously, through Islamic Cultural Institutes and Centres for Islamic Studies. Aware of such payments, America had been prepared to overlook them, preferring the status quo to political confrontation and a falling out with an Arab ally. The loss of American lives from an attack on one or more of its warships would leave them with little option but to strike back, especially in an election year.

The white van had closed up behind their car and although they had made good time along the coast it had not prevented the second van from joining the convoy. She wondered if, in some way, they were in communication with each other. Since getting into the car at the hotel her driver had communicated only with her, as far as she could tell, and yet the two vans seemed to know where the car was heading, without instructions. How had the second van known which way to proceed in order to join them? Had they extracted the information from Farhan? The car in which she was travelling appeared to be a standard rental model, with no extras. If there was some method of communication between vehicles and/or a tracking device, it had to be in one or both of the vans.

They were approaching the turn off for the Waterpark, some fourteen kilometres from the city, when she asked him to slow down. The residential area through which they were travelling had, like most of Dubai, sprung from the desert only recently. It seemed to be a most unlikely place from which to launch a destructive missile.

'What are we looking for?' he enquired.

'A line of storage units, where people leave their possessions when they go away for some time.'

'This doesn't look like the sort of area where you would find storage units. Are you sure he didn't feed you some crap on this?'

'Why would he lie? If we don't find the missile he doesn't get paid, and we could all be out of business.'

They had turned right off Al-Wasl Road into a short street that connected with Al-Jumeirah Road and the sea.

'There!'

The man in the cap had braked and pointed to a row of four storage units on the right, between two large houses each with a high surrounding wall. The units were metal containers, imported from Russia, on a plot of sand marked for development. A security guard eyed them from within a small shed that stood behind a wooden barrier, at the front of the plot. The two vans, meanwhile, had taken up position behind the car. At first she thought he was addressing her, but then she realised he was issuing instructions to the people in the two vans, in what she assumed was Hebrew. The absence of any visual cue meant that the car must be equipped with a sensitive communications system, as well as a tracking device for the vans to follow.

'What do we do now?' she asked.

'Look for the missile, what else?' He made to leave the car, but she stopped him.

'Shouldn't we first find out if it is still here? Let me talk to the guard. There is no point in our wasting time in searching. It might already have been moved.'

'OK. You have two minutes. If he doesn't cooperate, we'll join you.' He followed this with more instructions in Hebrew.

In spite of the hour it was still hot as she crossed the road towards the units. The guard, seeing her approaching left his hut, his eyes glued to her body. She could feel him undressing her with his eyes. It was her belief that most Arab men were either very hot-blooded or deprived of sex. In all her time in the Gulf she had never found out which. Once she had attempted to introduce the subject with a female Arab friend, only to be firmly rebuffed.

The guard was a young illiterate from the Yemen and eager to talk. The loneliness of his job and the appearance before him of a young and attractive Indian woman loosened his tongue. He told her that all of the units were full of the personal effects belonging to European teachers on extended leave, following the temporary closure of a language college in Za'Abeel. A consignment had been delivered, in the past few days, he couldn't remember exactly when, but it had not been stored. Upon its delivery it had been accepted and removed by three men, Arabs, in a white utility. He had seen it all. No, he didn't know where they went.

The man in the cap was not pleased. The utility, he explained, if used as a mobile firing platform, would be almost impossible to locate. He once more gave instructions to the unseen, after which all three vehicles drove onto the Al-Jumeirah Road, where one van turned left, the other right. Within minutes they were gone from view. The car had parked across the road from two apartment blocks between which she could make out lights on the sea.

'What are you going to do now?' she enquired.

'Wait. It could be anywhere. But, perhaps we will be lucky and find it. If you were an Arab and you had only a limited knowledge of how the Shahab–350 works, where would you go to fire it at a ship?'

'To the sea? On a beach?'

'Right. But why hasn't it already been fired? They have had ample time, but still it hasn't been fired. Why?'

'Maybe they don't know how,' she suggested.

'And maybe they're waiting for a target. Do you want to go back to the city? This is not your business. You have done all you can for us.'

'I will wait.' He was right. Strictly speaking it was not her fight, or that of India. Although, if the missile were to be launched, she, like all the other residents of Dubai, would be affected by the outcome. But trying to find it with such a small team would be, she agreed, almost impossible.

'We may not have long to wait. Do you know this area?'

'I have only been here once, to a party, although I have driven through many times. The Formula One course is close by and I often go to the Club Mina, further along the coast. With so much at stake, why aren't the Americans here looking for the missile? It's their ships that will be hit.'

'Do you think they would make a better job of finding it? Their methods would not work. Not in the time left to us.'

'Have they been told about the possible strike against them?' Previously he had indicated that finding the missiles, between Kuwait in the north to Dubai in the south, was an Israeli operation. But things had changed. Assuming the consignments in Kuwait, Qatar and Bahrain had been located and neutralised, there was still the matter of one on the loose in Dubai.

'The Americans, in this part of the world, are always ready for an attack against them. It is part of life.'

Seventy-five nautical miles off the coast the USS Goldrush, a 'Raleigh' class LPD, an amphibious transport dock and command ship for the US Navy in the Arabian Sea, was heading South, after minor repairs at the 5th Fleet's dock in Bahrain. Aboard, the crew of twenty-four officers and 400 non-coms, including ninety command support staff, were on state two readiness. At sixteen knots, her best range speed, she would meet up with the rest of the fleet, currently engaged in manoeuvres off Khasab, at the mouth of the Strait, the following day. Although over forty years old the *Goldrush* had undergone a number of refits and was considered good for another ten in her extended role as command ship. Equipped only with gun armament and no missile, torpedo or ant-submarine defence she relied upon other vessels for her protection. Her escort vessel, the frigate USS *Karl*, lay one nautical mile to starboard. The *Karl*, an 'Oliver Hazard Perry' class FFG, carried missile and anti-submarine armament, as well as gun armament and two helicopters. Like the *Goldrush*, her crew of thirteen officers, 193 non-coms and nineteen aircrew were on state two readiness. The sun had all but gone from the sky, sinking quickly over the unseen desert, when the alert went out for a possible blockade runner, a tanker, flying a flag of convenience, suspected of attempting to carry a consignment of Iraqi oil through the Strait of Hormuz, to an unknown destination. A Canadian Air Force Orion, part of the International Intervention Force, had been shadowing the vessel since picking it up on radar off the Iranian port of Bushehr. It was unlikely that the tanker would be able to slip through the fleet, undetected, nevertheless the crew of the *Karl* would welcome its painted profile on the bridge, along with the other trophies collected during its short tour of operations. To find and impound the vessel, before joining up with the rest of the fleet, meant that the crew of the Karl would move to the top of the league. When first sighted it was as a silhouette against the fast setting sun, hugging the shore attempting to merge with legal shipping out of Dubai. Still north east of the emirate, the tanker was making approximately eighteen knots in a east-south-easterly direction. The Karl, whose maximum speed was twenty-nine knots, altered course to intercept, leaving the *Goldrush* to continue its zigzag course. The tanker was still several nautical miles to the south-west of the *Karl*, its crew focused on the intercept, when electronics specialist, Helen Lopez, first saw the incoming missile on the screen of her SPS-49(V)5 air-search radar. At the same time an operator on the *Goldrush* picked up the incoming missile on his SPS-40 air-search radar. The Orion, having passed on the target to the *Karl*, had resumed its patrol to the north. It too picked up the missile fired from Dubai and notified fleet command aboard the *Goldrush*. The missile, a Shahab–350 streaked across the evening sky at 1.5 Mach. The crew of the *Karl* went to state one readiness and the order was given to fire a Flank MR-3 ant-missile. The MR-3 was new to the fleet and had been installed aboard the *Karl*, at Norfolk, just three months previously. It had been thoroughly tested and was considered to be the sharp end of one of the best anti-missile defence systems afloat. It failed to intercept the incoming missile and Helen Lopez watched her screen in disbelief and amazement as the Shahab and the *Goldrush* became one.

London

'Had a good flight back, George?' Summers asked, solicitously.

'Yes, thank you. The Gulf's a different world from when I was last there.'

'Time, George, everything has changed. Nasty business, that ship being hit like that. I don't suppose we know which group carried out the attack?'

'Not yet. Not our concern,' Dolby replied.

'True.' Summers sat on the edge of his desk and flung out his arms. 'Look at this place, we're just boarders, you and I. We're the last, you know. In a year or two, nobody will remember Thames House and the old service. This is a damned awful place to work, don't you think?' Summers moved to the window and looked wistfully out at the traffic below. Prior to the merger his rank and service would have qualified him for an office overlooking the river. Under the new, all-purpose security service, he was lucky to hold onto a room of his own. These days he was forced to share a secretary and file a report to Mary Stone every day, irritants he bore less than stoically.

'Thought the Americans had beaten us to it and spirited the old man off to the States. Seems they are as much in the dark as us.'

'So who has him?' Dolby replied.

'Your guess is as good as mine. We've traced him as far as Athens, after which the trail goes cold. The Americans will have other things on their mind now.'

'You got my message about him heading for the States?'

'Unverifiable, old boy.'

'It came from a reliable source, I can assure you.'

'I'm sure it did, George. I'm sure it did. But we need something more. If he flew from Athens to New York or Washington, there must be some record of it, a passenger manifest or something. I suppose we should be pleased that he has not gone to

Baghdad. But you would have thought somebody would know something.'

'He has switched his identity,' Dolby offered. 'There must have been a limited number of elderly Russians travelling between Greece and America around that time. Surely by cross-checking through all the flight schedules and passenger lists we could come up with something?'

'Quite. I've asked our colleagues in the CIA to cooperate with us on this one, George.' The volte-face did not catch Dolby by surprise. He had known the Convenor over many years, long enough to know when external pressure was being applied. He continued, 'If he has gone to ground in the States, as you say, they will soon find him.'

Such trust in an organization Summers would rather anathematise than praise, was less catatonic than opportunistic. In spite of his age and the limited years he had left to serve both Queen and country, Summers could play *Machtpolitik* with the best.

'They have a fellow coming over this morning, Alex Kelday. Do you know him?'

'No, don't think I do.'

'Batioushenkov is so old, in one respect it may not matter where he has gone now that we know he's not with Saddam, except that we are supposed to keep tabs on these BW people.' It had mattered sufficiently for Dolby to be sent half way around the world. What had changed?

'It would be good to tidy things up,' Dolby suggested.

'Absolutely. Let's hear what our American friends have to say.'

When Kelday entered Dolby immediately recognised him as being one of the two he had seen at Dubai International Airport. After introductions and the regulation serving of tea, with chocolate biscuits for guests, Summers opened the meeting.

'It's good of you chaps to respond so quickly to our suggestion, particularly under the circumstances. It doesn't seem to make sense, our duplicating the search for this fellow. Are you based in London?'

'No. Washington. I was passing through and the office asked me to pick this one up. Perhaps you could fill me in on the details.' Summers obliged, omitting those bits that were of interest only to Her Majesty's Government. There followed a languid exchange in which both sides feigned a lack of enthusiasm for or interest in Professor Batioushenkov.

'Well, that seems to be all. Are there any questions?' There were none. Summers closed the meeting by saying, 'I'll leave it to you two. Let me know the moment you have something worthwhile. Travers and Barrington-Brown are both away. You can use their office, George.' Dolby shared a small office with the ample Phoebe Strongman, who was never away, except when she travelled the short distance across town to one of the safe houses. It was an office, bereft of daylight, next to one of the communication stations. Entries in the security register testified to the fact that Dolby spent less time at Vauxhall Bridge than most officers, preferring, contrary to his instructions, to work from home or at one of the safe houses.

'How is the merger working out?' Kelday enquired, as they walked down the corridor.

'You mean between the two services? Oh, it's been a couple of years now. Still a few bugs to iron out, but we're getting there.'

'You know something, I can't imagine us and the FBI getting into bed together. Just wouldn't happen. And it certainly wouldn't work.'

'Is that so. Here we are, chez Travers and Brown.' Dolby led the way into a windowless room equipped with two desks, computers and a filing cabinet.

'They aren't exactly generous with the room, are they?'

'Not exactly. At least now everybody has a carpet. In the old days you had to head a section to qualify for even a rug on the floor.'

'Look. Do we have to work here? Can't we go out and talk over a coffee, somewhere?'

'Why not? Probably just as secure and infinitely more comfortable.'

As they walked under the five steel arches of Vauxhall Bridge, along the recently completed pedestrian clip-on, it began to rain.

'The Professor seems to have given us all the slip,' Dolby began.

'Where do you think he is?'

'We were rather hoping you would tell us.'

'Right. He obviously wasn't taking up Saddam on the job offer. The new boys now in control of Baghdad might have been interested.'

'We'll never know,' Dolby replied.

'Haven't your people down at GCHQ come up with something? Wasn't it them that got this ball rolling in the first place?'

'They have simply confirmed that he left Stepnogorsk for the Gulf. Do you know the Gulf at all?' Dolby innocently enquired.

'I've been through it a couple of times. Never spent long there. How about you?'

'I spent most of the fifties in the Middle East. All changed now, of course.'

Dolby pushed open the door of the small mock-Tudor coffee shop. A table became vacant as they entered, by a lattice window overlooking a small rain-soaked brick courtyard.

'I put some time in at our Embassy here, a few years ago. In those days it was damn hard to get a decent coffee in this city.'

'Not now. Coffee is the preferred drink of the young.' Dolby had attempted to sound like an advert, but failed.

'George. I think it would save a lot of time if we levelled with each other, don't you?' Kelday stirred his flat white and silently cursed his Director, Paul Damaskinos for interrupting his journey home and sending him to London. Now, as punishment for failing to bring home the Professor, he was having to work with the torpid Brits.

'There really isn't much more to tell,' Dolby lied. The invitation to 'level' was not one to which he was instinctively attracted.

'I think we both know more than we are letting on. Which is OK. But if we're to locate this guy we're going to be a damn sight more successful if we pool what we know. They aren't going to let me go home until I, until we find this old Russian. Now, much as I like London, I would prefer to be back in the States.'

'I think I understand. What about the NSA? Haven't they heard anything?'

'Not a damn thing. If they had I don't think I would be allowed to share, anyway.'

'You seem to have a problem, Alex. You want us to "level" with you, but you are not allowed to reciprocate.'

'Look. You know how it works. We know a little and you know a little. Between us we know a lot. Isn't that how it is supposed to be?'

'But in this case, "a lot" doesn't amount to very much. Does it?' Dolby could almost feel sorry for the man from the CIA.

'OK. How about this. We thought that you had him. That you were in the box seat from the moment he left Stepnogorsk. Now you tell us that you don't have him. Is that how it is?'

'I can assure you that, as far as I know, Professor Batioushenkov is not in the United Kingdom. We thought, at first, that you had taken him back to the States.'

'And what made you change your mind?' Kelday replied.

'Let us just say that we received information to the contrary.'

'Which doesn't push the boat any nearer the shore. George, you're holding out on me. Between us we can crack this thing and go back to whatever it is we should really be doing. But only if we work together.'

'I agree. Would you like another coffee?'

'No, thanks. So, we were both aiming for the same target, but neither of us made a hit.' Kelday stirred his empty cup with a plastic spoon. 'We know he is not in the Gulf. We also know that he left Dubai for either Athens or London. How does that sound?'

'Sounds OK to me,' Dolby replied.

'You say he is not in the UK, which leaves us with Athens.'

'Logic would seem to suggest so, but not necessarily. He could have gone on elsewhere,' Dolby suggested.

'We looked at that. Do you know how many flights leave Athens in a twenty-four hour period? We're checking them out. But supposing he took a boat to South America or a ferry to Italy? Really, he could be anywhere.'

'We have a report, not verified, that our target was heading for the States. That is why we thought that you had got to him first. Then we found out that you didn't know where he was, either.'

'If he has gone stateside I suppose we can discount the thought that his visit is benign?' Kelday proffered.

'I would imagine so. Who else would use his services?'

'The sort of stuff he's been working on reduces the possibilities, wouldn't you say?'

'One would hope so. If he has not been recruited by your government, and presumably you would know if he had—'

'Damn right!' Kelday interrupted.

'Then we are left with the unpleasant prospect of his working for a terrorist group.'

'Take your pick. After September 11 it's open season. But if he is in the States we will find him,' Kelday replied emphatically.

'That is what the Convenor said.'

'The last thing we want is for some aging Russian crazy unleashing his crap in the States.'

Washington State

Professor Batioushenkov sat huddled inside the ferry, away from the damp chill of the wind that blew down the inlet from the Pacific. A cold front was about to envelop Puget Sound, a time when the trees would roar and the white cliffs of Whidbey Island would disappear behind billowing puffs of saturated stratocumulus cloud.

The Sound extends almost 130 kilometres, from the Strait of Juan de Fuca in the north to Olympia, the State capital, in the south and takes its name from Lieutenant Peter Puget, an officer aboard HMS *Discovery*, under the command of George Vancouver. To the Indians the area is known as 'Whulge', but to the world it is Puget Sound, the generic name for the whole region. Such though, was not Captain George Vancouver's intention, when, on 7 May 1792, he landed at Point Wilson. It was foggy and he was forced to wait for a clearance before entering Admiralty Inlet, a body of water he intended should bear his name, which extends from Port Townsend to Tacoma. When at last he was able to go exploring he reported that, 'The country before us exhibited everything that bounteous nature could be expected to draw into one point of view.' He further reported, in his diary that, 'I could not possibly believe that any uncultivated country had ever been discovered exhibiting as rich a picture.'

The aging Russian biochemist, eager only for sleep, had never heard of Vancouver or his trusted Lieutenant Peter Puget. Nor was he appreciative of the many beaches and forests that were passing by, beyond the salt-sprayed window upon which the first drops of rain began to appear as the inlet turned a threatening grey.

The young Russian-speaking Canadian that had escorted him from Almaty, through Bahrain and Athens to America, who sedulously carried his cardboard suitcase, had provided both assurance and a new identity, before leaving him at Chicago. For a short while they had been co-conspirators in a struggle against frontiers and revenue hunters, before he was passed on to a middle-aged woman, much as an unaccompanied minor would be passed from one solicitous airline staff member to another, a heavily built woman who now stood beyond the glass, leaning over the ferry's rail, staring at the gathering invasion of bad weather from the ocean. She had been as silent as her predecessor had been loquacious, a condition he had at first attributed to an inability to speak Russian. An opinion dispelled when she explained, above the roar of two gas turbine engines thrust into reverse at Seattle, their method of transiting the city. Her East Slavonic was with an accent that was Baltic in origin, Latvian or Lithuanian and left little doubt as to her attitude towards his mother tongue, thus confirming her status as that of a refugee from the former Soviet Empire. About her there was a deep loss, which would not or could not be shared, much like his own. They could, he had thought, be an estranged father and daughter, the one mourning his wife, the other her mother, each alone in their loss, yet linked with a common grief.

The faltering start from Astana with Kazakh Air, the uncomfortable time between flights and the interminable hours spent in the air, crossing innumerable time zones, had reduced him to that of an exhausted, pathetic figure. The next sector of his long journey from Stepnogorsk would take one hour and forty minutes, aboard a ferry making eighteen knots, from Edmonds to Port Townsend. On a rare clear day it is as Captain George Vancouver described, aboard his four-hundred-ton sloop-of-war, *Discovery*. But on the day Professor Batioushenkov crossed Puget Sound, low clouds obscured the sky and the white cliffs of Whidbey Island were lost to view, as the vessel began to pitch and role with the rising storm.

'We will soon be arriving. The Mukilteo ferry takes just twenty minutes to cross over to Whidbey and then you can rest.' She looked down without pity at the small frail creature that sat staring at his feet and for whom she was responsible. A man who embodied a past she wished only to forget. The collapse of the Soviet Empire had bought little cheer to those like her, people whose life had been ruined before they had begun.

There had been so much preparation, so much planning to bring this bag of clothed bones so far and it was her task to see that he safely complete the last stages of his journey. Setting up the laboratory, as per his instructions relayed through a series of couriers over a period of months, had been something of a nightmare. To that end she, like others, had made a number of trips to Seattle and beyond, observing strict security throughout, each time returning with an ever increasing amount of equipment and materials. There had been a number of false alarms, times when they thought that they had been discovered, when she felt sure that she was under surveillance. Others within the group had felt the same, leaving each to wonder whether, at this late hour, they might yet be exposed. None were under any illusion as to what their actions involved. But now that 'the chef', as he was known, was at last with them, the odds against them safely completing their mission, had been greatly reduced.

Whidbey Island had been selected not for its remoteness, but for the ready availability of a farm, left to a member of the group by a father whom he had never known, and who had abused his mother, a father who had sought atonement for his failures through a bequest. Inland from Ebey's Landing it was away from the domestication that has turned so much of the island into a suburban beach estate. The farm was in a broad valley, the approach to which was down a winding track between two meadows, affording ample warning of any visitors, wanted or otherwise.

For the short ferry trip from the mainland she found herself joined, unexpectedly, by one of the younger members of the group whose job it was to drive them from the landing to the farm. The Professor was not introduced, she didn't see the need. Her companion took charge of the suitcase and stood regarding their charge with intense interest.

'He doesn't look very well.'

'It's been a long trip, for someone of his age. Once he has had a good rest he'll be OK,' she replied convincingly.

'Do you think we should get him looked at by a doctor? There's a lot riding on this guy.'

'We'll see how he feels after a good rest and some food. Is everything ready?'

'Yes. He can start work as soon as he wants. Finest laboratory west of Seattle.' The words froze on his lips as she looked at him with extreme disapproval.

'You should be more careful what you say.'

After a light meal, they put him to bed and gathered together in the large kitchen that served also as a meeting room. They were six in number. A more disparate group it would have been hard to find on the island, but it was one linked in solidarity and with a common cause.

Frank was the first to speak, Frank who had conceived the scheme, Frank who, over a relatively short period, had brought them together, Frank who had served the US DEA for twenty increasingly disillusioned years.

'You all know what we are here to do. You know why we have brought the Professor to Puget Sound and why we've built him the best damn laboratory for miles around. It's even more important, now that he's with us, to maintain security. We are well stocked with food and the farm's well provides all our water needs. If, for any reason, any of us has to go into Ebey or off the island I don't have to tell you how important it is not to mention the fact that we have a guest, to anyone! Let me or Jason know if you see any strangers in the village or around the area. The farm's telephone has been disconnected, we will communicate by cell phone when away from the farm, but keep any conversation brief and assume that your message is being recorded, that way you won't say anything you shouldn't. Also, until further notice, no more hunting. From now on it's eggs, chicken or frozen meat for all. The last thing we want is to draw attention to ourselves by firing off shotguns around the place. Any questions?'

'How long will he be here?' asked the young man who had driven the Professor the last few miles of his long journey.

'That depends. We won't know until he starts work. It could be weeks or months. He's a wanted man. They'll be pulling out all the stops to find him. So the sooner he can complete his work the healthier it will be for us all. If it goes well we could all be gone by winter,' replied Frank. 'Anything else? Good. Over to you, Jason.'

'Once he has recovered from his trip, the Professor must be allowed to work when and how he wants. Day or night. It might take him a while to get over his jetlag and to get used to living among us. Remember, he is not a young man. Let's make sure his stay with us is short, comfortable and constructive. I've drawn up a roster of all our various duties. Now that the Professor is with us we must keep strictly to it.' After a long pause he continued. 'I don't understand what makes a man do the sort of work the Professor has been doing for the past fifty odd years. It's something he will ultimately have to answer for, in this life or the next. But each one of us here, with the exception of Frank, has been robbed of someone we loved by cocaine and if he can eradicate it and put the people who pedal the stuff out of business, I am prepared to forget whatever else he has done with his life. The Professor speaks practically no English, which I admit, is something of a surprise, so Emma and Tony will have to translate. I think that's all. As Frank said, security is our main concern. We have the opportunity to make a difference, but that opportunity could just as easily be taken from us. Let's not let that happen.' Jason had been an Episcopalian minister until the death of his son from a cocaine overdose. His organisational skills, along with his age (he was fifty-two), made him a natural leader of Providence Two, second only to Frank.

It had arrived as a disk, left lying on Frank's desk one morning, along with a note that read, 'view and destroy'. He had come into his Arlington office early that day to catch up on some work, so early that some of the cleaners were still in the building. The disk had its origins within the DEA and had been taken off a 'Class One' Agency computer. There was no addressee or addresser. It concerned a BW biochemist, Professor Batioushenkov, in Kazakhstan and his work on the eradication of the coca plant. It spelt out how, working alone in a makeshift laboratory, he had done what no other biochemist had been able to achieve and, in so doing, put at risk not only the world's coca trade, but also the US anti-drug industry worth $19 billion a year, an industry that in one fifteen-year period spent $300 billion (three times what it cost to put a man on the moon) trying to keep drugs out of the country. What was clear, from the information contained on his computer screen, was that there were those within the DEA, who, threatened by such an upheaval in the drug industry, were prepared to go to any length to make sure that the Professor's achievement would never be put into effect. It did not spell out how or when they would achieve their aim. What was of most concern to Frank was the origin of the disk, how high within the system had a move against the Professor been sanctioned? There was no mention on the disk, of the Professor planning to leave Stepnogorsk in the immediate future. He spent a number of frustrating days cautiously attempting to uncover the veracity of the disk's content and how the DEA, with no known agents or even stringers north of Almaty, had discovered the Professor and his work. Had someone within the CIA leaked the information to a contact in Arlington? It seemed the most likely of explanations. As a senior enforcement agent with the Agency he had access to most of the material that would have exposed any interest in the Professor's work. But his labour was to no avail. If the Agency was engaged in a covert action against a Russian biochemist in Kazakhstan, it was at a level senior to his own. But, if an action was planned, such maleficent behaviour from his superiors would come as no surprise. He had, over many years within the Agency, become inured to their machinations. Disillusionment had given way to pragmatism. But it had not been easy working for an institution whose reports to Congress on coca production statistics were fictional, indicating year after year a drop to justify their policy, an agency whose mission had become a gravy train upon which rode so many to a respectable retirement, an agency that made its own rules, an agency that had perverted the reason for its own existence. There was a maxim within the Agency – 'Beat cocaine and the DEA were out of business'. It was a truth that was about to be tested.

At the centre of all human decisions lies a complex system ranking everything we encounter in terms of simple priorities. What did he want to do with the rest of his life? Without the binds of a family to hold him in bondage, concomitant with a stagnant career through his own probity, not to mention an exiguous pension which was thankfully supplemented by a wealthy wife, in the final analysis the decision to leave had been an easy one, but not before securing the names and addresses from central registry, of individuals throughout the country, whose lives had been torn apart by coca and who had expressed their disgust at the Government's failure to arrest the increase of drugs within the US. From there it had been a simple matter of selecting and collecting about him a small group of reliable, disaffected citizens, eager for a short but decisive fight. It seemed a fitting way to end a career that had been committed to fighting the spread of drugs. They were not the kind of team one would normally have selected to take on the world cocaine trade and the DEA, at one and the same time, presupposing that such a team could exist. But they were highly motivated and, by their very nature, less likely to be detected.

From the outset, the safety of the Professor was paramount. Once he was on the move, or even thinking about it, those that kept tabs on such people would be on the alert. The Baghdad ruse had been the Professor's one contribution to the scheme. It was not without risk. In accepting Iraq's offer to work for their regime, Western intelligence organizations, including Israel, would be on the lookout, and would move to prevent him ever reaching Baghdad. Those within the DEA, cognizant of the true meaning of his labour once they became aware that he had left Stepnogorsk, would do all in their power to eliminate him. And so the transporting of the Professor, from Hell's Kitchen to Puget Sound, had been meticulously planned and, in so far as his arrival at the farm was concerned, well executed, despite the best efforts of Kazakh Air to disrupt the stratagem. It seemed unbelievable, after all that had gone before, that they, an incongruous team of amateurs, had been so successful. The little old man asleep upstairs could now rest, while they kept watch.

Puget Sound

Through the small gabled window at the end of the long sparsely furnished room, in the fading light he could see clouds plunging across a sky in which gulls squawked their unfamiliar evening call in defiance of the rising wind. Deprived of the familiar he was unable at first to sleep. The walls and ceiling of rough boards, reminded him of a dacha in which he had once stayed near Kovzha, during the heady days of the Biopreparat Research Institute, in Leningrad. It had belonged to an apparatchik with Kremlin connections, a man later convicted of crimes against the state. Then, unlike now, there had been respect for his work and enough money for him and his family to live a good life. Now it had all come down to one sparsely furnished room and a suitcase, in the nation he had always thought of as the enemy. But the rough wood of the walls and ceiling were commingled in bewildering juxtaposition with thoughts of another room, in a building far less elevated than the dacha, in the Vector Laboratory at the Koltsovo Research Centre in Siberia. The winters had been bone-numbingly cold, the food sufficient only to keep them alive while they worked. Scientists in the USSR had been generally held in high esteem by the Party, they had been people of privilege. Not so those who worked at the Vector Laboratory. They were only one step away from the unfortunate in the Gulags. There had been so many acts of betrayal, against him, his wife, Dorcas, Russia, the Party. And now those whose fraudulent abjuration had destroyed everything that had ever held any meaning for him, were in control, picking at the decaying bones of a carcass that had once been an empire. But throughout, there had always been his work.

There had been no epiphany, no quest for eternal salvation, no inner demons to exorcise. What had driven Professor Vasily Batioushenkov was revenge, that most base of motives. Rather than inflict upon an unsuspecting world a plague of his own construction, something he was more than able to effect, he would rid it of a weapon that was as personal as it was universal. He would do so not from some latent regard for humanity, but as a way of simply getting even with those who had destroyed his daughter. From the time he had first seen Zoya Natalya in the Moscow clinic, he had resolved to act. It had taken years, but eventually he had constructed his method of revenge. The fact that others might be saved from destruction, through that which he had developed, was of no interest. He had seen few signs of man's love for his fellow beings, throughout his own life. Betrayal, both personal and institutional, was all that he could remember.

He had started where others had left off, with Fusarium oxysporum, or FO, a fungus from Kauai in Hawaii. It is a parasite specific to coca and, when first introduced by the US government into Peru, an act officially denied, it destroyed coca plantations across the country, turning the plant's leaves yellow and causing them to wilt and die. Because it is a living organism it is self-generating and even when spraying has stopped it will continue to spread. The locals had called it *seca seca*, dry dry. That had been in the early eighties. By 1995 the US Government had spent $15 million on its development, but the means of delivery were primitive. A cartridge would be shot from a helicopter, into the ground of a coca plantation. The cartridge would then explode and release the spores, a sequence known to the natives as *lluvia blanca*, white rain. A Professor David Sands of Montana University had been the man who turned FO into a herbicide. Later it is believed he developed a similar strain adapted for use against marijuana, but it was never used. Not surprisingly, he supported his Government's contention, that the existence of FO in Peru, was the result of nature rather than man. He, like his masters in Washington, could give no satisfactory explanation as to how a spore dispersal travelled from Kauai in Hawaii, to Peru, 8,000 kilometres away.

Batioushenkov had been tempted to share his findings with Sands, but in fear of betrayal, he had gone on alone, developing a further strain of FO. Following the original application of FO in Peru, pineapple, yucca and coffee plantations were found to be adversely affected by the herbicide, which lives in the soil for forty years. In order to solicit the help of others necessary for his plan, he would have to develop a strain that did not mutate. This he had been able to achieve, in part, through the introduction of basidium, a microscopic spore-bearing structure produced by only certain fungi. His strain would not affect other crops, a condition insisted upon by any group sufficiently concerned to risk helping him in the eradication of coca. In spite of the limitations of his laboratory, all his experiments had proven successful. The hard part would be replicating the spores in sufficient quantities. For this he would require a proper laboratory. He would leave it to others to spread the parasite throughout Columbia, Peru and Bolivia. Once it had taken hold in those three poverty-stricken republics, as a self-generating parasite, it would spread over the rest of the continent.

Providence Two, as they called themselves, had made contact with him at Stepnogorsk, through a courier. Aware daily of his own mortality, if he was ever to revenge his daughter's death he would have to act while he was able and accept their offer of cooperation, no matter how alien the concept of working in America. Prior to their contacting him, he had only obliquely addressed the need for the assistance of others, but had not processed the thought sufficiently to identify any particular group or groups who would be of value to his plan. Providence Two, no matter how distant or amateur, represented a chance, possibly his only chance of revenge.

The bed was comfortable and warm and he could smell the foreign rurality beyond the rough-hewn walls, as sleep eventually enveloped him.

Washington

Alex Kelday barely had time to shower and change before reporting to the Annex and his boss Paul Damaskinos. Wolfowitz and Weston were also in attendance.

'I have a meeting with the Director in five minutes, Kelday. What do I tell him?' Damaskinos sat at his desk, flanked by Wolfowitz and Weston, both of whom stood with their arms crossed.

'The folks in London were helpful, but they don't seem too sure where the Professor has gone. They think he came stateside, but as yet nothing has shown up from immigration to substantiate their claim. We have cross-checked every passenger manifesto out of Bahrain and Athens. Nothing. We're still working on London.'

'How can this have happened? How do you lose a geriatric Russian between Bahrain and Athens? Damn it all, he doesn't even speak English! Someone must know where he is.' Damaskinos had little or no concern for the well-being of Batioushenkov, but fear and loathing for the man he must now face without an answer. In a city where covering up your mistakes is deemed a prerequisite for a successful career, the Assistant Director had no intention of facing his superior empty-handed.

'We would know by now, if he had arrived in Baghdad, that's for sure,' contributed Weston.

'I think we can forget Baghdad. Even before those clowns seized control, he was never going there. The whole thing was a sham. OK.' It was time to take stock and prepare for the future. The Assistant Director of Operations was not the sort of superior to be bogged down by failure. 'Your stopover in London was a waste of time. Is that correct?'

'If they know where he has gone, the Brits are not letting on. But, for what it's worth, I don't think they have any idea.'

'What about the Israelis?' Damaskinos enquired.

'Yeh. That shooting at Bahrain airport. They may have been more successful a second time,' enjoined Wolfowitz.

'They didn't have the opportunity. I saw the Professor entering the departure lounge. Mitchell went in shortly after. Nothing.'

'There is another possibility,' Weston offered.

'It is?' enquired Damaskinos.

'They could have taken him back to Israel.' Weston suggested. 'We know they've got their own BW programme humming away. We thought that they wanted to eliminate him, right? But supposing they wanted him for themselves? Supposing that is where he was going, all along?'

'It's possible, but unlikely,' Kelday replied. 'They've got more than enough brains to run their own programme, without bringing in yet more Russian scientists. Unlike Saddam, they keep the ones they've got.'

'But you agree with Weston, it is possible that he has gone to Israel?' Damaskinos intoned.

'Possible, but unlikely. Why would they try to kill him?'

'We don't know if the hit you witnessed at Bahrain was Israeli. It could have been an attempted robbery, for all we know,' Wolfowitz suggested.

'I don't think so. The old guy they shot was a refugee, he had nothing anyone would want to kill for.' Conceding the possibility, Kelday continued, 'I suppose they could have gone to Israel. Bahrain, Athens, Tel Aviv, it wouldn't have been a hard thing to pull off. But we've checked all possible flights, as well as foreign military and freight aircraft movements around that time.'

'OK. Let's cut the speculation. If there is the remotest possibility that this guy is in the States then, we had better find him, and quick, before he starts something. If he's linked in with some terrorist group we could be in for a bumpy ride. But let's first make sure he's here, before we press the panic button. Any questions, Kelday?' Damaskinos was anxious to leave.

'If it turns out that he has come here, do we hand it over to the Bureau?'

Paul Damaskinos had left his chair and was walking towards the door, followed by Wolfowitz and Weston. Now, only centimetres from Kelday's face, he said, 'When we find out where he is, then, and only then, will we consider other possibilities. OK? Meanwhile keep looking. There is no room in our business for fixed thinkers. Until we know for sure that he is in the States, try to keep an open mind. Think global. I don't care what you do, just find the bum!' The door slammed behind the trio.

'Kate, is that you? Alex Kelday, we met recently, remember?' Since returning to Washington he had phoned her several times, only to be told by the Bureau that she was not available.

'Yes, I remember. How are things?'

'Fine. Why don't we meet for lunch?'

'Yes, why don't we. I think I'm free, just let me check.'

The phone went dead for a few moments, before she continued. 'That would be nice. Did you have anywhere in mind?'

'There's a place I go to called the *Rapid Grill*. Do you know it? It's on 7th Street, just north of Pennsylvania Avenue.'

'I'll find it. What time?'

'Twelve thirty OK?'

'See you then.' Her voice was relaxed and friendly. He had been right to contact her. Recently, his social life had been less than frantic. Perhaps Kate Cranley of the FBI would change that. In all truth, he had thought a lot about the woman, since leaving her in Dubai.

Jose Miguel, the manager of the Rapid Grill, greeted him like a long lost friend. Although the place was packed with the lunchtime crowd Miguel found him a table by the window. Across the road, in his absence, the construction site had become an office block close to completion, the sound of drills and electric saws still emanating from within.

At first he did not recognise the lady who walked towards him between the tables, wearing a smart blue suit, as being the same dowdy dresser he had last met in a police station at Dubai International Airport. She was taller than he remembered. The suit was flattering and the ease with which she moved pleasing.

'Hello. I'm glad you could make it.' Before he could move around the table to greet her, Miguel had seated her and presented the short luncheon menu. Although the Rapid Grill did not appear on any list of preferred places to eat in the capital, its name belied the quality of food presented.

'So this is where Alex Kelday is to be found, when he's not at home.' She smiled at him, trying hard to conceal the extent of her pleasure at their reunion. After his hurried departure from Dubai she had ruminated on the possibility of their meeting again, a meditation the excitement of which took her by surprise. Following her timely departure to the Gulf, away from the self-centred Dean Casey and his Jensen Mark 3 Interceptor, she had resolved to be more circumspect with her relationships. That which she shared with First Officer Casey, of Delta Airlines, had come too close for both her personal and professional comfort. She would, in future, prevent a repeat performance. But Alex Kelday had reappeared to undermine her resolve.

'Have you been back long?' he enquired.

'A few days. And you?'

'The same. I had to stop over in London, on the way home.'

'Nice.' Holding the menu aloft she said, 'And what does Alex Kelday recommend?'

They shared a more than creditable Australian Cabernet Sauvignon, a Cranswick Smith Reserve, 1996. It had been her choice. He had seldom met a woman who was both confident and brave enough to order wine. In his experience they deferred to whichever male was present. It was only towards the completion of their meal that they arrived at that point where some justification for their meeting seemed warranted.

'Did you ever find your missing Professor?' she enquired.

'Are you asking me out of professional or personal interest?'

'It could be either. I have something that might be of interest, if you don't mind mixing business with, what I hope has been, pleasure.'

'Not at all, and yes, it has been a pleasure,' he replied.

'After you took off for Bahrain, the Dubai authorities released those two rogue DEA agents, Bobrowski and McCone. They didn't know that much, anyway. A couple of chancers doing what they had been told. We had no further use for them and they were fired from their agency, so there didn't seem much point in hanging onto to them.'

'That was very generous of you.'

'We would probably have had trouble extraditing them back here. Letting them go seemed the easy option. It was suggested that they stay out of the States. Yesterday they both arrived by ferry, in Seattle, from Victoria, British Columbia.'

'And you are wondering why they have come home, when you told them to get lost?' He found it hard to suppress his interest. If they had returned to complete their mission, it would mean that the Professor was somewhere in the States.

'I just thought that you might be interested.' She smiled at him from behind an extravagant glass.

'Have you any idea where they are now?' he enquired.

'Now that is interesting. Once we were alerted by immigration that they had entered the country the Bureau office in Seattle thought it might be nice to keep an eye on them. Remember, this only happened yesterday. I checked, just before leaving the office to meet you. It seems that they got off one ferry and then boarded another for some place in Puget Sound. Why Puget Sound?'

'After their experience in a Dubai slammer, maybe they wanted some rain and fog?'

'You're not interested. And I thought that it would buy me lunch.'

'You mean you would sell Bureau material for lunch at the Rapid Grill? I must remember to tell Miguel. Have you ever been there?'

'Where?'

'Puget Sound?'

'Never. I'm an Eastern girl.'

'I can see that. Where do you think they are going?'

'You are interested. I thought you might be.'

The more time he spent with her the more attractive he found her to be. She had a natural sophistication, a demeanour not in abundance among the women of Washington. Her feminine allure was disquieting. He must have been blind in Dubai, not to have seen her for what she was.

'If I'm paying for this lunch I want value for money,' he playfully whispered across the table.

'Really. It was a nice lunch. And, if I say so myself, the choice of wine was excellent.'

'So?'

'So what?'

'Where did they go from Seattle?'

'Who?'

'Ms Cranley, it's possible that by merely meeting me for lunch you have compromised yourself with the Government of the United States.'

'I won't tell if you don't.'

'You don't seem to realise that Bobrowski and McCone could lift my career out of the swamp,' he pleaded. 'So, where did they go?'

'Oh, I see. Mr Kelday lost his Professor, a fact that has not gone down well in certain circles. And now he wants to win back favour by hunting down two unemployed public servants. Or could it be that Mr Kelday thinks that if he finds them he might also locate his peripatetic Professor?'

'Why does such a smart lady work for the Bureau, when she could be working for McDonald's?'

'Nobody ever asked me. Do you think I should transfer?'

'Not if you continue to withhold information that is prejudicial to the national interest.'

'Now there's a thing. If I can have another coffee, I'll tell you. How's that?'

'Done. Miguel? Another two coffees and the check, please.'

Puget Sound

The three-hour time difference between Washington and Seattle, in addition to the flight time, provided the opportunity for Kelday to catch up on some much needed sleep, a rare condition since his return from the Gulf, exacerbated by a late evening of dining at the *Iron Gate*, 1734 N Street, with Kate Cranley. They had chosen to dine inside rather than al fresco under the trellis, along with most other patrons, both circumnavigating most of the evening without once discussing their respective employment. Each finding the other companionable and interesting.

Damaskinos had reacted in a manner that was as predictable as it was questionable when confronted with the facts, a commodity rare in the world of intelligence. What should have become a Bureau prerogative would remain an Agency interest. Kelday would fly to Seattle to monitor the situation and protect the Agency. Whether the Bureau would intervene before Messrs Bobrowski and McCone were able to complete that which they had failed to accomplish in Dubai was problematic. Having gone freelance since their dismissal from the DEA, both could be relied upon to act not in the best interest of law and order, but possibly on behalf of errant senior officials within the Administration. Not for the first time did Kelday ask himself how it was that they had been able to locate the Professor when the CIA had not? An inter-governmental investigation was already under way, into the operational procedures of the DEA, to identify those responsible for the attempted assassination of Professor Batioushenkov and once found, the connection between the Professor's work and the DEA would no doubt be revealed.

On the left-hand side of the ferry, piling stubs of an old dock projected out into Admiralty Inlet, victims of the shipworm, their protective creosote having been washed away by unrelenting tides. A stiff in-shore breeze blew past Fort Casey creating a chop on the waters of the Sound as light rain began to fall. It had been a number of years since Kelday had stood on the deck of such a small vessel. The freshness and the brooding beauty of the Sounds along with the movement of the ferry beneath his feet released in him a feeling of youthfulness and freedom, reminding him of another ferry trip, when, as a young student touring Europe, he had crossed the Bosporus under a cerulean sky and admired the approaching domes of Europe. It seemed, then, that the whole world was his for the asking and that he had only to reach out and take it. Now, still on the right side of middle age, the years that stretched ahead would be inextricably linked with the Agency. Such a thought, on such a day, in such a place existed as a cloud, every bit as dark as those now gathering to the west, beyond the Quamper peninsula. Kate had told him that Bobrowski and McCone had purchased tickets in Seattle for Ebey's Landing on Whidbey Island, a destination, he reasoned, ill-suited for the release of a biological contaminant. The absence of a densely populated area, along with a climate that was less than conducive to the spread of a toxic killer virus, meant that, whatever the Professor was doing on Whidbey Island was for release elsewhere. Maybe Seattle was to be the recipient of his endeavours. The Assistant Director of Operations had instructed him to remain clear of the FBI, unless circumstances dictated otherwise, an instruction he felt inclined to respect, for the present. Rather than seek accommodation on the island, where his presence would be more noticeable, he would stay in Port Townsend, a picture-book town replete with artists, craftsmen and small boat builders, but once, in less genteel times, a place where press gangs roamed to fill the hammocks of trading vessels, and Indian traders drank hard grog, after coming to town, laden with pelts.

Early the following day he hired a car and drove onto the little Whidbey ferry for the twenty-minute trip across Admiralty Inlet to Ebey's Landing. The largest of the Puget Sound Islands, Whidbey, has been inhabited for over ten thousand years and was among the first to be settled by Europeans. As well as being host to many town folk, eager to retreat to an earlier lifestyle to which they pay only lip service, it is home to farmers and artists, promiscuously scattered throughout the island's interior, among the lush forests and cultivated landscape. Port Townsend, with its largely transient population, had yielded little in the way of information. There had been no sign of Bobrowski or McCone. Also, the Bureau was not in evidence, which, within the geographic and social confines of the town meant that they were, in all probability, ensconced in Ebey's Landing, where their presence would be even easier to detect.

After driving off the small vessel he found a café from where he could observe those leaving for and arriving from Townsend. Northern Whidbey Island is also connected to the mainland by the Deception Pass bridge, through Fildago Island. However, it is the long way around for anyone travelling from Seattle, a fact Kelday reasoned for maintaining a watch at the southern point, Ebey's Landing. Most visitors, having arrived from Townsend, leave the ferry to either hike off into the interior or up the coast to Fort Ebey State Park. Those passing through or seeking a more sedentary method of viewing Whidbey, take Highway 525 North, up the centre of the island.

There are a number of military air stations, including Whidbey Naval Air Station on the island's north-west coast, that compete for air space with civilian air traffic, including helicopters and light amphibians, over the land that was once the hunting ground of the Swinomish and Suquamish Indians. To the east, near Seattle, is Boeing City, where, until its hegemony was shattered by a European consortium, most of the world's airliners were built and tested. Visual sightings of these leviathans is often limited by either low cloud and rain or fog, but there is ample auditory confirmation of their existence. Kelday watched as two veteran Jet Ranger helicopters flew in formation north over the town, just below the cloud, the noise of their Allison 320 engines momentarily drowned out by an invisible Boeing 747–400 on a test flight, their lazy rotors rotating mutely, as they disappeared from view behind a clapboard church. Their profile was not unfamiliar. They were the sort of machine favoured by the Bureau for moving teams of operatives around the country on close support operations. Any alternative explanation for their presence above Ebey's Landing he was not prepared to even countenance. To the trained observer, paranoia is not a consideration, when assembling visual evidence. Each related piece confirms the hypothesis. There may be one or even a number of clues that indicate when an operation is in place. Along the road from the café was parked an innocuous US postal van, its doors shut, the cab empty. It was another clue. He had seen such vehicles many times, parked innocently beside the road, his own agency often used them as cover. Inside would be one or two communication agents seated behind a battery of sophisticated equipment to eavesdrop on the innocent as well as the guilty. Two helicopters and a seemingly innocent postal van, along with any other physical evidence, do not, in themselves, complete the picture. There is also a feel about a place, an expectation that is percipient to the initiated, something that defies explanation. Kelday knew, beyond doubt, that the Bureau was alive and well in Ebey's Landing.

To the great US public, if a deadly virus was about to be unleashed upon the nation it seemed only logical that both his own agency and the Bureau, along with other affined government bodies, should work in concert to combat the threat. There is, however, much that is illogical in the antithetical and competitive world of intelligence. There are empires to protect, careers to be enhanced and egos of gigantesque proportions to be fed, none of which Kelday questioned. He had lived too long among the mirrors. There would already be in place plausible deniability as to why, one or other of the various agencies concerned, had not been included, should the necessity arise to defend a corner. In time, at some level within the system, right up to the National Foreign Intelligence Board, which is chaired by the CIA, minds would be brought together, united in the common cause, if only for as long as the threat persisted. Meanwhile he would continue to work alone, informing Washington only of that which would not come back to hurt him.

Kelday was aware that Bobrowski and McCone would not expect their presence to go undetected for long and that they would carry out the elimination of the Professor, if that was still their aim, as quickly as possible, effecting their escape with commensurate speed. Perhaps they had already done so, leaving the lead-footed Bureau to explain all. Unable to face another cup of indifferent coffee he left the café, turned right and walked towards the US postal van. There grew within him, as he approached the vehicle, an almost irresistible urge to bang on the metal side of the van as he passed by. Drawing level he saw, seated in the passenger seat of a large black four-wheel drive parked behind the van, the profile of Kate Cranley. The windows were tinted and she was looking down at something on her lap. Her companion, behind the wheel, was busily eating a hamburger, paying little attention to those on the sidewalk. Walking past, Kelday ducked into the first shop, a hardware store, the kind that caters for those who feel compelled to remodel their home, irrespective of their talents. Moving to the back of the store he was able to keep a watch on the vehicle outside, with little risk of being seen by anyone casually glancing in through the window.

After a while it moved off and Kelday was about to leave the store when a young female clerk emerged from a room at the back.

'May I help you?' she asked.

He turned to look into the smiling face of a young Indian girl, possibly a descendent of the Suquamish, no more than fifteen.

'No, I was just looking around.' The bell over the front door rang, indicating that someone else had entered the shop. The young girl glanced expectantly past him at the new customer. Kelday again turned to leave only to be confronted by Kate Cranley.

'Mr Kelday, I do declare,' she said, in mock surprise.

'As I live and breathe, it's Ms Cranley. Fancy meeting you here.' She was wearing a lightweight brown jacket over a white blouse, along with beige cord slacks and tramping boots, blending perfectly into Ebey's Landing.

'Can I help you?' asked the clerk.

'No, thank you. I'm just browsing.'

They both moved away from the counter to the other side of the shop, an area given over to various books on 'how to'.

'How did you know I was in here?'

'Put it down to superior training. I saw you leave the café.'

'You didn't mention the other evening that you would be coming out west,' he said.

'No. I didn't know then that I was. They hit me with it the next morning. They think I would be the best person to ident our two villains from the DEA.'

'Why didn't you call and tell me?'

'I haven't had time. Anyway, may I remind you that it is Bureau business.'

'Who is your friend?' he said, indicating the road, outside.

'Someone from the Seattle field office. The National Security Division is also involved. This island is humming with our people, or hadn't you noticed?'

'I had. And have you found your two delinquents?'

'Not yet, but they are on the island and the place is about to be sealed tight. The State has just drafted in the troopers. Soon you won't be able to move for law enforcers.'

'Well, that's a relief. What about the Professor?'

'So far nothing on him. Bobrowski and McCone will lead us to him, assuming he's here. They're not here for the weather. What other reason would they have for coming back to the States? They're taking a hell of a risk, and for what? Where are you staying?'

'I thought it might be better to leave my things in Townsend,' he replied.

'I can't stay long, he thinks I've just come in here to buy some things. Why couldn't you have chosen a book shop? What am I going to buy?'

'May I recommend these small brass hinges, Madam. Good for every occasion.'

The suggestion of some collusion between them spoke also of an intimacy he found more than pleasing. He knew then, as he had known all along, but until then had denied, with Kate Cranley the possibility of an adventitious relationship was specious. Any unauthorized contact with an agent of the CIA, if exposed, would do nothing to improve her career and yet she had put herself at risk by meeting with him.

'Thank you. Just what I was after, a set of hinges. What are you going to do now?' she asked,

'Probably follow you.'

'Not a good idea.'

'What would you like me to do?' he replied.

'Meet me again for dinner, when we get back to town.'

'It's a date. If you can, keep me informed. You have my number. I want to be there for the kill.'

'An unfortunate turn of phrase, wouldn't you say?'

'It may come to that. Will you leave first or shall I?'

'I'll pay for these and leave. Give me a few moments.'

He watched as the young clerk struggled with the computer to record the sale and diligently put the hinges into a bag, after which Kate left the shop.

Whidbey Island

The breakthrough came with the sighting of someone who looked like Allen Bobrowski, in the township of Coupeville on Penn Cove. The sighting was uncorroborated, but the owner of an anglers' shop had positively identified Bobrowski from a photograph of the two ex-DEA agents being circulated around the island. Bobrowski had come into the shop and sought directions to the farm of a deceased island identity. A son, from off the island, had inherited the property and recently moved in, along with a group of others. It was locally thought that it had been turned into some kind of commune. The Sounds had, in the past, attracted people of that kind. From such a story the Bureau assumed that the two ex-DEA agents had joined a cell and that the farm had become a launching pad for a terrorist attack, and all without having first established the true whereabouts of either Bobrowski or McCone. It was a factoid, the acceptance of which was to be critically challenged in a subsequent enquiry, carried out by the Justice Department.

The Bureau's Special Agent in Charge (SAC), the head of the Seattle field office, had left his desk on Second Avenue and taken personal command of the operation on the island, along with a supervisor to head the squad. He had set up a command centre, courtesy of the US Navy, at the Whidbey Naval Air Station. Since the operation had been deemed to fall under the heading of domestic terrorism, the SAC would also have officers of the Bureau's National Security Division to assist. The Strategic Information Operations Centre, on the fifth floor of the J Edgar Hoover Building, in Washington, was being set up for a twenty-four hour observation of the operation, codenamed Northwind. Following the use of excessive force by the FBI at Ruby Ridge, in August 1992 and at Waco, April 1993, Northwind would be conducted with the utmost caution. The rules of engagement were to be precise, circulated to all and strictly adhered to. The fallout from both Ruby Ridge and Waco had a profound effect on the Bureau and its method of operation. SACs across the country were now as circumspect as they were emulous.

Following the possible sighting of Bobrowski, Kate Cranley had been ordered to Coupeville, where she arrived late in the afternoon. Before leaving Ebey's Landing she had rung Kelday and informed him of developments. A SWAT team and sharp-shooters greeted her arrival at Coupeville, confirming that, whatever else may transpire, the Bureau would not be outgunned. They had been flown into the Naval Air Station and spirited across the island in a fleet of four-wheel drive vehicles. The supervisor, an ascetic with military pretensions, had been less than friendly, as he briefed her on the possible sighting of Bobrowski and the location of the farm. As with other government security organizations, there remained, among a dwindling few within the Bureau, the archaic view that women had no place in the field under such a man Kate Cranley was now placed. It was spelt out to her that her presence would be tolerated only because she had been sent to the island by Washington and that, given the opportunity, once she had identified Bobrowski and McCone, her services would no longer be required. Kate Cranley decided, in the interest of the Bureau and her career, that she would keep as far away from the supervisor as was possible.

It takes less than half an hour to drive from Ebey's Landing to Coupeville, under normal circumstances. Alex Kelday had barely left there before running into the first line of State troopers at a hurriedly prepared roadblock. After much persuasion they let him through. The next checkpoint, less than a mile from the first, proved impassable, even when he reluctantly showed them his CIA pass. Whidbey Island was fast becoming a prison. Holding him at the checkpoint, an officious trooper phoned ahead. Within minutes a large off-the-road vehicle approached, at considerable speed, from the direction of Coupeville. It came to rest, its brakes screeching, ten metres from the road block and there it sat. So dark was the tint of the windshield that Kelday was unable to see into the cab. After what seemed like ten minutes, a dark-suited figure, his face masked by MacArthur sun-glasses and wearing a blue FBI cap, got out of the passenger side of the cab and walked slowly towards Kelday, who was standing by his car. If the melodramatic arrival was designed to impress or intimidate it failed at the point where the Special Agent trod in a rural deposit, left by a Labrador out for his daily walk. There followed a pantomimic performance by the officer, trying to remove the deposit from his right shoe, while the State trooper and Kelday, standing side by side, looked on without exchanging a word. Eventually the agent, satisfied that he had removed all that was possible, approached the intruder.

'Are you the guy from the CIA?' he growled.

'Alex Kelday from the Washington office. I'm looking for agent Cranley,' he lied.

'What for?'

'I told him nobody was going past here,' contributed the trooper, a statement ignored by the Special Agent.

'We have an operation going down. Do we know about you?'

'I shouldn't think so,' replied Kelday.

'Why don't we know about you?'

'Because nobody told you? I'm sorry about your shoe.'

The agent looked down at his shoe and then at Kelday.

'Are you here officially?'

'I could be. Would that help?'

'You're damn right it would!'

'Why don't I speak to your supervisor?'

'What for?'

'So that I can be here officially.'

'Since when has the CIA taken to employing comedians.'

'We try to cover every field. Just get your supervisor to check with Washington, that should get things moving.' Damaskinos would not be pleased. Wolfowitz and Weston would whisper tendentiously in his ear and the Agency would be forced to explain its involvement in a domestic operation.

It took half an hour before confirmation came through that would allow Kelday to drive on to Coupeville, during which time the agent sat in his vehicle, leaving the trooper and Kelday to wait by the road. The first hastily erected roadblock was clearly effective, since no other vehicle approached the second. Overhead a bald eagle circled in search of a late afternoon meal. Far off, to the west, a ship's horn sounded out at sea, beyond the Whulj and, for the first time since arriving in the Sound, Kelday felt the sun on his face. It was brief and weak but it was there. Eventually the agent left the hidden comfort of his vehicle and again approached Kelday, ensuring, while doing so, that he did not step in anything that might be deleterious to his shoes.

'Follow us and don't stop until we do. The super will see you at Coupeville.'

'Is agent Cranley in Coupeville?' he called after the departing officer.

'I wouldn't know,' came the reply.

The light was beginning to fade as they entered the small community of Coupeville. The FBI had set up a command post beside the old weatherboard school hall, and large ugly vehicles, some bristling with aerials, were placed in a crude circle, as if in expectation of a raid by the Haidas or Suquamish Indians. Kelday could not help but notice the absence of specialist chemical containment or dispersal vehicles.

The supervisor turned out to be a man roughly his own age who, mindful of the Bureau's record, wanted to array matters, not only to the satisfaction of his SAC, but also the media, whom he suspected were already lurking behind every tree. There was about him, something military, a trait Kelday had thought no longer fashionable within the Bureau. He wore dark blue overalls and body armour.

'Are you Kelday?' he enquired.

'Yes. I didn't mean to gatecrash your party.'

'William Shapiro. I'm the supervisor here. We didn't know the Agency was involved. Nobody seemed to know you were coming,' he said reproachfully.

'Our interest is more in a certain Russian professor than the two ex-DEA guys. I hear that you have identified one of them, here in Coupeville?'

'Who told you that? Was it the media?'

'I just heard it, somewhere.'

'Not from me, you didn't. Until the Bureau identifies them they don't exist. We are trying to keep the thing low until we're sure what we're dealing with. It could be a terrorist cell, right here on the island. Can you imagine that? In Puget Sound?

'A terrorist cell?'

'Yep. God knows what they plan to do here.'

At this point it occurred to Kelday that the FBI may not have linked the two ex-DEA agents to a missing BW scientist. If such was the case then they would be woefully unprepared for what could happen in the event of the release of a hazardous substance.

'What do you know about the guy these two jerks are after? Professor Batioushenkov?'

'I haven't been briefed on any professor,' he replied. 'Is there something I should know?'

A shiver ran down Kelday's spine. Either the right hand in the FBI was not in communication with the left or there had been a failure, on the part of someone, somewhere, to properly identify the nature of the threat to which this particular corner of the nation was now exposed. Either way the result could be the same. Nothing short of catastrophic.

'You mean you haven't been briefed at all on what could happen here, if Professor Batioushenkov has teamed up with some terrorist group?' he replied incredulously.

'As far as I know we're mounting an operation to flush out two ex-DEA agents, wanted for a bucketful of misdemeanours, who may have joined up with some local terrorist cell.'

'Do you have an agent, Kate Cranley, with you?'

'Yep. She's from Washington too. They want her to ident these two guys. Seen them in the Gulf or some such place. We could do it from the snaps they sent, but no. They want her to confirm or deny. Damn waste of Federal funds, if you ask me!'

'Where is she now?'

'We're just about to make a move on the farm. She'll be at the briefing I'm about to give.'

'Can I come along?'

'I don't see why not, since you're here. I'll have to clear it with my SAC, first. Shouldn't be a problem.'

After the briefing, as the SWAT team and the sharpshooters moved off to their vehicles, Kelday managed to pull Kate Cranley into his car.

'Are you attempting to highjack me, Mr Kelday?' she impishly asked.

'Kate. Do you know what the hell is going on?'

'I thought Supervisor Shapiro just told us. We're going out to the farm to arrest Messrs Bobrowski and McCone, if they are there, and anyone else who gets in the way.' Her vocal imitation of the supervisor, although accurate, was sufficiently flippant to irritate Kelday.

'Your friends in the Bureau seem oblivious of the fact that we have the potential for a toxic or chemical release that could wipe out who knows what. And they are going in with guns blazing.'

'Alex. We don't even know if the Professor is here. Nobody has seen him. There was a sighting of somebody similar, an old man on the ferry, from Everett. But he was travelling with a younger woman who could have been his daughter. So until we know for sure—'

He did not let her finish. 'But you put it all in your Gulf report, didn't you? What the hell is the Bureau playing at? Why do they think Bobrowski and McCone have joined up with a terrorist cell? Those two clowns aren't terrorists. They're not the type.'

'What is the terrorist type?' she replied.

'Not Bobrowski and McCone. They're opportunists, here to kill the Professor and for money. They're bounty hunters.'

'That doesn't mean that they can't join a terrorist cell. Does it?'

'No, but it isn't very likely. They're after the money for hitting the Professor.'

'You mean, chasing someone who may or may not be on Whidbey.'

'Right. I think I should have a few words with the SAC. At least he should know what might happen, before it all blows up in his face.'

'I don't think you have the time. We're off.' She left his car and walked towards a black, high wheelbase, four-wheel drive vehicle that shuddered under its own power, waiting to be released, like a fighting dog on a short lead.

The Farm

The Model 21 Winchester that Max carried from the farm had belonged to his father and his father before him. The latter had purchased the double-barrelled shotgun in 1933, from the Winchester Company, at a time when most Americans were having trouble putting food on the table. Of all the Winchesters ever made the 21 is the most coveted by collectors. The Tournament Grade 12 Gauge, with a 32-inch barrel length, had been custom-built with fine wood to metal finish. The engraving on the metal was tasteful but not profuse. It had selective ejection, which meant that, when the gun was opened either or both of the shells would be automatically ejected according to whether one or both shells had been fired. He had inherited the gun, along with the farm, from a father he never knew. Both gun and farm should have gone to his older brother or at least been shared. That they were not was due to cocaine.

His brother, an aesthetic youth, was both musician and painter and had become a cocaine addict while working in a New York club. Dependence on the drug is psychological rather than physiological since there are no characteristic withdrawal symptoms when the use of cocaine is ceased abruptly. The effects of cocaine on the brain come from a chemical neurotransmitter, known as dopamine. The limbic areas of the brain, the region that deals with emotion, contains dopamine. Cocaine blocks trans-porters to the brain, increasing dopamine concentrations in regions associated with pleasure and the result is an intense wave of euphoria, known as 'the rush'. 'The rush' is followed by 'the crash', when the cocaine is eventually flushed from the system, made worse because the body's natural level of dopamine is depleted and there is a strong urge to return to 'the rush'. Cocaine makes you feel good so you take more, when it wears off there is less dopamine so you feel bad; so you take more cocaine to make you feel good again. When Max's brother first took cocaine, sniffing the drug in a broom closet between sessions, it artificially boosted his dopamine count, prolonging the pleasure he felt. From sniffing a daily dose of 0.4 gram, he quickly graduated to injecting himself with a daily dose of 5 gram, until that was not enough. The lethal single dose of 1 gram, following a drinking bout with some fellow musicians, induced convulsions before his lonely death, on a subway.

A wild cat had been causing havoc among the farm's chickens to the extent that, despite Jason's order to the contrary, Max resolved to hunt down the pest. After all, was it not his farm now? Was it not his responsibility to hunt down and exterminate such vermin? No one had seen him slip away with the shotgun and, the handful of Super X shells in his pocket would be all that was needed to protect their egg and meat supply. He knew where the animal would be at that time of day and, if asked about the sound of a shotgun being fired, he could always blame the Clansys on the neighbouring farm. Had he been raised in the country, as his father had wished, or simply spent more time away from the cloistered suburbs of Seattle, he would have detected something different about his environment that evening, as he walked in the gathering dusk. There was, among other indicators, an absence of rural sound. He had almost crossed the small yard that separated the house from the first barn, when he heard the sound of something moving behind an old plough, off to his right, close to the hen house. The fowl remained undisturbed, which meant that, whatever he had heard, it had not been the cat. Putting a shell into each chamber he walked towards the plough.

Bobrowski had seen him leave the house, silently closing the door behind him. With McCone in close attendance he had positioned himself as far from the main building as possible, keeping to the fast growing shadows. They could hear music emitting from within and the sound of uninhibited conversation. When the youth furtively appeared, with a shotgun under his arm, they both retired deep into the shadows. From the previous day's observations they had established the layout of the farm complex and in particular the location of the laboratory, where the Professor spent most of his time, returning to the house only for his food and sleep. Both men were armed. They were skirting around the house, in the direction of the laboratory, when they saw the youth walking towards them. Both men quickly crouched down. So still was the evening air that each could hear the other breathing. They watched as the youth stopped, loaded the shotgun and then began walking towards them. The one staring into the Stygian void behind the plough, the two, at a silhouette against the illuminated farmhouse. An owl hooted, at the same time the chickens in the chicken house to their left, became agitated. From their right a large black feral cat appeared crawling on its belly, like a stalking lion, towards the hen house, intent on an evening meal, oblivious to the human drama about him. Both Max and Bobrowski saw the cat, McCone did not. Crouched behind and to the left of Bobrowski, near the chicken house, he could see only the plough and the armed youth. Bobrowski turned towards McCone to make sure the latter had seen the cat.

With both barrels already loaded Max had only to raise the shotgun to his shoulder and fire. The cat was directly in front of him, less than six feet away and moving from left to right. Raising the gun and with the right barrel selected, he took up the first pressure on the trigger. Before he could apply more and eliminate the threat to their food source, he was blown off his feet by two bullets from McCone's Heckler and Koch MP5 rifle. Falling back, Max's right finger tightened on the trigger, discharging the shotgun harmlessly into the trees beyond the barn. He fell to the ground, the evening light becoming dimmer with every dying breath.

Both Bobrowski and McCone broke cover and sprinted past the barn towards the laboratory, less than fifty yards to their right. A number of people emerged from the house. A woman screamed, another called for a first-aid box. Bobrowski and McCone had almost made the distance to the low wooden building that served as the Professor's new work room, when another shot rang out, followed by a fusillade. Those from the house that had run out into the evening quickly turned to seek shelter back behind its stout door, but not before two had fallen, having come into the line of fire between the two fleeing men and the SWAT team that had been taking up position among the trees.

Supervisor Shapiro was in the process of moving his team into position when Max unwittingly flushed out Bobrowski and McCone. Shapiro was checking on the deployment of his team, moving along the line, when the first shot was fired. The second, a shotgun blast that ripped through the trees, removed the scalp of a SWAT team member who had been adjusting the legs of his bipod, to lift his rifle above the tall grass and steady his aim. Believing themselves to be under attack, and so within the rules of engagement, the order to fire that never came, became redundant. In the fading light people could be seen, first leaving the house and then fleeing back inside for cover. A number were seen to fall. Shapiro attempted to stop the firing, since none was returned, but before he was able to regain control of the situation McCone, to cover Bobrowski, had turned and fired into the dark, narrowly missing the Supervisor, after which all semblance of control was lost. Bobrowski burst through the laboratory door flinging himself on the floor, as heavy calibre bullets ripped through the thin timber walls. Equipment and glass containers blew apart, their contents spewed into the air, as rounds of fire raked the room's interior. For one second, before the lights were obliterated, Bobrowski saw the small figure of Professor Vasily Batioushenkov standing, like a pillar, in the far right-hand corner of what had been the one-room laboratory.

As well as the Professor, Bobrowski saw a way out, a door at the end of the room, which, once he had dispatched the Professor, would be his escape route. McCone was still managing to hold their attackers at bay, but not, he thought, for much longer. Crawling forward towards where he had last seen the target, the Glock 22, still with its magazine of fifteen rounds in his right hand, Bobrowski made his way through the broken furniture and splintered glass, that had been until a few minutes earlier, the means by which cocaine could be, if not eliminated, greatly reduced throughout South America. Resting on his right elbow, he fired three shots into the bundle that now lay in the corner of the room. They penetrated the body of an old man who had died a second before from cardiac arrest, an old man who, at the very end, felt betrayed.

As Bobrowski reached the door he lay on his left side and fired a further three rounds into the dead body of Professor Vasily

Batioushenkov. McCone was unlikely to survive and he had to be sure that, as the sole beneficiary of their evening's labour, he had fulfilled the contract. Rounds were still being fired into the laboratory, but he could no longer hear any return fire from the yard. Pushing the rear door open with his hand, the handle and locking mechanism having been blown off with the first rounds that struck the lightly built shed, he eased himself forward on his belly, down a short flight of stairs, into the fresh evening air. As he rose to break for cover behind an adjacent barn, he was struck by a fusillade from members of the SWAT team that had moved around the other side of the house, to block off any escape. Bobrowski died instantly, McCone, after receiving several hits, lived only long enough to see the small leather boots of a woman standing inches from his face.

'That's McCone,' Kate Cranley informed the supervisor. 'Is he dead?'

'As good as. Let's see.' Shapiro kicked the rifle from the dead man's grasp and knelt down beside the stretched out body. 'Yep, he's dead. You had better see if you can ident the other one.'

They walked in silence the length of the bullet-riddled shed to the rear door. Crumpled on the ground, at the bottom of a short flight of steps lay a second body. A Glock 22 lay a foot from the outstretched right arm. With the area now lit by large arc lights, a stillness settled on the scene, made more extreme by that which had gone before. The supervisor gestured to a member of his team who turned the body over. The lower half of the face had been blown away, there remained enough, however, for a vomiting Kate Cranley to identify the body as that of Allen Bobrowski. She staggered back from the body into the arms of Alex Kelday, who led her away towards the house.

'There's another one in here,' someone called out from within the shed.

Before Kelday could caution Shapiro about entering the shed he had mounted the steps and disappeared inside.

'What the hell does he think he's playing at? There could be bacteriological or chemical agents in there enough to write off the entire State.'

It took some time for the body of the Professor to be bought out of the shed, but only a moment for Kelday to identify it as being Professor Vasily Batioushenkov, one of the world's most experienced BW scientists.

As Kelday helped Kate Cranley into a vehicle, Shapiro appeared, a shotgun slung over his left shoulder.

'A Winchester 21 and in mint condition. Been looking for one of these for years, but I guess I'll have to hand it in, it's evidence. I guess the media will be here any time soon.'

'What about the others?' Kelday enquired.

'What others? We took out the two we were after.'

The media, both national and local, made much of the story, how two international terrorists had attempted to establish a base in Puget Sound. No mention was made of an elderly Russian scientist, or who the disparate group were who had taken over the farmhouse. Forensic experts failed to identify the various substances found on the walls and floor of the shed, and the investigation into the illegal workings of the DEA came to nothing, after being smothered in a welter of conflicting evidence and bureaucracy The subsequent Justice Department investigation, into the raid on the farm house, slammed the management of the FBI and its handling of events. Kate Cranley and Alex Kelday met for dinner in Washington, at the Iron Gate, on 1734 N Street. That evening they dined under the trellis.